New E

A Nov

by

Robert Cubitt

(The Magi Series Book 3)

© **2017**

Having purchased this eBook from Amazon, it is for your personal use only. It may not be copied, reproduced, printed or used in any way, other than in its intended Kindle format.

Published by Selfishgenie Publishing of, Northamptonshire, England.

This novel is entirely a work of fiction. All the names characters, incidents, dialogue, events portrayed and opinions expressed in it are either purely the product of the author's imagination or they are used entirely fictitiously and not to be construed as real. Any resemblance to actual persons, living or dead, events or localities is entirely coincidental. Nothing is intended or should be interpreted as representing or expressing the views and policies of any department or agency of any government or other body.

All trademarks used are the property of their respective owners. All trademarks are recognised.

The right of Robert Cubitt to be identified as the author of this work has been asserted in accordance with sections 77 and 78 of the Copyright Designs and Patents Act 1988.

Other titles by Robert Cubitt

Fiction

The Deputy Prime Minister

The Inconvenience Store

The Charity Thieves

The Warriors Series

The Warriors: The Girl I Left Behind Me

The Warriors: Mirror Man

The Magi Series

The Magi

Genghis Kant

Non-Fiction

I'm So Glad You Asked Me That

I Want That Job

Contents

Foreword
1. The Dead Hand Of Bureaucracy
2. Intruder
3. Missing Person
4. Deception
5. Prison Break
6. A Step Back In Time
7. Susikins
8. Peeling The Onion
9. The Bank Robber
10. The Solicitor
11. The Kelp Workers
12. Bomb Disposal
13. The Golden Garter
14. Coddled Eggs
15. The Hideaway
16. The High Price Of Eggs
17. Gunfight At The Hideaway
18. Mind Mapping

Appendix
Author's Note
Preview
And Now

Foreword

In writing this series, The Magi, I have described a galaxy in which many strange things exist and many stranger things happen. Some of these things are real and some of them I made up. If you know which is which then you had a good science teacher and you paid attention in school. For the rest I have provided a short glossary at the end of each chapter to help you.

If, after reading the glossary, you still aren't sure which things are real and which are made up, then please can I come and live in your galaxy?

Some of the more common terms are shown below, just to get you started.

c - A constant, the speed of light in a vacuum, which is 299,792,458 m/sec. As used in the expression $e=mc^2$. In this book speed is measured in comparison to c, i.e. 0.95 c = 284,802,835.1 m/sec. This produces a standard for the measurement of speed to compensate for the many and varied measurements that are used throughout the galaxy. See also 'time'.

Li - A unit of measurement of distance roughly equivalent to 5 Earth metres.

Met - A unit of measurement of distance. Plural Mett. 5 Mett = 1 li.

Nuk - A unit of currency that is exchangeable throughout the galaxy. One nuk is sufficient to buy two Big Macs on any planet except Earth, where they cost 5 nuks each, but that's Earth for you.

Sim - A unit of measurement of distance. Plural Sims. There are 50 sims to a met.

Tea - A generic term referring to all non-alcoholic beverages consumed by public servants across the galaxy. Although they differ greatly from planet to planet in terms of their ingredients, most of these beverages are brown in colour and taste like they need less sweetening in them than they actually have, even if they have no sweetening in them at all. They are never as good as the beverages that are made at home.

Time - With so many variations in the rate at which planets revolve and the duration of their orbits around their stars there was no standard unit for the measurement of time before the Magi took on the governance of the galaxy. Indeed, one of the many wars that had raged was known as the war of the 23 hour day, which had gone on for two years or 933 days, or 1072.95 days if you had a 20 hour day. One of the first acts of the Magi was to introduce a standard unit of time based on the extremely accurate pulses produced by an atomic clock located on the planet Greenwich. Currently no one in the galaxy is aware of the irony of this.

1 - The Dead Hand Of Bureaucracy

"So this is it, eh? New Earth." An Kholi's voice was suitably awed.

"Yup, what did I tell you?" Den had a smug grin on his face.

"It is amazing. Have you been here before Den?"

"Let's say I had some business interests here at one time. I'd rather not talk about them. You'd heard of New Earth, of course, I mean before we decided to come here?"

"How can you not hear about a planet that got so screwed up that the occupants had to build themselves a whole new planet."

"Good point, but they didn't start out by building a new planet. They tried colonising their moon first, then the fourth planet, which they call Mars. That didn't work out. It was easier just to build a planet. Technically it's actually a space station."

"Some space station. I've seen moons that were smaller. Why didn't they just go somewhere else?" Gala asked.

Den continued the story. "They couldn't. At that time they hadn't had any contact with other species in the galaxy, so there had been no transfer of technology, particularly the wormhole technology needed for inter-stellar travel. So all they could do was build within their ability to travel. Their big breakthrough came with the space elevator."

"What the heck is a space elevator?" An Kohli asked.

"I've heard of them." Gala said. "There was an engineer on Artsutanov Beta who messed around with the idea, but it didn't get very far."

"That's right," Den replied, "and he wasn't the only one. It was an idea that was tried out in a few star systems, but it had loads of technological challenges, so in the end they all reverted to developing better technology for their shuttle craft and abandoned space elevators."

"But these humans made it work."

"Well, it makes sense if you have archaic technology like the humans." Gala, the engineer, said. "Their use of rockets to lift loads from the surface of a planet cost huge amounts in terms of energy, for just a small payload. That also made them very expensive to build. But once you have an elevator up and running it's almost free in energy terms. You load up something at the top end, like minerals mined on the Moon or from asteroids, and that acts as a counterweight for whatever you want to lift up into space."

"That's right." Den picked up the story before Gala could steal his thunder. "Once you have the first elevator working, you use it to build more of them. You manufacture the components on the ground, then send them up in the elevator to be assembled in space. There's no limit to the size of ship you can build; as you can see from what's in front of us."

"It can't be that easy or everyone would be doing it." An Kohli scoffed.

"No, it isn't. The big challenge is to find a material that's strong enough to lift a load, but light enough so it doesn't pull the space station end out of orbit and send it plummeting to the ground. These seemingly backward humans seemed to have cracked that problem."

"So why do we have to go to New Earth to get down to the planet. Why don't we just use one of these elevators." An Kohli was always in a rush and always looking for a shortcut.

"They aren't used for passengers any more, only for freight. Food grown on New Earth is sent to the elevator by shuttle, then sent down using the elevator. Then supplies for New Earth are sent back up the same way." Den pointed towards the viewing screen where they could see an ugly freight shuttle craft that was just leaving the huge satellite. "See. They had just about finished building New Earth when they made first contact with other star systems. In the resulting exchange of technology they learnt about advanced engines to power shuttles, so they decided to go that way for passenger transport."

"But still," An Kohli said, admiringly, "Building that was a huge achievement."

"Of course it didn't start out that size." Den continued. "The first unit was about the size of a shed, just big enough for the team, what they used to call astronauts or cosmonauts, who were going to assemble the first few units. There were only a dozen of them. Then it just started to get bigger. In hardly any time at all it was so big it was in danger of being dragged out of orbit and crashing, so they moved it out to where you see it now. It shares an orbit with the moon, only on the opposite side of the planet."

"Wouldn't that affect the tides?"

"Of course, but they didn't think of that until it was too late, which is pretty typical of humans; they call themselves 'people' sometimes. It's so big that it has its own gravity and everywhere on the planet that has a coastline now has four high tides a day. It plays havoc in some of the low lying areas."

The spacecraft Adastra drifted towards the gigantic myriahedron, floating in space, its angles, tubes, and globes sparkled in the sunlight. It seemed impossible that any species could build such a massive object. It seemed even more impossible that the species that did it would be the technologically retarded humans of Earth.

"So what happened, Den? Why did they have to build it?" Amongst the small crew Gala was the only one not to have heard the story.

"The way they lived, centuries ago, they threw billions of tons of carbon dioxide into their atmosphere every year. They seemed to be unaware of what that was doing, or they were so stupid they didn't care. Anyway, as we all know, when you do that, the heat of the sun becomes trapped inside the atmosphere and the temperature starts to rise. And it did. Slowly at first, barely noticeable, then a little bit more, then it started to accelerate. The polar ice caps went within a generation, weather patterns changed dramatically. Land that was previously used for agriculture started to dry up because of the heat. The people were starving. That's when they started playing around with settlements on the Moon and Mars, but they proved impractical. Mars was too far away and half of the moon was in darkness for half the time, which made it difficult to power using solar energy. So they started building this. It's home to about ten million people now."

"Wow, that's impressive. Is that the whole population of Earth?"

"Good grief no. Down on the planet there are twenty billion people, but the majority depend on New Earth for their food. It's where they grow it and process it, then they send it back down to the planet using the elevator system."

"Where do they get the water from?" Gala asked. "You can't synthesise water. Well you can if you have enough hydrogen and oxygen, but it's not something you could do on the scale they need here."

"No, you're right. You can't see it from here at the moment, it must be round on the far side of the station, but they have a huge slab of ice the size of a planetoid. They blast it out from the moons around the planet they call Jupiter and they tow it here. It's connected to the space station by a pipe so big you could walk through it. One end is heated so it melts the ice and the water flows along to storage tanks on the station. They still have to recycle the waste water, though, to conserve it and even then they get through one of the slabs every ten Earth years or so."

"Wow, you seem to know a lot about this place, Den" Gala rarely paid Den a compliment, so the fact that she did now was significant.

Den laughed. "Too many late nights in front of their media stations with nothing better to do."

"We're almost there." An Kholi broke in.

"How can we be sure that Su Mali came here to hide one of the Magi?" Despite numerous conversations on the subject, Den Gau was still unconvinced.

"She spent several days here. According to the galacticnet, it takes six days to get a permit to descend to the planet's surface. She didn't spend all that time here just because she had a thing about myriahedrons."

The ship gently docked itself and An Kholi went through the shutdown procedures. If they were to be here for a week or more, she had no intention of wasting fuel by keeping all the ship's systems running.

Carrying small travel bags, they left the Adastra and followed the signs to Immigration. This rankled with all three of them. Nowhere else in the galaxy did you need to prove who you were before you were allowed to land on a planet. "It's because, technically at least, New Earth isn't a planet, it's a space ship." The galacticnet had informed them. "However," it had added "Earthlings are lovers of bureaucracy and if they hadn't been able to use that excuse they would have come up with something else." An Kholi was surprised that the Galactic Council In Exile (GCIE) hadn't chosen to base itself on New Earth. Srumphrey *(see The Magi, Genghis Kant)* would have felt right at home.

They arrived in the immigration hall. In the far distance they could see a line of ten booths, each housing a uniformed Earthling. Above nine of the booths hung signs that said "Citizens of Earth only." Above the tenth hung a sign proclaiming "Citizens of all other planets". Taped lanes zig-zagged away from the nine positions where the Earth citizens could queue. The lanes were empty. Similar taped lanes retreated from the tenth position but here the lanes were occupied by hundreds of members of different species, all waiting in line for their turn to have their travel documents examined.

Den let out a sigh of resignation and was about to head for the back of the queue when An Kholi stopped him. "Let's try something else first."

She turned and walked towards a uniformed official who was propping up a wall with her bulky body.

"Good day." An Kholi said with her brightest smile. The official scowled back; clearly she wasn't going to be fooled by good manners. "My colleagues and I are Guild bounty hunters and we're here on official business." She produced her Guild ID to back up her claim. "I wonder, is there another way onto your planet that avoids all the queuing?"

The official examined An Kholi's ID with all the care she would give to examining a donut, in other words a great deal of care.

Satisfied, she looked up. "Wait here." She commanded before walking down the side of the taped off lanes to consult one of the officials in the booths.

A human walked past the small group and entered the lanes that would take her to the booths reserved for the citizens of Earth. She carefully negotiated the taped lanes, her suitcase following obediently behind. When she reached a yellow line she stopped. Nine sets of eyes examined her from behind the safety of their armoured glass shields, before returning to whatever important tasks they had been engaged in before the human had arrived.

The human was clearly used to this, as she stood uncomplainingly behind the impenetrable barrier of a layer of coloured pigment. Time ticked away and more humans joined her. Clearly a passenger ship had just docked. For every five or six new arrivals one of the officials would leave his or her booth and disappear through a door marked 'Staff Only'. When the queue had grown to around fifty humans the last remaining uniformed official, positioned in the booth furthest from the front of the queue, stood up behind his armoured glass protection and shouted over the top. "Next".

The female at the front of the line walked forward and spent the next five minutes rummaging in her bag and patting all her pockets to find her travel documents, while the lengthening queue behind the yellow line shuffled its feet and muttered.

Officer Donut returned to An Kholi and pointed towards the line for non-citizens of Earth. "Join the queue please, Madam." Was all she said, before returning to her important work of wall propping. An Kholi knew she was defeated. This sort of bureaucracy always has the upper hand and any further attempt to subvert it could only end up with her in a booth with another uniformed official pulling on a latex glove.

Without a word she led Gala and Den across to the queue, which was now several beings longer.

* * *

Warrior, aka Tiny Blur, took out his earpiece and leant back in his chair, rubbing at his eyes and temples. The morning election conference with the Fell had gone well. All was set for polling day. His party, The New Peoples' Party, were standing at 52% in the polls and now his team of software engineers were toiling away to make sure that no matter what button the voters pushed the result would conform to that prediction. No one would be able to accuse him of rigging the election. After all, if he had rigged it he would have given himself more than 52% of the popular vote, wouldn't he? For once the polling organisations were proving to be invaluable, which wasn't always the case.

In the end, it hadn't been difficult to blacken the name of his nearest rivals, the Etonories. He had resurrected a demon from their past: Snatcher! She had been dead for several centuries but her memory cast a long shadow. Just the whisper of her name was enough to make normally rational beings start foaming at the mouth and tearing at their hair, assuming that they were a species that had hair in the first place. Or were capable of foaming at the mouth for that matter.

So, in just a few days he would hold the reins of power. The Fell believed it would be they who called the shots, but of course they didn't know that they had placed the reins in the hands of one of their own; one so devious that he made a corkscrew look as though it could be used for drawing straight lines.

He would go through the motions, of course. The Fell would hold their virtual meeting every week and decide what orders to give their new government. But between their agreement and his implementation there would be some subtle changes. It was something he was adept at, having done similar things before as President of Earth. To get elected he had promised that there would be no increase in direct taxation. How he had laughed at that one. He had simply found a whole raft of things to which he could apply indirect taxation.

Of course what he told the voters didn't matter anymore. With complete control of the electoral system he would never be required to leave government, ever again. When it became time to retire he would choose his successor and then work with them to make sure they would get elected, at the same time as making sure that they became a full member of the Fell. Unless it was Gridiron Broon, of course. He could go fuck himself.

Automatically his hand stretched out to his communications console, intending to contact his old pal George Bush the 125th. Old habits die hard; George was one of the Magi and seven of them were still missing. He had to assume that George was one of the seven.

How they had laughed over that one. Brilliant! They had insisted that the election in their sector of the galaxy for a place on the Galactic Council had used proportional representation. Of course George had been few people's first choice candidate, but he had been a second and third choice for people who couldn't bring themselves to vote for THEM (whoever their personal THEM might be), so George had sneaked in when none of the other candidates had achieved an overall majority after the first count and the second and third preference votes had come into play.

Tiny patted himself on the back over that one. He had made a killing with the bookmakers as well as seeing his old pal go to Polaris Beta, the seat of the Galactic Council.

Which brought him to his current conundrum. Many people still regarded the Galactic Council as the legitimate government and the GCIE as the caretakers until the Magi could be found and restored to their rightful place. So how was he to make sure that his new government was seen as legitimate?

There was a quiet ping from the array of viewing screens, arranged above the front of his aircraft carrier sized desk. He selected the one that had announced the incoming call and saw the face of his Communications Director, Alison Fakescottsman. "Hi, Alison. What can I do for you?" Tiny Blur had found it useful to make Alison think he was calling the shots. It was a typical ruse he used when manipulating people.

"Just thought you would like to know, An Kholi and her crew have just docked at the inter-stellar space port."

"What do they want here?"

"No idea, but they said they were on official Guild business. If I were a gambling man I'd say they were here to find another of the Magi."

"Do you think that's likely?"

"If they're not then I'll eat my kilt."

Tiny Blur almost blurted out that Fakescottsman didn't have a kilt, but thought better of it. Besides, he'd made that promise before and not stuck by it.

"OK, I'll give some thought to what we do, if anything. While you're here, I've been giving some thought to the Galactic Council In Exile. What do we do about them?"

"We eliminate them, of course."

"Sounds a bit drastic."

"Remember what we always used to say in the old days, when election time came around and we had to pretend we were something we weren't if we wanted to have any chance of being elected. At the end of the day it's all about the greater good. In this case the greater good is that the GCIE isn't around to get in our way."

"I suppose you're right." Tiny Blur conceded, grudgingly. "But in that case, how do we find them? No one knows where they are."

"The Guild of Bounty Hunters do. Our sources there tell me that every time An Kholi finds one of the Magi, she takes it to the GCIE. If she finds another one, we simply let her lead us to them."

"So if she's here, on New Earth, and she's looking for one of the Magi, it would be in our best interests to help her find him...her... er, it."

"It probably would be. We would need to make sure she didn't suspect. I doubt she's in favour of our new government being formed."

"So how do we follow her?"

"Her ship is docked at the inter-stellar space port. We send someone along to plant a tracker on it. Seemples."

"OK. Well we can find out where Su Mali landed when she visited 'down there'." Tiny Blur used the expression that was always used by the inhabitants of New Earth to refer to their former planetary home. "Then we can guide her to it. You take care of the tracker on her ship and then make arrangements for her planet pass to be granted quickly."

"I'm not sure that would be such a good idea. She might suspect something was up if she wasn't treated like everyone else."

"Fine, scratch that then, make sure she gets messed around as much as an inefficient bureaucracy can arrange."

"No problem. I'll let the health service take care of it. They're the most inefficient part of the planetary government."

Tiny Blur grimaced. He wouldn't wish that on his worst enemy. Of course the nurses were all angels who weren't paid enough and the doctors did a marvellous work. That went without saying, despite the fact that everyone kept saying it, but the administrators and managers? They were a different kettle of fish.

* * *

To apply for their permit to travel down to the planet's surface took them half a day. That was twenty minutes to actually complete the application and five hours to travel to the Planet Management offices and queue to complete the application. Queuing was an art form on New Earth, An Kholi observed. An official who overheard her told her not to be so silly. It was far more serious than that. An Kohli noted that many of the humans carried portable entertainment systems to help them pass the time spent queuing.

The completion of the application was something that could have been done over the galacticnet, but for some reason it had to be completed there, in the offices of the Planet Management Department. No one could tell them why, only that they had to do it if they ever wanted to set foot on the planet's surface. In the box where it asked 'purpose of visit' An Kholi had entered 'I don't know' and this seemed to be acceptable.

For some reason they were then sent to the health department where they completed more forms, each of which seemed to require them to complete yet another form. When An Kholi asked if this was normal, again no one knew. The officials they dealt with had simply been told to give them the forms to fill in. Someone would contact them within the next six months, but no one said why.

An Kholi was somewhat suspicious about the diversion to the health department. No one else in the queue had been sent there, and there were several species from off-planet in the queue, so that wasn't the reason. However, she kept her thoughts to herself as they took the monorail journey back to their hotel. It was an unassuming place which provided rooms for people on a tight budget. An Kholi could afford better, but she always looked for bargains and the Spaceport Travel Inn was the cheapest that New Earth had to offer.

"So what now?" Den had asked.

"Now we wait, apparently." An Kholi replied.

Gala excused herself from the waiting and returned to the Adastra to carry out some routine maintenance tasks. It was nothing that couldn't be done at the next scheduled service, but sitting around in enforced idleness was something she couldn't do. Den, on the other hand, thought all his birthdays had come at once. He excused himself to return to his room with a bottle of something that An Kholi thought might be paint stripper, a pile of dubious looking entertainment discs and a happy smile on his face.

An Kholi decided to take a guided tour of the artificial planet.

It started with an audio-visual presentation about how New Earth had been constructed. Despite looking like a large solid mass it was in fact hollow, the outer skin being built around two giant crosses set at right angles to each other. Where the six arms of the two crosses intersected was the heart of the construction, its power plant was a giant nuclear reactor.

Most of the rest of the galaxy had stopped using nuclear power several centuries earlier. They preferred much cleaner and safer cold fusion or natural sources such as that produced by the light of their closest star, but for New Earth only nuclear would do. An Kholi thought that if the power plant ever failed they would probably see the explosion several galaxies away.

The outer surface of the planet was made up of solar panels that harnessed the sun's energy, but solely for the purpose of growing crops. Wherever two angles of the myriahedron met there was a globe shaped structure where crops were grown. It was the same crop in every globe, a type of kelp. The original plant had only grown in the salt waters of the planet below, but this genetically modified version was able to be grown using hydroponic systems. Despite the giant icebergs that supplied water, much of it was recycled from the urine of the population of the artificial planet, something that the majority of the population didn't realise, the commentary told her. An Kholi could understand why the fact wasn't highly publicised.

Once harvested the kelp was processed into a range of foodstuffs which contained all the nutrients that humans needed. The majority was shipped down to the planet, while fresh meat, fish and eggs were sent back on the return journey, along with manufactured goods. An Kholi was surprised by that, thinking that agriculture was no longer viable on the planet's surface, but it appeared that in the newly created savannahs there was plenty of scope for raising animals. It was vegetables they could no longer grow in any quantity because of a lack of water.

On completion of the presentation they were introduced to their guide who herded them onto a monorail which whizzed them across an interior arc of the myriahedron to one of the growing globes. It had clearly been set up as a tourist centre because the area was skirted with viewing stations large enough to accommodate parties of the size that An Kholi was in.

The atmosphere was steamy and smelt strongly of something An Kholi couldn't quite put her finger on and if she knew what it was, wouldn't want to, she thought. Here the tour guide explained the growing cycle of the kelp, the methods used to keep it supplied with water and the methods used to harvest it. One of the most significant by-products of the kelp was oxygen, which kept the occupants of New Earth alive without the need to transport air from the planet below. Carbon dioxide scrubbers were also used to supplement the natural efforts of the kelp.

Above their heads, cages holding workers were suspended from cables as they pruned the kelp to keep the main shoots growing strongly. Others were harvesting the kelp, cutting it off its supporting frames and dropping it into even larger cages suspended below the work cages.

"Come, come." The tour guide chivvied them, as tour guides across the galaxy are prone to do. "We go to see where the kelp is processed."

Between each globe ran a connecting tunnel, which provided a perfect linear production line for converting massive quantities of kelp into edible, or so An Kholi was told, substances. To fool the eater into thinking that the kelp was actually something else it was shaped and coloured into whatever it was supposed to imitate. Off white spheres were something called potatoes, red spheres simulated tomatoes, flat green leaves were called cabbage or lettuce. "The only food we don't simulate is broccoli." The tour guide announced. "No one likes broccoli." This brought a knowing laugh from the humans on the tour and looks of puzzlement from everyone else.

From the production line, the tour continued through a gift shop to another of the connecting tubes. This one was lined with cafes and restaurants where the party stopped for lunch. An Kholi assumed she was eating kelp, it certainly didn't taste like anything she had ever eaten before. She left most of it on her plate.

"Come, come," the tour guide chivvied once again, using heavily accented Common Tongue to communicate, even though she had allowed them more time for lunch than was really needed. "Now we visit carpet factory and jewellery shop. Later we go to leather goods outlet."

An Kholi had no use for a new carpet, hardly ever wore jewellery and though she liked leather she didn't fancy paying Earth prices for more. She excused herself and caught a taxi back to her hotel.

She was amazed to find that the taxi had a real, live, driver, something she hadn't seen before. Everywhere else in the Galaxy that she had ever been, the taxis were fully automated. On some planets they were fitted with a droid, who wasn't really needed, but that was more of a marketing ploy. As the taxi pulled up at a red light to let traffic across an intersecting tube she made the rookie mistake of engaging him in conversation.

"You don't see taxi drivers very much these days, not where I come from." It was an innocuous sort of comment but the lights had hardly changed to green before she regretted making it.

"Bloody droids getting in everywhere these days, taking people's jobs. And they're crap drivers. I've been driving this cab man and boy for forty years and never had an accident, but I hear there's people dying in their millions in taxi's driven by droids." An Kholi was about to interject to correct him on this gross factual error when he was off again. "I blame all this bloody artificial intelligence. You know, I can finish the crossword in the Daily Scum in ten minutes, but it would take artificial intelligence two days to do it? Eh? Eh? Did you know that, Eh?"

An Kholi started to bless the existence of artificial intelligence for making sure she didn't have to deal with a lack of intelligence such as this more frequently. When the taxi got back to her hotel she fled with the driver's voice ringing in her ears. "Oy where's my tip?"

What in the galaxy's name was a tip?

Glossary

Common Tongue - A language that evolved gradually as the various species of the galaxy started to encounter each other and discovered that communication worked better if both parties understood each other. The most extreme example of what happens when both sides fail to communicate was when the Andromeda system went to war with the Antaries system after an Antarian said "Good morning, that's a nice hat" but was interpreted by the Andromedan as having said "Your mother is a twenty toed agravarg who has sex with donkeys". 95% of all known species now use the common tongue to communicate. The remaining 5% don't have the necessary vocal equipment to actually speak the language but are able to use universal translation programmes to interpret, though occasional failures resulting from incorrect use of context still leads to misunderstandings similar to the one described above (users of Moogle Translate will be familiar with this problem). Planet Earth is one of the few in the galaxy where different languages are spoken in different parts of the planet and Common Tongue has been used to overcome this shortcoming with varying degrees of success. The people of some countries, such as The Netherlands and Denmark, are so fluent that they often use Common Tongue in preference to their own languages. The French are fluent but refuse to speak it and the British rarely get past "Two pints of beer and a packet of crisps please, Tonto".

Galacticnet - A vast network of data connections that means that, for a price, just about any source of information can be connected to any other source of information and can be accessed by anyone with the means to do so, legally or illegally, across the galaxy. Broadband speeds may be limited on planet Earth, please consult your broadband supplier if you can get them to answer the phone.

It can also be used as a form of communication, including use as a virtual meeting room. Popular amongst teenagers as a medium for socialising as, let's face it, anything is better than actually talking to your mates.

No one owns the galacticnet, though several major corporations own individual components of it which gives them the right, they feel, to spy on your e-mails. Warning: 99.9% of all information stored on the galacticnet is inaccurate and I know that because I found that statistic on the galacticnet.

Gau - A shape shifting species from the Flage star system. They have a telepathic bond with each other which means they can sense the presence of another Gau in the vicinity and they can identify each other by sight.

Myriahedron - A polyhedron with 10,000 or more faces. The resulting angles and planes are so slight that from a distance the shape appears spherical

Wormholes - Physicists had long theorised that wormholes in space could be used as short cuts that would provide travel in excess of the speed of light without all that dangerous $e=mc^2$ business. It is akin to running round the outside of your house to get from the front door to the back, or taking a leisurely walk along the hall to get to the same place. However, turning theory into practice was something of a challenge.

It was solved one day when a research assistant accidentally dropped his pencil and when he bent over to pick it up found himself in the changing rooms of a women's basketball team several light years from his lab. Hardly had the screams started when he dropped his pencil again and when he picked it up he found he was back once more in his lab. At least that was the defence he relied on in court.

After that it was only a matter of reverse engineering the moves the lab assistant had made to be able to find one's way back to the changing rooms… sorry, to solve the riddle of travelling through worm holes. Wormholes are also used to achieve speedy communication through space and are the foundations on which the galacticnet was built.

Space elevator - See the author's note at the end of the book for a genuine explanation of this concept.

2 - Intruder

Den climbed out of his bed and rubbed at his eyes. His head throbbed and he looked accusingly at the bottle that lay on its side on the floor. An Kholi had been wrong, it wasn't paint stripper, but after what it had done to him Den suspected that it may have been something far worse.

He croaked a command for the curtains to open. He had to squeeze his eyes shut against the sudden glare, but when he opened them he was surprised to see a cityscape outside his window. He recoiled from the view and started to panic as his brain told him New Earth was about to crash into old Earth, but then a more rational part of his brain told him there must be another explanation. It took him a moment to work out what it was, and then he pointed the remote control at the room's viewing screen and brought up the menu.

Clicking on the Window Settings option he accessed the list of views that he could select for his window. The setting he was on was called Paris Cityscape, which he should have worked out for himself based on the huge phallic tower that formed the most prominent landmark. A toggle to the side told him he could choose between day or night views.

He scrolled down and found a view titled Tropical Beach and selected it. The view of Paris melted away to be replaced by one of a long arc of silver sand. To one side palm trees swayed gently in the breeze while on the other an azure sea lapped at the shore. In the mid distance a man and a woman walked, hand in hand. Despite their obvious movement they never actually got any closer to the foreground of the scene. It was still too bright. Den returned to the menu and scrolled down, looking for something a little more hangover friendly.

At the bottom of the options he found Torquay Hotel Room. Selecting it he found himself unexpectedly looking at herds of wildebeest sweeping majestically across the plains.* He blinked, decided his hangover was making him hallucinate and went back to the view of Paris, though he used the toggle to switch it to a night time view to protect his weakened retinas.

There was a knock at the door. He ignored it. It was too early for visitors, he decided. The knock became a banging and rather than force his poor head to suffer any more he went and answered the summons.

"We've been called back to the Planet Management offices. Apparently the health department want to interview us. Is there anything I should know before we get there? Any little.... problem you haven't told us about?"

"What are you implying?" Even in his hungover state, Den was able to take umbrage at this slight.

"Nothing. Nothing at all. Anyway, Gala and I are ready to go. We'll meet you in the foyer in five."

Den slammed the door and staggered towards the bathroom, hoping that a shower might save his life.

* *Fawlty Towers; Series 2, Episode 1. Writers: John Cleese and Connie Booth.*

* * *

An Kholi finally put an end to the nonsense from the health department when she challenged the young doctor to describe what it was about Den Gau's physiology that allowed him to change shape. She had no idea, but neither did the doctor. With no one qualified to examine them, there was no way they would allow themselves to be examined. So the officials had to reluctantly allow them to leave, but only after they had signed a myriad of waiver documents.

"We're just being messed around here." She told Gala and Den. "Someone wants to delay our departure for down there and they're using spurious health checks as an excuse." She stalked back towards the monorail station, her anger evident in every stride and the thump of her elegantly booted feet onto the synthetic rubber surface of the tube along which they were walking.

"I don't know if it's related, but I think someone has been aboard the Adastra, as well." Gala informed them.

An Kholi pulled up short, almost causing Den to collide with her. "Are you sure?" They started walking again as they discussed the possibility of an intrusion.

"Not one hundred percent, but when we leave the ships unattended for any period of time I always place a few security tell tales of my own. Alarm systems and intruder detectors are fine but they can be overcome…."

"Yes I know." An Kholi snapped impatiently. "So what makes you think someone has been on board?"

"One of my beautiful blond hairs stuck across the exit door of the airlock with a little bit of spit. It wasn't there anymore. Then I checked the security camera images and a section was blacked out. Not wiped. That would be a dead giveaway, but subjected to some sort of interference. It could be natural, stellar radiation or something like that, but I don't think so."

"Were there any signs of a search? Anything missing?"

"No. If there was then they were the tidiest thieves in history."

"In that case the only other reason for sneaking on board would be to plant something, a bug or a tracker. Maybe both. But if it's a tracker it's not so they can follow us down to the planet. Foreign ships and shuttles aren't allowed down there. We have to use one of the official transfer craft."

"Which means they want to follow us when we leave." Den joined the dots.

"Precisely. I think whoever planted the tracker wants to find out where I take the Magi when we've found them. Well done Gala."

"But you've always used the Pradua to deliver the Magi eggs."

"I know that, Den, and you know that, but whoever planted the tracker doesn't know that."

"That's assuming it is a tracker." Gala reminded her that they didn't as yet have conclusive proof that a tracker had been planted.

"We'll know as soon as we've been over the ship with a fine tooth comb."

"Best not to attract attention. I'll do it. I went on board yesterday, so if I do the same again today it won't look unusual." Gala volunteered.

"I thought there was a fail-safe to prevent the ship being entered illegally." Den reminded them.

"I didn't arm it. If it went off it would take half of New Earth with it and perhaps us as well."

"OK. Thanks Gala. If you find anything, don't remove it, just come back and tell us. I think we should also assume that our rooms are bugged." Den looked a little alarmed at the thought. "Just be careful what you say. If we want to discuss anything important we go and find a nice noisy bar somewhere."

* * *

Once Gala had confirmed the presence of a tracker aboard the Adastra, An Kholi convened a meeting at the noisiest bar she could find. Travelling independently they had criss-crossed the network of broad tunnels that made up the framework of New Earth, getting in and out of taxis, going into bars and hotels through one door and immediately leaving through another, doubling back, stopping suddenly to look in shop windows and generally making it difficult to follow them.

It made little difference, they knew. There were security cameras everywhere and anyone who had access to their images would be able to find them whenever they wished. But at least they had tried. Their main protection against eavesdroppers was the noise in the bar. It was deafening.

It was clearly a young person's hangout. An Kholi, Gala and Den stood out like a sore thumb. Blue predominated in the current young person's styles. Blue hair, blue eye shadow, blue lipstick and nail varnish. They wore baggy blue jumpers or shirts and, of course, blue skirts. The females were dressed in a similar style.

A band was playing loud and very bad music to which none of the youngsters were listening. They were either busy with their communicators and ignoring their companions, or they were shouting at each other. Anywhere else this shouting would be seen as a precursor to violence. Here it was just conversation.

"Not only did I find the tracker, but I also found bugs on the command deck, the lounge and in the shuttle. There was also a spy camera in the shower in my room, but not in anyone else's."

An Kholi saw Den give a guilty start at that last revelation, but she decided not to act upon her instinct. That would be a private conversation between her and Den, to be saved for another day.

"So", said Den, after he had recovered his composure, "The question is, who planted them?"

"It has to be the Fell, or at least one of them." An Kholi chewed on the inside of her cheek as she thought the matter through. "Anyone know who the local Fell member is?"

Den pulled out his communicator and tapped something into it. The response came back quickly. "A contact of mine suggests it's someone who uses the alias 'Warrior'. Not much is known about him or her, as far as my contact is aware. He's thought to be a current or former politician, and an important one, but she doesn't have any more than that." An Kholi decided not to ask what the relationship was between Den and his contact. There are some things about which it is best not to ask.

"Shouldn't be too difficult to track down." Gala shouted across the tiny distance between their heads."

"You have to be kidding." Den shouted back. "This is Sector One. It's the most highly politicised sector of the galaxy. To top that, Earth, or rather New Earth, is the most highly politicised planet. Everyone seems to be involved in politics in some way. They spend months, even years, talking about elections, and then after the elections they talk about how stupid the voters were to elect whoever they elected and why it all went so badly wrong for the parties that didn't get elected. The media in this sector can't think of anything better to do, so they fill the galacticnet with endless speculation and when they get it all wrong they fill even more of the galacticnet by analysing why they got it so wrong, without ever admitting they did get it wrong, of course. It's why so few other species bother to visit this sector. It would drive any normal species insane."

"So what you're saying is that there are plenty of candidates for the person we believe to be Warrior?" An Kholi summarised.

"Isn't that what I just said?"

Actually it wasn't, but again An Kholi let it slide. Shouting made argument difficult.

"But we still have to try to work out if the Fell…"

At that point the band finished its song and the only sound that could be heard was the word 'Fell' echoing around the room. An Kholi quickly recovered. "And then he fell as well." She shouted. She looked around to see if anyone was paying attention and was relieved to see that the teenagers were all doing what they had previously been doing, which was mainly ignoring each other, as well as ignoring the three 'oldies' in the corner booth.

Gala had been working on her communicator while An Kholi and Den had been talking, or rather, shouting.

"I've found a list of nearly a million current and former politicians active in the politics of Sector One." She announced dismally. At that the band started up a new song, indistinguishable from the previous one, so they had to resume shouting at each other.

Den punched a drinks order into the small terminal set into the top of their table and a few moments later a waitress appeared carrying a tray of drinks. She placed one in front of each of them as they raised a finger to indicate which was theirs. Den was struck by a thought.

Placing a gently restraining hand on the waitress's arm he shouted at her.

"If you were taking a guess at which politician was a member of the Fell, which one would you choose?"

The waitress paused for a moment, deep in thought.

"Either Tiny Blur or George Bush the 125th." She answered at last.

"Why them?" Den followed up.

"Look them up." The waitress hollered. Den paid the drinks bill, adding a little extra so the waitress could buy herself a drink of her own. He didn't know that, using local terminology, he was tipping her.

Gala was already tapping furiously at her communicator. Den shouted a question at her and then started tapping at his own communicator. Gala got her answer first and passed her communicator to An Kholi to read what she had found. It was a Frickingpedia entry for Tiny Blur. As she read An Kholi drew the conclusion that anywhere else in the galaxy Tiny Blur, formerly the President of Earth, would now be doing serious prison time, but here on New Earth there were people who still took him seriously as a politician. He had even been put in charge of organising the election of the new galactic government. That revelation stopped An Kholi in her tracks.

The one question that no one knew the answer to, anywhere in the galaxy, was by what authority were these elections being organised? But of course, if you were the Fell, you didn't need any authority. You just imposed your will and you found a useful fool to do the imposing on your behalf. But what if the useful fool was also…. No, it couldn't be true, could it?

An Kholi passed the communicator back to Gala and took the one that Den was offering her. George Bush the 125th she was already familiar with. Anyone who knew anything about the Magi knew the name, as Bush was one of the nine. The wisest beings in the galaxy, or so it was assumed, though Bush was the exception that proved the rule. Well, that rule had certainly been tested with his election, but of course, under the rules of the galaxy, his appointment had to be accepted.

But as she read through Bush's biography she realised something of which she was previously unaware. Bush and Blur had been close buddies. Blur had been Bush's campaign manager when he was elected to the Magi. An idea began to form in her mind. No; it was preposterous, but then again?

"I'll accept Blur as a candidate." An Kholi shouted at her companions. "But Bush is Magi and he's one of the seven that are still missing." She hadn't totally discounted the possibility that Bush was both a member of the Fell and a member of the Magi, but with him missing and his intelligence, for want of a better word, stored in a memory egg, he had to be dismissed for practical purposes.

"So how do we prove it?" Gala asked the question that they were all thinking.

Author's note: 2020 update. This book was written before the 2016 Presidential Election in the USA. Had I been writing it now, the character of George Bush the 125th would have been given a different name.

3 - Missing Person

An Kholi, Gala, and Den took on the roles of typical tourists. In truth there was little else for them to do until their permit to go down to the planet was granted, but it would also give them the opportunity to try to see if they were being followed. If they were then it might offer the opportunity for them to turn the tables, either following the follower or even making a grab for them and indulging in a little bit of light interrogation.

Other than the guided tour, the bars, restaurants, and shops, there was very little for tourists to do on New Earth. As an artificial planet, it had no scenery, no historic sites, and no places of interest that they could visit. The Earthlings who had travelled up from the old planet seemed delighted to traipse around the shops and bars, but none of the three of them quite saw the attraction.

An Kholi and Gala, located a spa that accepted day visitors and spent time in its gym and swimming pool, before submitting to the awesome array of massages and treatments that might, but probably didn't, improve the way they looked. The treatments were designed for use on humans and their off-planet physiologies weren't really compatible with the ingredients used. However, it made them feel good to be pampered.

Den found a bar where some Sutrans had established a nice little business for themselves adopting the visual features of well-known Earth celebrities from both the present and the past. He found a beer he liked from the many hundreds that were on offer, and flicked through the electronic catalogue, watching snippets from film and TV until he found someone he liked. The trouble was, they were all human and even the most attractive couldn't really hold a candle to an Aloisan or a Sabik female. Even the Towians were better looking. Still, beggars couldn't choosers, he decided pragmatically.

It was late at night when an attractive young woman sat down beside him and offered to buy him a drink. Den was immediately on his guard. In his experience the young women who sat down beside him asked him to buy them a drink, not the other way round and then only as a precursor to more serious business. However, she was pretty…

The woman wasn't Sutran. As a species of Gau he would have felt her brain patterns if she had been. That made her more interesting for him. They exchange some small talk, the ritual moves of early courtship, at least that is what Den believed them to be, but she clearly had a different agenda. She introduced herself as Gaga Sullivan, an employee of New Earth Consolidated Kelp (a subsidiary of Gargantua Enterprises), or NECK for short.

"Someone told me you were a Gau." Gaga carefully lifted Den's hand from her knee, where it seemed to have fallen of its own accord.

"That's true." Den artfully draped his hand across the back of the bench seat they were occupying, so that it was millimetres (fractions of a sim in the galactic measurement system) from her neck and shoulders.

"Is it true that Gau can change their appearance?"

"More than just our appearance. I can look like anyone that you want me to be, within certain physical limits."

"Could you look human?"

"The only thing that could be easier would be for me to look like a Gau." Den chuckled at his own joke. "Would you prefer me to look like someone else? A celebrity perhaps? Is that what does it for you?"

The woman moved away, half turning so that she was both facing him and also out of easy reach. "No, nothing like that. Look, how would you like to earn some money? Easy money."

Part of Den's brain told him to run away. Very far away. The other part, however, was already in Jarrods spending the money she was offering. The Jarrods side of Den's brain won.

"Well, how can I refuse a pretty girl in distress." Den's leer was enough to put a Sutran off her lunch, but the woman ignored it.

"My boyfriend has gone missing. That is, he's on New Earth somewhere, but I don't know where. You can change yourself to look like anyone, so you can get into places where others couldn't."

"What sort of places?"

"Police stations, the prison, the Space Force HQ. Those sorts of places."

Den had sobered up as she spoke, the thought of danger acting on him better than an ice cold shower. "What makes you think your boyfriend might be in one of those places."

"Well, he's not been very discrete in talking about the Fell. He thinks the Fell are behind this election that's coming up and he's been trying to organise a demonstration to get people to boycott it. It might have got him arrested."

"On what charges? I thought New Earth, and old Earth for that matter, is a democracy where free speech was not only allowed, but encouraged."

"Before the Fell, maybe. Even now, if the cause for which you are speaking doesn't upset the Fell you'll be allowed to get on with it, but he was directly attacking the Fell. Only verbally, you understand. Anyway, he's gone missing and the protest isn't going ahead. I don't think that's a coincidence."

"So why not just go to the Police?"

"Because the Police are probably behind him disappearing. Either them or the Space Force. They were set up shortly after the Fell came to power. Nice smart uniforms and big guns. No one really knows who they're answerable to, though they're paid by the government; That's our government on Earth. As for the Police, these days it's cheaper to let yourself be robbed than to pay the police to investigate a crime."

"You have to pay the police?"

"Not officially, of course, but if you turn up at a police station without any cash you can expect a long wait to fill in a form and then probably nothing will happen."

"A lot has changed since the last time I was here." Den commented enigmatically. Some basic instinct set off alarms in his head. Here he was, sat in the bar of what amounted to a bordello, when a pretty girl who has no business in such a place except, perhaps, monkey business, comes up to him seeking a favour. This wasn't normal. When something abnormal occurs it is best to tread with caution. It was a lesson he had learnt the hard way.

"You seem a little bit out of place in here, so how did you find me?" Den hoped the question sounded innocuous.

"By accident really. I was sitting in a café across the way when you came in here." She looked at her watch. "That was hours ago. Anyway, you caught my eye because you clearly aren't from around here. Anyway, you also caught the eye of two guys sitting at the next table. One wondered what species you might be and the other knew you were a Gau, so he told him all about what Gau can do. It set me to thinking that you might be able to help. I've been sitting across there ever since trying to pluck up the courage to come in here and speak to you. I've drunk so many cups of coffee that I probably won't sleep for a week. Not that I've had much sleep since Beckham went missing, of course."

"Who's Beckham?"

"My boyfriend. Sorry, I forgot to tell you his name. It's Beckham United. That's not his fault, his father was a big football fan."

Den had heard of football. The game had even made its way further afield in the galaxy, with leagues springing up in a number of star systems, especially in Sector One. The revelation of the name allayed his fears a little. If you were going to invent a name for someone, then that wouldn't be the one you would invent.

"Do you have a photo of him?"

"Of course." The woman took out her communicator and searched its memory. Finding what she wanted she flicked it across to Den's communicator. He saw a good looking, by Earth standards, young man of around twenty five, with a bright smile and an open, honest looking face. He and Gaga would have looked good in wedding photos.

"Where did you last see him?"

"Do you know Kelp Bed 140 East, 60 North?"

"Can't say I do." Den quickly worked out that the numbers related to some sort of longitude and latitude system. He had seen numbers such as those displayed at the entrances to the tubes that connected the kelp globes, obviously an aid to navigation in a place where most locations looked very similar. In recreational areas, such as the one he was now in, the tubes also had names, but in the industrial areas he guessed that names wouldn't be as much use.

"Well, that's where we both worked. He was supposed to meet me in the Eastwards exit, after work. He didn't show up. That was two days ago."

"He worked for NECK as well?"

"Yes. Practically everyone up here works for NECK, except for the administrators and the police. Oh, and the Space Force of course."

"Look, I don't know if I'm going to be much help to you. I'm only expecting to be here for three more days, then we should get our permits to go down there. When we come back up we'll be leaving New Earth straight away."

"Who is 'we'?"

"I'm here with two friends. We're…" Den searched for words which describe their presence without giving away their mission. "we're looking for someone."

"Another missing person?"

"You could say that, though not in the way your friend, er, Beckham, is missing."

"You could do a lot in three days." The woman cajoled.

He could do a lot, Den admitted to himself. He could party for three days solid. He could have fun, he could get drunk, he could get laid. Or he could help this attractive young woman.

Gaga gave Den her most appealing smile.

Dammit. Why did she have to do that?

* * *

Den wasn't a sophisticated sort of person. He would be the first to admit that. His school teachers had said that he was not one of the galaxy's great thinkers, and that had been from the teacher that had liked him the most. He tended to think in straight lines, which was all you needed when you spent your life running away. Your primary thought was 'how the hell do I get out of here?' and the answer to that was generally a straight line between wherever you were and the nearest exit.

So it was that Den decided that the best place to start looking for a missing person was the police station nearest to where he had last been seen. Cut backs in policing had meant that there were fewer police stations than there had once been. There was also more crime than there had been, but the planetary government denied any connection between the two statistics. So it was that Den was several Earth miles from kelp bed 140 East, 60 North when he walked into the police station. It was an unusual experience for him, to be walking into a place like that without the heavy weight of handcuffs on his wrists.

Behind the armoured glass was the sort of bored looking police officer who was clearly counting the days until retirement. They can be found all over the galaxy and are immediately identifiable by their bulk. Too large to run after criminals, but also too well connected to more senior officers to make it worth the effort needed to get rid of them.

"I'm looking for a missing person and wondered if you might have had any report of him. You know, maybe a victim of a crime, or an accident perhaps." As he spoke he slipped a ten nuk note through the gap under the armoured glass that allowed documents to be passed. Gaga had told him that was the basic entry fee into any sort of dealings with the police.

The note disappeared so fast it was as though it had never existed. Den held up his communicator so that the officer could see the photo. "His name is Beckham United." Den added.

The officer made a show of looking up the name on his computer terminal.

"No one arrested by that name, as far as I can see. No one involved in any accidents, either and no one of that name listed as a victim of crime. Now, let me see; missing persons. No, no one by that name reported missing. Do you want to report him missing?"

"No, thanks. Any unidentified bodies?"

"We don't have any unidentified bodies anymore. Not since the DNA data bank was established. You wouldn't know that of course. Being foreign, like." The final words were said with the sort of down turned mouth that indicated disapproval. Den let it go. He wasn't here to antagonise anyone by accusing them of being speciest.

"We have DNA banks where I come from too. I just hadn't realised that Earth had caught up with the rest of the galaxy."

The police officer folded his arms across his chest, which suggested to Den that he had caused offence anyway. "Yes, Sir. And we're just getting around to inventing a new thing called a wheel, as well, and we're almost finished with a prototype for fire." He laboured the point.

"Sorry, officer. I didn't mean to imply anything." Den lied. "I wonder, could you check your photo archives to see if this chap turns up?" Den fed another ten nuks through the glass partition while smiling sweetly, or what passed for sweetly for him.

The officer grudgingly returned to his computer terminal. "Flick the phot across then."

Den did as he was asked. They waited while the photograph was compared to all those in the police database. A self-satisfied ping announced that the computer had found a match.

"Well, he's on our records. Bit of a political agitator. Nothing serious, just a couple of demo's and some name calling. One arrest for disturbing the police, sorry, I mean peace. Now let me see… Oh yes. He called a police officer a fascist pig. Let off with a caution. But nothing more serious than that. Are you sure you don't want to report him missing?"

"No. I'm sure he'll turn up."

The officer tapped at some keys on his terminal. "Now, Sir, I'll just need a few details about you for our records." But when he looked up he found there was no one standing in front of him and the door to the street was gliding gently shut.

That had been informative, concluded Den when he was outside in the street, or tube as it actually was. Beckham United not only existed but he was also as described by Gaga Sullivan. That didn't mean he, Den, wasn't being set up in some way, but it did mean that if he was then some thought had gone into the matter. If it was a trap then he still couldn't see what the aim of it was.

On the taxi ride to the police station he had checked out the Space Force. According to their own site on the galacticnet they were established to combat terrorism, but there was a lack of information regarding the terrorist threat they were supposed to combat.

According to many other sites on the galacticnet they were a bunch of licensed and uniformed thugs who bashed heads in first and asked questions afterwards, if at all. If they wanted him they would have him by now, Den knew. They were also the most likely people to have lifted Beckham United. The question now was how to establish whether or not they did have him.

Den hailed another taxi and asked the driver to take him to the Space Force HQ for their sector of New Earth. The taxi driver's eyes opened wide with surprise and he made it clear that it was rare for anyone to ask to be taken there.

Den got the taxi to pull up short of his destination and he found a vantage point from which he could observe the entrance without being observed. He quickly morphed into a human shape, making him look remarkably similar to the taxi driver who had just dropped him off, though his Gau clothing style wouldn't stand up to close examination. A man running for a bus wouldn't look twice though, which made the disguise good enough for the time being.

Space Force HQ took up one whole block on a transverse tube between two kelp bed globes. It was remarkable only for the fact that there was a single door half way along and a total lack of windows. Oh, yes, and it had half a dozen armed guards pacing up and down in front of it.

Other than the police officer he had recently talked to, they were the first weapons he had seen anyone carrying since arriving on New Earth. A large sign at the space port had stated quite clearly that all weapons had to be surrendered to the authorities on arrival and that the carrying of weapons was prohibited. Heavy penalties applied for the breaking of these rules. He, Gala and An Kholi had left their weapons on board the Adastra rather than surrender them.

He watched for some time and nothing much happened. The only new revelation was that there was a second access, for vehicles, close to the entrance to the globe where he was standing. A pair of large doors slid apart and an unmarked hovercar drove out, turning away from Den to disappear along the tube.

It was getting late and the amount of beer he had drunk was making him more tired. He decided to call it a day and start again in the morning. Perhaps some sort of inspiration might strike while he slept. He turned and trudged along the tube that provided a route through the kelp beds. He had no idea where he was or where the nearest taxi rank might be. There was no one around he could ask, though through the plexiglass sides of the globe he did catch sight of people tending the kelp. He waved at them but they ignored him.

At last, near the exit from the kelp bed, he found an all-night café where the bored looking waitress used the galacticnet to get him a taxi in exchange for him buying a cup of coffee. Slumping down on the back seat of the taxi, he slept all the way back to the hotel.

Glossary

Hell - Belief in deities has died out on most planets with higher level intelligence, but there is still an almost universal acceptance that evil lurks in the galaxy and its source may be found in a place called Hell. Quite where that is, is something of a mystery, but legend has it that there is a place called Swindon and Hell may be close by.

Jarrods - A department store with branches on Earth and New Earth that operates on the principle that some people will always pay more for the things they want because they have no idea what the real cost should be. Jarrods markets itself on its exclusivity, even though anyone can wander in off the street. If you want to see how stupid rich people can be, make a visit to Jarrods and see how much they charge for a packet of tea.

Sutra - A planet in the Flage system that is purported to be the home of the most beautiful women in the galaxy. Like the Gau they have the ability to shape shift to appeal to the different subjective opinions of what constitutes beauty.

4 - Deception

Den went through his usual morning ritual of waking up, cursing his hangover, wincing at the artificial daylight, coughing, farting, and retching. Then, feeling much better, he showered, dressed, and went in search of An Kholi and Gala, intending to partake of breakfast while he brought them up to date with the previous evening's events.

Answering the knock on her bedroom door it was difficult to make out An Kholi in the darkness. Den strained his eyes trying to pierce the gloom, but even in the dark he could see that something was wrong.

"Can we have some light?" he asked, puzzled as to why An Kholi should be stumbling about in the dark.

"No we can't." An Kholi's voice was muffled, almost distorted.

"You may as well tell him." Gala's voice came from within the room. At least Den assumed it was Gala's voice. It too was muffled. "He's going to find out eventually."

The lights came on and Den almost physically recoiled at what he saw. An Kholi's whole head seemed to have swollen to twice its size. Not only that, but her skin was covered in ugly red blotches. So swollen was she, that it had caused her hair to spring out at odd angles, like purple coloured straw from a broken bale. Although An Kholi's body was covered by some sort of robe it was clear that the rest of her was as swollen as her head.

She stepped aside and allowed Den to enter the bedroom. Sitting on the bed, looking pretty miserable, was Gala. She was equally as swollen.

"Good grief. What in the name of the galaxy happened to the pair of you?"

"We're assuming it's an allergic reaction." An Kholi filled him in on their day at the spa, especially the treatments that had involved a wide range of creams, lotions, and unguents. "We've communicated with them, of course, but they won't accept any liability. They say we should have told them that we weren't human, as though lilac coloured skin is normal on Earth. Anyway, they're sending a dermatologist to take a look at us, though they say it's as a favour, not an admission of liability."

"You poor things. How long are you going to stay swollen up like that?"

"No idea until we see the medic. It could be hours, it might be days or even weeks."

"What if the swelling doesn't go down before our permits arrive?"

"That isn't a problem. They're valid for six Earth months, so we've got plenty of time."

"So, are you planning on hiding yourselves away in your rooms until you're better?"

"That's about all we can do. There's no way I can go out looking like this." One of An Kholi's few faults was her vanity. She was never seen anywhere at less than her best. If she was forced to dress in an old sack she would accessorise it, slap on her make up, and make sure her hair looked good. For her the term 'dressing to kill' wasn't just a cliché.

"I'm with An Kholi on that." Gala added. "I look like a freak and knowing my luck I'd run into an old boyfriend the minute I walked out the door. Or maybe worse. Maybe I'd run into the female for whom he'd left me."

"So, Den, what was your day like? Maybe I shouldn't ask."

"Well, I did have one interesting experience."

"Spare us the details." An Kholi muttered.

"No, I don't mean that sort of experience." Den made allowances for An Kholi's delicate emotional state and didn't take offence at the implied criticism. He brought his two colleagues up to date with the events of the previous evening.

"Did you think that it might be some sort of trap?"

"I did, but the story checks out, as far as it goes. Of course I only have Gaga Sullivan's word for it that this Beckham United is really her boyfriend, but I can't see any motive for approaching me if she was making it all up. If someone wanted to grab me then all they had to do was wait till I left the bar I was in. If they wanted you as well I doubt I was in any sort of state to prevent them following me back here. Beside, this address is on all the forms we've filled in over the last few days. Mind you, right now they would have trouble recognising you. Your own mothers would have trouble recognising you."

"Very funny." Snapped An Kholi. "So, what does this woman think she could do even if you can track her boyfriend down?"

"I don't really know. We know that the police are probably useless. If this is political then they won't want to get involved. But the legal system seems to be working still, so maybe, with a good lawyer, she could force whoever has him to let him go."

"That's if it's a legitimate part of the Earth government that's holding him. If it's criminals working for someone else then they won't exactly trip over themselves to obey a court order. You think it might be Space Force that has him?"

"Seems most likely. No one argues with them and I doubt anyone would do anything if they saw someone being arrested by them. Everyone seems to give them a wide berth if they can."

"And if it was them?"

"The simplest thing would be just to shove Beckham United into a garbage chute and eject him into space. He'll either drift off into the galaxy or get pulled down into Earth's atmosphere and burn up. It doesn't matter which."

"In which case you're wasting your time."

"Maybe. But I thought that looking for him might give us a line into the Fell…"

An Kholi frantically signalled him into silence, pointing at the ceiling mounted lights. Of course. The room may be bugged. Best not to use the F word.

"OK, yes, well it may give us a lead in to some of the things we would like to know."

"So what's your next move?"

It was Den's turn to point at the ceiling lights. "I'll make a few inquiries, see if I can find out anything of interest, but I'm guessing

I'll hit a wall. Unless I can find someone who saw him being snatched, or if I can get inside Space Force HQ, I've got nothing to go on." He changed the subject. "Now, anything I can do for the two of you before I leave?"

"No. We've ordered breakfast from a local take-away. It'll be here soon. We've got access to the galacticnet and the hotel's media systems, so that will do for entertainment. As for the rest, we'll see what the medic has to say."

With that, Den composed his face into a sympathetic look and made his farewells, stifling his desire to make fun of their predicament. The Earthlings had a word for it that didn't exist in Common Tongue: schadenfreude; the delight taken at the misfortune of others.

* * *

First order of the day was for Den to look a little less Gau-like. Physically that wasn't a problem. He could look like almost any male being in the galaxy providing they weren't too big, but he couldn't change his clothes the same way as he could change his body.

There were clothes shops near to the hotel so a quick visit to one of them allowed him to buy the sort of clothes that would let him to blend in. Plain worker's overalls with a pair of boots and a peaked hat with a strange logo on the front. He had seen many of the workers in the kelp beds wearing those sorts of clothes. He also bought a second set of clothes for evening wear, the sort of thing he had seen the men wearing in the Sutran bar the night before. Nothing fancy, but with a hint of 'got dressed in the dark with no wife to advise me'.

If you want to know what's going on, Den had always thought, ask people who gossip for a living. He headed back to the café where, the night before, the waitress had helped him to get a taxi. It was a different waitress on duty now, but no less bored. This was one of the industrialised areas of the space station and there was little business for a café at that time of day. Even Den's company seemed preferable to what she had been doing, which was mainly staring out of the window.

After ordering a cup of coffee and exchanging a few meaningless phrases about the lack of weather, he ventured further. "I saw a Space Force building just along the way. Do you get many of them in here?"

"Yeah. It's regional HQ. Some of them come in, mooch for free coffee and donuts." She said in her broken Common Tongue. "Boss plays hell with me if I give anything, but it's not him that is standing here faced with four of them. I give them coffee free and donuts half price. They happy." She gave Den an odd look and he realised that his human appearance didn't fit with his speaking Common Tongue. He hoped she would assume that he was from another part of New Earth.

"Four at a time. That seems a lot?"

"You know what say: one to read, one to write and two to beat a confession out of a suspect so first two have something to write and read."

Den knew he was supposed to chuckle, so he obliged. Almost on cue a hovercar pulled up outside the café and parked in a 'no parking' zone. Four officers sauntered into the café. There was a dark skinned one with stripes on the sleeve of her uniform, she seemed to be in charge, a slightly less dark skinned one and then two pale skinned ones. They gabbled something at the waitress in a local language and then went over to a table to wait for their order. The waitress looked at Den and rolled her eyes in a 'see what I mean' sort of way and started making coffee.

When Den wanted to get into somewhere he shouldn't really be, he had often used the simple but effective method of bashing someone on the head, stealing their clothes, and adopting their looks. It had worked countless times and it was why the Gau were such useful people to have around. The one thing he couldn't do, though, was speak languages; at least languages other than his own, Common Tongue, and the words necessary to order beer in just about every star system in the galaxy.

Planet Earth was almost unique in the galaxy. It had several hundreds of languages and if you spoke the wrong one in the wrong place, it marked you out as a stranger. Common Tongue was used almost universally across the galaxy, except perhaps in the home, but on Earth they still clung to their old ways. In different parts of the giant space station they spoke different languages and only spoke Common Tongue if they really had to, and then they spoke it badly. Unless, of course, they were Dutch or Scandinavian in which case they spoke it perfectly, which annoyed the hell out of everyone else.

So, with the 'bash them on the head and steal their clothes' option not available to him because of the language barrier, Den had to try something else. He opted for a direct approach. He tried to look casual as he wandered through to the toilets at the back of the café, changed into his Gau clothes and Gau form, then slipped out of the back entrance and came back into the café through the front door. He spoke to the waitress as though he had never seen her before and ordered himself a coffee.

Pulling his communicator from his pocket he brought up the picture of Beckham United and nervously approached the group of four Space Force officers.

"I'm sorry to bother you." He said in Common Tongue. "But I'm trying to track down an old friend. He said he would meet me here, but he hasn't shown up. I don't suppose any of you know him?"

He passed over his communicator. The most senior one made a show of examining the picture and then passed the device around the table. The two pale skinned ones took a brief look at the picture and shook their heads, but the fourth one took a longer look and gave Den a hard, knowing stare. It's not the sort of look that anyone wants to get from an armed official, but especially not from the sort of officials with a reputation for casual violence. The officer was clearly trying to work out why Den was really asking about the person in the picture. "I never see him." He said, finally, before handing the device back to his senior officer. "Sorry, help we cannot." She announced, handing Den back his communicator.

Den thanked them and returned to the counter to finish his coffee as the suspicious Space Force officer drew his friends into a huddle. Glances were cast in his direction as he told his colleagues something.

Den decided it was best if he was no longer there. Quickly he left the café, doubled around the back, changed his clothes and his looks once again and returned to the café from the direction of the toilets, where he resumed his seat and exchanged a few words with the waitress. One of the officers was no longer present, but he re-entered the café a few moments later, shaking his head in a 'no, I can't see him anymore' type of gesture. Den was relieved to see that none of the four were paying him any attention.

The four officers finished their coffee and donuts then left the café, but Den noticed that they didn't return to their vehicle. Instead they split up and headed in opposite directions along the broad tube. No doubt looking for a Gau, he decided.

"So who is bloke who you look for?" Clearly she hadn't been fooled by Den's disguise. Perhaps she had even caught a glimpse of him changing. Or maybe two customers speaking Common Tongue within a few minutes of each other was too big a coincidence.

"He's just a guy who's gone missing. Do you know him?" he showed her the picture, which she examined at length.

"Yes. I know. He always shouting about democracy and freedom and shit like that. He on local TV news." She indicated the antiquated viewing screen that was mounted high in one corner of the café. Den looked up half expecting to see Beckham United's face appear, but it was showing some sort of sporting event. Well, it was showing images of a number of men standing around a large green area doing very little, so Den assumed it was a cricket match. It could as easily have been the world paint drying championships.

"Have you seen him recently?"

"Yes, but not on TV. Last week, I working late shift. He comes in with girl. They arguing. He leaves, she stays and cries for a bit, then she leaves as well."

"Is this the girl?" Den had managed to snatch a photo of Gaga Sullivan as she had left the Sutran bar, just in case he had needed to show her picture to An Kholi and Gala.

"Yes. That her. Very pretty, but not when crying. Then only red eyes."

"Had there been any sort of demonstration around here? You know, crowds, shouting, placards and stuff."

"No. They don't do that here because Space Force come out of HQ and bash heads. They do it down Trafalgar Square."

Den had been there. It was one of the large open spaces contained within some of the globes, where people gathered and sat around when they had nothing better to do. It would also seem that it was the place where demonstrations were held.

It wasn't a great leap of the imagination for Den to work out what Beckham United had been doing in the café. He was on his way to Space Force HQ and Gaga Sullivan had been trying to stop him from going. But why hadn't she told him that? Because if she had told him where Beckham United was then he wouldn't have agreed to help, that's why. She had been playing him all along. She knew that as a Gau he could change shape and therefore he might be able to get into Space Force HQ. But the only way he would go in there would be to find out if Beckham United was inside. If he already knew he was in there then there was no reason to go in. Once inside he was, Den assumed, supposed to take the opportunity to get the young man out.

The treacherous little… No, that was unfair. Would he have behaved any differently? Probably not, under the circumstances. So, different question: why was Beckham United going to Space Force HQ? But the answer to that wasn't his business. The woman had hired him to find her boyfriend. That had been the basis of their agreement. Nothing had been said about springing him from a maximum security paramilitary headquarters. That was a whole different ball game. He used his communicator to send Gaga Sullivan a short message. "Meet me. One hour."

* * *

While Den would be quite happy to spend his entire life in idleness, neither An Kholi nor Gala could stand being idle for any length of time. The dermatologist had come and gone without being able to offer any meaningful assistance. He had an anti-allergy injection he could offer, but it hadn't been tested on non-humans, so…

They had politely declined and sent him on his way. Now they were trawling the galacticnet for any information they might glean on Warrior, Tiny Blur, and George Bush the 125th in an effort to tie the three names together. Of course there was no end of information on Tiny Blur and George Bush the 125th. Even after Blur had resigned the Presidency of Earth they had remained close friends and often appeared in images together; at charity events, at political gatherings, at state occasions and so on. And of course there had been Blur's assistance in getting Bush elected to the Galactic Council as the Magus for Sector Nine of the galaxy.

None of that, however, suggested that Blur was Warrior. An Kohli Moogled Space Force and read their history. Interesting. Although they had been set up by the current President, the idea had come from Blur. Of course, the connections might be more historical than she had imagined.

Slack Hay was the current President, taking over when Blur had stepped down. They had been old party comrades, in lock-step throughout Blur's career, so it had come as no surprise when Blur stepped aside and let his old friend take over the leadership of the planet. Blur had said that he wanted to spend more time with his family, though as soon as he resigned most of his family found reasons to emigrate to the far side of the galaxy. It had also been Blur who had masterminded the political campaigns that had resulted in Hay being re-elected time and time again. Blur seemed to have a knack for such things. It didn't matter how badly Hay actually governed the planet, come election time the opposition seemed unable to dent his majority. No matter who the pollsters said would win, Hay's party always managed to scrape through.

There had been accusations of vote rigging. A reporter had made claims before the last Presidential election, but these had been rebutted and when the reporter committed suicide it was assumed it was because he had lied and it had destroyed his reputation.

Then the Space Force had been set up to counter the growing terrorist threat. No one was quite sure which had come first, the threat or the Space Force. An Kholi had found speeches in the archives of Blur announcing a war on terror, though there had been no terrorist atrocities at the time. Blur had declared war on three different star systems, but no wars had actually been fought. With the galaxy at peace no government thought that having a strong military force was necessary, which made it impractical to fight inter-stellar wars. However, states of war had existed, so peace conferences were arranged and peace treaties signed. This was when the first talk of terrorism had arisen.

Continuing her search An Kholi found media reports of terrorist acts. Mainly bombs on New Earth that had failed to detonate. Anyone from outside of the Sol system wishing to visit Earth had to go to New Earth first, which made it the easiest target for terrorists. However, she could find no record of any attack that pre-dated the establishment of the Space Force. Had she known of the old Earth cliché she might have asked 'which came first, the chicken or the egg?'

As far as Blur was concerned, far from spending more time with his family, he was spending most of it getting other people elected and now he was the man behind the election for a new galactic government. Everything pointed to him either being a member of the Fell, or at least very close to someone who was. But as far as smoking guns were concerned, there was a complete absence.

* * *

Den poked around at the food on his plate. He was unsure what it was supposed to be, but regardless of shape or colour it all tasted the same. Had he not been so hungry he would have left most of it.

He saw her enter the café , looking around trying to spot him. Of course she had been looking for a Gau and Den was still in his human disguise; It was safer now that Space Force officers were interested in what a Gau was doing asking questions. He half rose from his chair and beckoned her over.

"Den, is that really you? Wow, I know you're able to change shape, but…. well, anyway, you look so different." When Den and Gaga had last parted he had told her that any message from him that said simply 'meet me' meant the café opposite the Sutran bar where she had been sitting when she had first spotted him. Messages can be intercepted and there was no point in giving people the opportunity to arrange welcoming committees by telling them where you would be.

"Well, I'm pretty sure that I know where Beckham is. He's in the local Space Force HQ. But you knew that already, didn't you?"

"I don't know what you mean." Her flustered appearance told Den she was lying. "How could I know that?"

"Because you were seen in a café close to the Space Force HQ a few nights back. You were arguing. He left and you were crying. It doesn't take much to join the dots, Gaga. So, was I supposed to get myself in there and then get your boyfriend out for you?"

"I'm sorry." She started weeping, which made Den feel uncomfortable. "Look, I didn't plan it. Not really. I just heard those two guys talking about you being a Gau and how you can change your shape to look like anyone you want, and I thought…"

"You thought I might be able to make myself look like a Space Force officer and bluff my way past their security."

"I guess so."

"Right, let's start again. What was Beckham doing, walking into Space Force HQ? He must have known he was asking for trouble."

"One of our members, one of the protest movement, had been arrested for something. We're not sure what but it doesn't really matter. Space Force only need 'suspicion' to lift anyone they want off the street. Beckham was going to try to persuade them to let him go."

"But he never came out again." Den concluded for her. "Did it occur to either of you that the arrest of the nobody was bait to catch a somebody?"

"Set a sprat to catch a mackerel, you mean."

"I have no idea what a sprat or a mackerel are, but if one is small and the other large, then yes, that's what I mean. What was your next protest about, that might make the authorities want Beckham out of the way?"

"If you look at the election results for President over the past few years it's pretty clear that there is vote rigging going on. No one knows how it's done, but the polls can't be that wrong all the time. The one thing they can't control, though, is the turnout. If people don't vote then it will prevent the election being regarded as legitimate, and that's what our demonstrations are about. We want people to boycott the election for the new galactic government. The demonstration wasn't going to take place just in New Britain. It was going to be right across New Earth and even across the galaxy, a whole series of them between now and election day. We have contacts in all the democratic star systems and they are all deeply suspicious of what is happening and they are all going to demonstrate against voting in the election. Of course Beckham is only one of the organisers, but he's important here on New Earth. Without him it will be harder to get things organised."

"Where's this New Britain place you mentioned?"

"Oh, sorry. In that disguise it's easy to forget that you aren't from around here. New Britain is what this section of New Earth is called. This area is New London."

"I knew that. We docked at New London Space Port."

"Right. This space station is organised into countries, just like down there. It's to help with language differences. When they planned the station everyone up here was supposed to speak Common Tongue, but that didn't work out too well. The French hated the idea and refused to agree to it. The British weren't that keen, either, nor the Americans and the rest of the English speaking countries. Everyone thought that if there was to be one language then it should be theirs, and no one voted for Common Tongue. The argument went on for decades, so long in fact that the space station was ready to go into operation and they had to do something to sort things out. So, to the north of us" she pointed out the café window, "Is New America, then there's New Russia, New China, New France and so on."

"I have to say you speak Common Tongue very well."

"That's because I'm a language teacher. I'm employed by NECK to teach the kelp workers, but they only get an hour a week of tuition so it's slow going. The first half of every lesson is spent trying to remember what they learnt the previous week. This whole language thing is a giant cock-up, but no one will admit it."

"In the meantime the workers get lessons to learn Common Tongue."

"And almost none ever properly learn it. The kelp workers are all on twelve month contracts and an hour a week isn't enough to learn the language. There isn't enough accommodation for families, nor schools or hospitals. The only permanent staff up here are the NECK managers, the police, Space Force of course, the maintenance people who keep the station in orbit, and the government and civil service. Perhaps fifty thousand people in all. Even the shop assistants, bar staff and taxi drivers are limited to twelve month contracts. They all live in hostels close to where they work."

"I didn't know that. It all seems very complicated and inefficient." Den was thinking, *"But that sums up everything I know about humans,"* He didn't say out loud. "So the demonstrations in New Britain won't go ahead… not without Beckham?"

"Actually, since I last spoke to you we've had a meeting and we're going to try to hold them, but it's going to be so much harder without Beckham. Look, it really isn't about the demonstrations."

"So what is it about?"

"The vote rigging, or rather the cover up of the discovery of the vote rigging. Just before the last Presidential election a reporter broke a big story about how he had the inside track on how the vote rigging was done. The government denied it all, of course, and the election went ahead. After the election the fuss died down a bit, mainly because witnesses were leaned on, or that's what everyone suspects. Then about a year later, once it was over, the reporter died."

"What has that to do with Beckham?"

"It was the way he died. There are these places where you can take recreational space walks. They call it a space-walk experience. You get suited up and sent outside to float around on a tether for an hour or so, pretending to be an astronaut, like they were back in the old days. The reporter was supposed to have gone out on one of those and then just opened his visor. The verdict was suicide."

"I still don't get…"

"Hang on, I'm getting to it. Anyway, on the news there were video reports of one of the operators of the space-walk experience saying how tragic it all was, and how everything was normal right up to the reporter going out through the airlock and how he must have over ridden the safety lock on the visor as well. Then a few weeks later we were out on a demo and there was a bit of a scuffle with the Space Force. Nothing serious; just the routine pushing and shoving, the sort of thing they do to intimidate us. Anyway, one of them lost his face mask, they all wear them so they can't be recognised and reported for hitting us, but Beckham recognised him. It's the one they interviewed on the video reports who said he was one of the space-walk experience operators. Beckham recognised him straight away and called out to me and some of the others to come and take a look. But by the time we got through the crowd he'd gone."

"So you think that Beckham was lifted to shut him up."

"It seems to fit. They couldn't just lift him off the street, because that would look like they were guilty. So they pick up Jenson instead, that's the kid who was arrested, and then Beckham just walks in off the street."

"Did he really go there to plead for the kid's release?"

"Not really. It was going to be a straight swap; Jenson for him. You have to get him out of prison for us. Please Den." Gaga looked at him beseechingly and it was hard for Den to resist. "We can't pay you much, but there are other ways…"

Den was taken aback by the veiled suggestion she was making. This must mean a lot to her if she was prepared to go that far. Well, maybe it wasn't the cause that meant so much; maybe it was Beckham.

"That won't be necessary." He said hurriedly. "Let's stick to our original agreement." He found himself saying. Damn, he thought to himself. Why did seeing a pair of gooey eyes always end up with him doing things he really didn't want to do. He had fully intended to tell her he was no longer going to be involved, and here he was now more deeply embroiled than ever.

Den had a thought and pulled out his communicator, calling up a photo he had taken earlier that day. He flicked it across to Gaga's communicator. "Do you recognise anyone in that image?"

She examined the image of the four Space Force officer's that Den had met that morning. Her eyes widened with surprise.

"Yes. The one on the left sitting next to the Sergeant, she's the one with all the stripes. He was the one who said he was employed as an operator at the space-walk experience."

5 - Prison Break

"Your head looks less swollen." Den told An Kholi as she answered the door. It wasn't true, but it might make her feel a little bit better.

"Thanks. Well, you haven't gotten yourself arrested, so how have things gone?"

"Confusing, really. Things weren't as simple as they seemed." He told her about his discoveries that day.

"I read about the vote rigging scandal." An Kohli commented. "I must admit I was suspicious. The galacticnet is full of conspiracy theories, but then again it always is. According to one of them this space station isn't real, it's just a hologram beamed into space to make the people of Earth think it's real."

Den chuckled. Since its inception, the galacticnet had been the home of the conspiracy theorists: the sad people sitting alone in their bedrooms eating cold pizza and believing that the Illuminati were the real rulers of the galaxy. Nowadays they were closer to the truth than they knew, with the growing influence of the Fell across the galaxy, and the forthcoming elections serving to give them some legitimacy.

"So what's the plan?"

"I don't know. That's why I've come to talk it over with you and Gala. You're usually the ones with the plan."

"Gala's gone back to her room for a sleep. I'm not sure how we can help though."

"I need some way of getting into Space Force HQ."

Am Kohli frantically pointed at the ceiling lights to remind him about the possibility of the room being bugged. He shrugged, but kept his voice to a whisper, leaning in close to An Kohli so as to keep the volume as low as possible.

"I need some way of getting into Space Force HQ." he repeated himself.

"Can't you morph yourself into something that can get through the air-conditioning ducts and into his cell? Something like a snake."

"Oh great, so I end up stark naked in his cell and we're both stuck in there because even if I can get back out, he can't."

"You don't have to get into his cell. You only have to get inside the building. If you can get to his cell maybe you can get the door open and get him out."

"OK, I see where you're coming from, but I need more information before we can go with that plan, like how the door locks work and where the guards are stationed."

"In that case we do need Gala." An Kholi used her communicator to waken Gala and summon her to the meeting. Den noted that the sleep induced puffiness had done nothing to improve her bloated features, or her temper.

"One of these days you're going to be able to look after yourselves." Gala grumbled, rubbing sleep from her eyes. An Kholi stifled a smirk and Den had to look away in case he, too, burst out laughing at her outburst.

Den gave her an outline of his problem and she started to search the galacticnet for answers. Gala was a borne engineer. Give her a schematic diagram and enough time and she could solve most problems.

"The solution lies in the design of the space station. Instead of going through the front door, you look for the back doors that the engineers inadvertently created. Now, the builders of this space station were incredibly proud of their achievement and quite rightly so. In its day there was nothing to match it and it's been used as the model for much bigger stations elsewhere in the Galaxy. It's amazing that humans could come up with something as sophisticated as this, and they owe it all to an engineer by the name of Bernard Runel. He was years, possibly even centuries, ahead of his time Anyway, he uploaded all of his designs and diagrams onto the galacticnet, so we should be able to find what we're looking for." She paused and examined the results of her search.

"Here, we are. From this mega-schemtatic we can click on any bit we're interested in to bring up the detailed diagram that will show us what we need to know." She showed the others a display,

"Now, as you know, each of the globes where they grow the kelp are connected to the globes around them by rigid tubes. The connections form triangular structures. That creates a rigid matrix which has very high structural integrity. A meteor could smash into one of the triangles and it probably wouldn't even buckle the neighbouring ones, they're so strong. The triangles are filled in with solar panels, which provide about forty percent of the electrical power for the station; the rest comes from the nuclear reactor that is in the middle of the six cross arms that the station is built around."

Den was about to ask Gala to tell him something he didn't already know, but remembered the current state of her temper and decided to exercise a little bit of patience.

"Now, the nuclear reactor also powers the motor that makes the whole station rotate, which means that the solar panels all get about 12 hours of sunlight each day. That also creates a centrifugal force to push us all outwards and keep our feet on the floor. Because there are no windows it's difficult to see how we're oriented, but in comparison to the surface of a planet you're actually upside down; your head is pointing inwards towards the core of the station while your feet are planted on the outer skin of the station.

"So the floors are really the walls then." Den said.

"Well, actually, they aren't. Because the tubes are cylindrical they would provide a curved floor, which is inconvenient. So the flat floor you walk on is a false one. That then provides space underneath for pipes, cabling, air circulation ducts and that sort of thing."

"So I get in by going under the floor then."

"No, that would be too difficult to navigate. You get in by going outside. The whole station is basically a hollow sphere, well not quite a sphere because there are actually thousands of flat surfaces, but from a distance it looks like a sphere, but it's hollow and the inside is the same pressure as the outside, in other words it's a vacuum. That's another safety feature. It means the force needed to make the sphere explode out into space is the same as that required to make it implode and therefore a state of equilibrium exists."

"You're starting to lose me, Gala." Den knew that left to her own devices Gala would start to wander off into the realms of higher physics and mathematics.

"Sorry. Anyway, the point is it's hollow. All that's inside is the cross arms, the nuclear reactor core, and the high speed monorail tracks that connect up the cities. But maintenance has to be carried out on the tubes, the globes, the monorails, and the rest of the gubbins, to use a technical term, which is how you get in. At various points in each tube are inspection-come-escape hatches. If an accident occurs then air tight doors slide shut, closing off any air leak, but just in case the primary doesn't work there's also a secondary system. That can leave people trapped, able to breathe, but unable to get out until the leak is fixed, so these hatches are the way they can be rescued." She smiled, "They're also the door by which you get in."

Den nodded, "So how do I gain access to these hatches."

Gala brought up an image of a small space craft. "With one of these little babies." At one end of the pictured craft was a curved aperture.

"This is what the maintenance engineers use to get at the hatches. The curved end fits over the hatch and forms an air tight seal. Open the airlock on the craft and then unbolt the hatch and voila, you're in."

"Sounds easy, except for one thing. Where do I get my hands on one of the engineering craft?"

"The same way as you usually get your hands on things you're not supposed to. You morph yourself into one of the engineers, borrow the right clothes and then just walk in and take one."

"You make it sound so easy. How do I know which hatch to go through."

"That's where we need to go back to the schematic." Gala navigated back to the right page. "Now, what are the co-ordinates of Space Force HQ, the ones they show at the tube entrances?"

"Well, the nearest globe is 140 East, 60 North. The tunnel designation, if I recall correctly, is 140E slash 60N alpha."

Gala entered the co-ordinates and they watched as the schematic zoomed in to show the tube Den had named. "So, there you are. Of course the schematic hasn't been updated since the station was occupied, so the description just says 'office units'."

Den pointed out the exact unit that housed Space Force and the schematic zoomed in to show the floor plan.

"From front to back we have a reception area leading to some offices, probably for managers as they have windows that look out onto the roadways. Then there's a large open plan space. Then at the back, against the wall of the tube, we have toilets, a kitchen area, a store room, an equipment room, probably intended to house IT gear and finally a couple more small offices. I'm guessing that some of those rooms will have been converted into cells, but it's anyone's guess as to which ones."

"That's assuming he's still in there at all," suggested An Kholi. She'd stayed silent as Gala had talked them through the stations structure, but now felt the need to make a contribution. "You could be going to a whole lot of trouble for nothing, not to mention the fact that you could end up as the prisoner."

"Well, think positive for now," continued Gala. "There are two inspection hatches that you can use. There's the one that gives access to the kitchen or the other that goes into one of the offices."

"I guess. I'll be going in at night, so the office will probably be empty. The kitchen, on the other hand, is probably in use twenty hours a day."

"Twenty four hours a day, actually," An Kholi corrected Den. "We're on Earth time here, remember."

"Well, that hatch is designated one five seven seven zero green. I guess the green means it's on the starboard side of the tube."

Den made a note. "Anything else I need to know?"

"It would be good to get a look inside the premises, to see how the layout has changed, but I doubt if that's possible."

"There's no virtual tour of the local neo-fascist HQ that we might take then?" quipped An Kholi.

"We should be so lucky." Never the less, Gala did a search, just in case. "No. Mind you, if they have had work carried out on the premises then someone will have had to undertake it, and there will have been schematics done for it. Leave it with me for a while, I'll see what I can come up with. Den, you need to go to this address." Gala pointed to the screen and he scribbled down the co-ordinates. "It's the local maintenance depot for this sector. That's where you'll get your engineer's ID and uniform. You can also do a reconnaissance to work out how you're going to 'borrow' one of the maintenance ships."

Seeing Gala immerse herself in her work, Den drew An Kholi away so that he couldn't be overheard.

"If I manage to get this kid out of Space Force HQ, I'm going to have to get him off this space station. It will be too easy to find him if he stays here. Can I borrow the Adastra?" It was a sensitive issue, Gala regarded the ship as her personal fiefdom, hence the need for broaching the subject out of her hearing.

"Yes, I guess so. Look, Den, You're a free agent and all that, and I have no say over anything you decide to do."

"I sense a 'but' coming."

An Kholi gave him a wry smile. "Yes, but, you've become part of the team and I don't want to lose you. There's no need for you to get yourself mixed up in this thing. It's not your business."

"I know. I started off just to get myself a bit of easy money, but … I don't know, it just seems wrong that these Space Force goons can just pick people up off the street."

"Well, I never. Den Gau: Freedom Fighter."

"Don't mock. I know you well enough to know that you'd do exactly the same in my shoes."

"Yes, and I know you well enough to know that you don't usually risk your neck for others." She laughed to show she was just joking; well, almost. "OK, but you look after yourself, you hear? And look after the Adastra. Oh yes, and don't forget the girl. She can't stay here either. They'd just use her to get to him again."

* * *

It takes an hour and a half to ready a Meteor class ship like the Adastra for departure after it has been fully shut down, so it was to the spaceport that Den went first, after leaving the hotel. Gala had been busy, he noted. Although the ship was never messy, it now had a bit of extra sparkle and the odds and sods had been tidied away, laundry hampers emptied and viewing screens polished. On the control console, the finger marks had been cleaned from the touch sensors. Gala loved the ship almost as much as if it was a sentient being and Den knew that if he damaged the Adastra then his life would hardly be worth living when she caught up with him.

He sat in the command seat and went to work to bring the auxiliary systems up to the levels needed so that when he initiated the engine start sequence all would be ready. He could blow the air lock emergency release and send the ship drifting into space if need be; it would then only take a few minutes for the engines to run up to full power. He had no idea what sort of craft Space Force had at their disposal, but there was nothing visible in the local area and by the time anything arrived to pursue him the Adastra would be accelerating away past Mars and towards a wormhole of its own making.

Before leaving, Den made a visit to the ship's armoury and selected a small pulsar. It didn't have much stopping power, but it was easy to conceal and the material it was made from would fool most detection systems. To carry anything larger would be risky and if a weapon was detected on him he would soon find out what prison food tasted like on the space station. The food served in the restaurants was bad enough so the prospect was less than appealing.

The engineering offices for the New Britain section of the space station occupied three complete tubes, forming a triangle. Den took up a position opposite the main entrance where he wouldn't attract attention while he watched the comings and goings.

It soon became apparent that not all the people that worked in the engineering section were directly employed. As well as the green overalls with the gold coloured logo worn by the engineers there were plenty of people wearing a multitude of other types of clothing, much of it stained by grease, paint or the other effluent of their trades. He spotted a small café where a lot of these visitors stopped off before going into the building, or after they came out. It was a typical worker's café, smelling of greasy food and sweat. He bought himself a cup of something brown that was described as tea but could equally have been used to weatherproof fences. From a seat by the window he was still able to observe the main entrance, but could also observe the café's clientele.

Den's Gaudar put him on the alert as he sensed the presence of another member of his own species. He quickly scanned the occupants of the café and his eyes bored into the back of a new arrival standing at the service counter. She finished punching her order into the automated service point and then turned, obviously looking for the source of the tingling that she, like Den, had felt.

Her eyes lit up as she spotted Den. She said something to her companion and then sauntered over to a neighbouring table where she took a seat with her back to Den. "Don't say anything." She muttered in Gau, just loud enough for Den to hear. "No one knows I'm not human. In a couple of minutes I'm going to go through the back, to the toilets. Wait a few moments then follow me. There's a door leading to a service area. I'll meet you there."

Den sat in a relaxed pose, apparently uninterested in anyone around him. The Gau was joined by two companions, all three of them dressed in stained work clothes. The female said something in what Den now knew to be English and headed for the toilet area. As instructed, Den waited for as long as his patience would allow and then followed her, finding the door and passing through it to an enclosed yard. The outer wall curved from the roof of the café down to where it joined the floor, showing that it was part of the outer skin of the station. High walls closed the yard off on either side. Large empty food containers were strewn around and Den thought he saw the tail of a rat disappear inside one of them.

The female stood with her back to the café wall, doing her best not to look suspicious while at the same time looking very suspicious.

"Well, you're the last person I expected to see around here." Den offered as an opening.

"Me in particular? Or a Gau in general? It doesn't matter. You came as a bit of a surprise to me as well."

"I meant a Gau in general. I don't think we know each other. My name is Den Gau by the way."

"My name is Ka Mera" She extended her hand and Den took it, shaking in the human manner. "I've heard of you."

"In a good way, I hope. Anyway, what brings you to New Earth?"

"A male Gau. Unfortunately when we got here he managed to get himself arrested for something or other and was kicked off the station, leaving me behind. I didn't have any money, so I adopted a human disguise and got myself a job until I can earn enough to buy a ticket out of here. What about you?"

"I'm here with friends. We're waiting to go down to the planet to … on business. In the meantime, I'm doing a bit of freelance work up here, helping someone out. That's why I'm in human form. So why don't you want your friends to know you're a Gau?"

"Have you heard the way this species talk about beings from other star systems? I've never heard such bigotry. It's easier to appear like one of them, blend in so to speak. I'll be glad when I can get out of here."

"You speak very good English." Den observed.

"You wouldn't think that if you heard them mocking me." She jerked her thumb towards the interior of the café to indicate the 'them' to which she was referring. "I tell them I'm Russian and that seems to be an adequate explanation."

"Perhaps we can do a deal in exchange for a free ride.

"I'm not having sex with you." She took a step backwards, putting space between herself and Den.

"No one's asking you to, and don't flatter yourself." Den wondered what it was about females that always made them jump to the wrong conclusion. Then he remembered that it usually wasn't the wrong conclusion. "What I meant was that you can help me with my little project and I'll give you a free ride out of here. All I need is some information and perhaps someone to watch my back for a little while."

"Is that all? It doesn't sound like much in exchange for a free ride. Where will I end up?"

"I don't actually know. I haven't got that part worked out yet, but it will be civilised and several light years from here."

"What sort of risk would I be running."

"You might get kicked off the space station, like your former boyfriend. At worst we're probably talking about a little bit of jail time." Den actually had no idea what the risks were, but hoped he was right.

"That will do me. What information do you need?"

"I need to know how to get hold of an engineer's uniform and ID and how to get to the maintenance shuttle craft. Then I'll need you to keep watch while I borrow one for a short while."

"I can get you the uniform and ID. That won't be a problem. I work on the cleaning contract for the building, so I come and go as I please and no one asks any questions. One of the engineers is really hot for me and I know where he keeps his spare overalls. Getting his ID won't be difficult." Den decided not to ask how she might go about doing it. It was probably better for him not to know. "I can take you through the building to where the shuttles are docked as well."

"When's the best time?"

"Tonight, about midnight. The shifts change over and there's always lots of people milling around. Half of them don't know the other half. I'll put an 'out of order' notice on one of the shuttle docks. Half of them are broken at any time so no one will be suspicious, and it'll make sure that one's free when you need it. Now, I've got to get back to my work colleagues before they start wondering where I gone. Meet me here at about eleven thirty tonight."

She turned and went back inside the café before Den had the chance to ask any more questions.

He couldn't help but marvel how complete strangers are sometimes prepared to take each other at face value simply because they're from the same species. He wondered if he would have been so willing to help Ka Mera if it had been she that had been seeking his assistance. He concluded that he probably would have.

* * *

Gaga Sullivan was already waiting in the café when Den arrived. He bought himself another mug of the brown fence stain and went to sit with her.

"I need you to do exactly as I tell you." Den said without any preamble. "If all goes well then I'll have Beckham out of Space Force HQ within the next couple of hours." He didn't add the caveats that Beckham might not still be alive or that even if he was still alive he might have been moved somewhere else. "If I succeed then I'm going to get both of you away from Earth and to somewhere safe."

"We can't just go. There are people… family … friends…"

"If you stay you will both be locked up within hours, days at the most. There's nowhere to hide on a space station like this and there's security cameras everywhere that record your every move. As it is I'm taking a huge risk; I have to get you off and then I've got to come back for my friends. If the police or Space Force work out that I'm involved in Beckham's escape they'll stick me in a cell and throw away the key. You've got to make your mind up. It's either do it my way or I walk away right now."

Gaga started sniffing, close to tears once more. Den was starting to feel his sympathy for her ebbing away. He was more used to dealing with self-reliant females like An Kholi and Gala. Even the stranger, Ka Mera, was less of a wimp than this human.

"OK. I guess if it's the only way to make sure Beckham is safe."

"That's better. Now, go and pack a small bag for yourself and Beckham, and I do mean 'small'". He used his hands to indicate how big he meant. "We haven't got time to wrestle large amounts of luggage on board ship. Besides, it will look more suspicious to have big bags. Then get whatever travel documents you need, including those for Beckham, and whatever cash you can get your hands on. The authorities will freeze your bank accounts as soon as they work out what has happened, so transfer the rest of your money to this account." He handed her his communicator and she copied his account details. "When you get where we're going you can open a new bank account and I'll give you the money back, less my fee." Den was experienced at making quick getaways so he was able to offer some sound advice.

"When you've got everything you need, come back here and wait for me. Be here no later than twelve thirty. I don't know how long I'll be, but I when I get here I won't be stopping for a chat."

Ka Mera had arrived and sat at another table, not wishing to reveal her association with Den until she knew it was safe to do so. When Gaga Sullivan left the café, she came across and sat next to Den, so they could converse without being overheard.

"Who was that?"

"You'll meet her properly later, I hope, but she's paying the bills."

"What is this all about anyway?"

"Better you don't know. I'll need you to look after these." He handed her a bag containing his spare set of human clothes. "When I come back from where I'm going I'll need to change into them." 'If I come back,' he thought to himself. "

"What's wrong with the clothes you're wearing now. I've got you the engineer's overalls, so you'll have two sets…. Oh, I see. There's someone else."

"Like I said. Better you don't know. Now, are you ready to leave as soon as I get back?"

"Yes. Everything I need is in my locker, which we pass on the way out. If you need a taxi to get us to the spaceport you'd better order it now and tell it what time to be here, and to wait until we come out. It will cost a bit in waiting time, but if you're in a hurry it's better than having to stand around waiting for a ride."

Den was impressed. It sounded as though Ka Mera was also no stranger to running away.

Ka Mera nodded her head towards the flow of people streaming towards the entrance to the engineering site. There were already twenty or thirty people heading towards the doors. "Time to go to work." She said, standing up. Den rose and Ka Mera handed him a set of green overalls and a matching cap. "Go through to the toilets and change into these. The ID tag is in the pocket. I'll wait outside, but be quick. If we arrive by ourselves we'll be more noticeable."

Den was back outside the café in less than two minutes. "That was quick." Ka Mera commented with raised eyebrows.

"I've had plenty of practice getting dressed in a hurry." She turned the corners of her mouth down in unspoken disapproval but said nothing. She led him across the road to join the queue of workers waiting to pass through the security gates.

"This set works just by waving your ID card in front of the scanner." Ka Mera told him. "The more sensitive areas require a retina scan, and if you need to get into the nuclear reactor area you get a whole body scan. I don't go there because of, you know…" she tapped her chest in the area above her two hearts.

The queue moved forward and Den had his ID card scanned. The security guard sitting inside the armoured glass booth didn't even look up from whatever he was doing below their eye line. Even if he had looked up it wouldn't have mattered. Den's face now matched the image on the ID.

Ka Mera led him through a maze of corridors that divided up offices, workshops, drafting rooms, plant rooms and rest areas until they reached a long line of ports set into the outer skin of the tube. Several had 'out of order' signs hanging above them, just as Ka Mera had predicted.

She led him past the first three ports and stopped in front of the fourth, quickly removing the sign and concealing it within her overalls.

"You'll need this." She handed him a sheet of paper, on which she had copied various English words and their Gau translations.

"They're so lacking in enthusiasm for Common Tongue that nothing is labelled in it. Those are words you'll need to identify to operate the shuttle's controls."

Den thanked her and climbed through the small square opening that led to the shuttle's interior. He waved her a quick goodbye and closed the hatch in the space station's skin, before shuffling backwards to close the shuttle's own airlock door. The command and control panel was set into the side wall of the craft, at right angles to the entrance door. The seat was worn and the fabric torn and scuffed by the tools that the engineers festooned themselves with. There were also some suspicious looking stains that Den tried hard not to think about. He settled himself onto the chair and compared the symbols on the sheet of paper with those on the control panel.

He found the one labelled "engine start" and passed his hand over it. He was glad that the ship was so old that it wasn't commanded by thought patterns. That would have made it impossible for him to operate without being able to think in English.

He checked that the airlock light showed red to indicate that the airlock now contained a vacuum and he could safely disconnect from the tube, then tapped the number of the inspection hatch he wanted to get to into the small navi-com terminal. The shuttle automatically disengaged itself and started to head in a straight line across the arc of tunnels and globes. Having to rely on the ship's own guidance system Den had no idea if he was going the right way, but he would find out soon enough. He watched with some trepidation as the arc of tubes flashed by outside the observation port.

After a thirty minute journey, the shuttle attached itself to the side of the space station once again. The light above the airlock door switched from red to green, indicating that it was safe to open the airlock, which he did.

The shuttle's docking port was securely wrapped around a square hatch, in the centre of which was painted the numerical identification '15770 Green'. There were eight clips arranged around the hatch, two along each edge. The one in the top right hand corner was painted green, the other seven were red. From Gala's briefing Den knew that he had to unclip the green one first, which he did. There was a soft hissing, which lasted only a second, as the air pressure inside the shuttle was matched with that inside this part of the space station. It was now safe for Den to undo the remaining seven clips.

As he worked Den noticed the amount of corrosion visible around the clips, no doubt caused by some sort of chemical reaction. It was an indication of age, but also of poor quality manufacturing. When he had finished he tugged at the handle mounted below the painted number. The panel was reluctant to move, probably having been in place since the tube was assembled down on the planet's surface, prior to being launched into space to be incorporated into the growing structure of the space station. He pulled harder and the panel came away with a sound like a sticking plaster being removed from a hairy arm. Around the edge, where the panel had been secured, Den saw a residue of synthetic rubber where the air tight seal had stuck to the metal of the tube.

Den laid the panel to one side and peered into the darkness inside what he knew to be an office. He had dreaded opening the hatch to find himself face to face with a member of the Space Force wondering what the hell he was doing, but that threat hadn't been realised, probably because it was the dead of night, at least nominally, and even Space Force reduced its staffing levels at night.

He stuck his head through the hatch and was startled by bright lights coming on. He quickly withdrew his head, expecting pulsars to start blasting away, but he had no need to worry. Motion sensors, he realised, possibly even heat sensors that switched the lights on.

Den took a moment to let his heart rates settle back to more normal levels, then eased his lower body through the hatch until his feet made contact with the floor. He rolled over onto his stomach and walked his feet backwards until he could straighten up.

The office had an empty, abandoned look, as though it was rarely used. A thin layer of dust covered the desk except for a small square bare patch, which suggested that something had been lying there until quite recently.

Den stuck his head out into the corridor and again hidden sensors detected his presence and switched on the lights. He was ready for them this time. The corridor stretched away from him for about a li (about five Earth yards) before it reached a corner.

Den struggled to recall the briefing that Gala had given him.

"A company called Buzzcock Engineering carried out some modifications on the HQ shortly after Space Force took it over. Fortunately they're part of Gargantua Enterprises and I've been in and out of their computer systems several times over the years. Buzzcock always use parts supplied by other Gargantua subsidiaries for whatever jobs they do, which is even better." Gala explained.

"The second office of the two, the one without the escape hatch, was converted into a holding cell. It's the only one. Buzzcock used a lock supplied by Clubbe Locks, another Gargantua subsidiary. Fortunately for us I once went out with one of their engineers. Clubbe Locks operate on an eight digit combination, which gives it ten million combinations including the default setting of all the zeroes. Clubbe were fed up getting calls from customers who had forgotten the combination because even with a plug-in computer to crack the combination it still took quite a long time and the customers didn't like paying. So they pre-programmed a short code into all the locks, which only the engineers know. My boyfriend used to like showing off by unlocking any doors that we encountered that used the same sort of lock. By the time he'd done it three times I'd memorised the number and the company have never changed it, so far as I know. If they have then you're going to have to find another way in."

"I bet he could have made a fortune if he ever decided to go into crime." Den commented, with more than a hint of envy in his voice.

"Funnily enough that's exactly what he did, but he got caught after his very first job. He forgot that Clubbe held DNA records of all their employees. He left a tiny trace of dribble behind him at the crime scene and he was arrested before he had time to get rid of the loot. He was sent to prison for ten years."

"Poor bloke." Sympathised Den.

"Don't waste your sympathy on him. They locked him up in a prison built by Buzzcock Engineering, with the same type of lock throughout. The first night he was in prison he walked through every door between his cell and the main gate and was never seen again."

Even in their swollen headed state Gala and An Kholi were able to join in with Den's laughter.

"Anyway, that's the code." Gala showed Den the numbers and he memorised them.

Now Den crept along the corridor to the end, where it turned at right angles. It opened out into the large open plan office space he had seen on the schematic. The room was deserted, lit only by the eerie light of holographic computer viewing screens. Den avoided putting his head inside in case he triggered any more sensors. On the far side of the large open space the only other source of light was rectangular, created by an open office door. It suggested that the only person on duty was inside that office. Den turned and bumped painfully against something hard before recognising it as one of the solid metal doors that swing into place to seal off the corridor if an air leak occurred in the tube.

Rubbing at his jarred elbow, Den retreated back along the corridor until he was standing outside the door of the holding cell. Quietly he slid back an inspection hatch and peered through. Opposite the door, against the outer wall of the tube, stood a bed. Lying on the bed was a young man. He lay with his hands behind his head, staring at the curve of the ceiling. Occasionally his lips would twitch, as though he was speaking. Perhaps he was engaged in some sort of internal argument and the twitching lips indicated the extent of his inner turmoil. Even from where he was Den could see bruise marks on his face which suggested some sort of violence had been used against the young man.

Den punched the eight digit code into the keypad and there was a thunk of bolts being withdrawn. The door slid open and a new sound started up. A steady and disconcertingly loud bleeping to indicate a door that shouldn't be open was now open. Damn. Gala hadn't warned him of that. Perhaps she didn't know about it.

Den threw himself into the cell and grabbed the man by his sleeve. "Come with me, quickly." He commanded.

"What happens?" The man was sufficiently alert to recognise Common Tongue when it was being shouted at him.

"Later. Hurry." Den knew he had to keep his words short and simple so Beckham could understand him.

He pulled the boy out into the corridor and turned him towards the office, which allowed him to push and guide at the same time. He propelled the lad through the office door and pointed towards the open hatch. "Emergency" he told him.

Den turned his attention back to the corridor and heard feet thudding across the office. The pace was slow, so whoever it was approaching wasn't running. A raised voice said something, but Den couldn't understand the English words, although he guessed it wasn't a welcome and an invite to stay for tea. Den made a dash for the cell door and slammed his fist against the 'close' button. The door slid obediently shut and the bleeping stopped. Two paces later the unseen feet also stopped. More words were spoken, the intonation making it clear that a question was being asked.

Den turned back to the office and hurried after Beckham, throwing himself through the escape hatch and into the shuttle. He replaced the hatch cover and was about to start to secure the clips when a thought struck him.

Using one of the tools he found inside the shuttle Den hammered one of the securing clips free from the hatch and dropped it inside the office. It might confuse someone for long enough to buy him some time.

Den laid the hatch panel down on the floor of the shuttle's airlock and retreated inside the craft, securing the inner door behind him. He took a deep breath in preparation for making the gamble of his life and checked the sheet of paper to identify the symbols that spelt out 'emergency release.'

He located the button, which was surrounded by black and yellows stripes and had a red safety guard over the top of it to prevent accidental operation. He could have guessed at its purpose, but better to be safe than sorry. He flipped the cover away and pressed down firmly. The shuttle craft was propelled backwards and Den was thrown into a heap on top of Beckham, who had taken refuge on the floor at the far end of the small craft.

In his mind's eye Den imagined the chaos his actions caused inside Space Force HQ. The sudden loss of air pressure would have sent any unsecured objects flying towards the escape hatch, propelled by a screaming rush of escaping air. The emergency door would have slammed into place, to prevent further damage and to protect the integrity of the rest of the building, at the same time saving the lives of anyone not already on the wrong side of it. If the damage was deemed by the automated system to have been significant then the whole tube might be sealed off and would remain so until the source of the leak could be identified and repaired. Den wondered which side of the door the approaching Space Force officer had been. If it was the wrong side then he was now dead, or as good as.

However, Beckham's status was now that of Humdinger's Cat. He was, to coin a phrase, Humdinger's Prisoner. Only when the cell could be accessed once again would it be possible to state whether the prisoner was dead or if he had escaped. Alive definitely wasn't an option if he had still been in his cell.

The furore caused by the air leak would no doubt cause the engineers to spring into action, so Den couldn't allow himself to be found in the vicinity. He used the manual guidance to take the shuttle deep into the interior of the space station's sphere, passing beneath one of the many sets of monorail tracks. Only when he was satisfied that he was far enough away did he tap the symbols for 'home' into the navi-com. The shuttle obediently changed course and guided itself back to its dock at the engineer's base.

Den handed Beckham the spare work clothes that he had brought and mimed changing into them. The young man did as he was bid, and then completed the look by pulling a cap down low over his eyes. His footwear was wrong, soft sportswear with rubber soles rather than the stout safety boots that workers wore, but Den hoped that no one would be looking at the man's feet.

As they approached the shuttle docks Den could see that most them were now empty as the engineers had rushed to the scene of the air leak. The craft's on-board system identified one of the vacant docks and attached itself, automatically completing the process by pressurising the airlock and opening the shuttle's door. The door into the tube had to be opened by hand, a precaution against some technical fault opening the door by accident and creating the sort of chaos that Den had so recently initiated.

On the far side of the corridor, Ka Mera stood with a mop in her hand, a bucket of water by her feet and a damp patch on the floor in front of her. Once again, Den marvelled at the lack of droids to do the manual, unskilled work, but decided that he didn't have time right then to pursue the matter.

"What the hell happened out there? What did you do? This place just went mad. It's like someone kicked open a wicki nest. I've never seen panic like it."

"No time for questions now." Den answered, swinging himself through the hatch. He was closely followed by Beckham.

"Beckham meet Ka Mera. Ka Mera meet Beckham United." Den made cursory introductions. "No time for more, let's get out of here before people start asking questions."

They hurried to put as much distance between themselves and the shuttle docks as was possible in the time available. Ka Mera made a brief diversion to retrieve a small travel bag from her locker.

As in so many places, security was arranged to make it difficult for people to get in. Getting out was far simpler. Doors opened to their touch and they went unchallenged by the few people who were wandering the corridors. As they passed open doors they could see people working away at computer terminals or standing arguing; the typical aftermath to any sort of crisis. Occasionally someone would hurry past, usually in the opposite direction to the one in which the three of them were travelling, more intent on getting to where they were going than paying attention to anyone who crossed their path.

Finding themselves in the street, Den looked across the road to the café and was relieved to see a hover taxi bobbing by the kerbside. He hurried across, his two companions following in his wake. Gaga must have been watching from inside the café because she came running out and threw herself into Beckham's arms.

Den prised them apart. "No time for that now. Get in the cab. Ka Mera, tell the driver we want to go to the spaceport." Den almost physically threw himself into the rear of the cab behind the two younger people, followed closely by the Gau female.

Ka Mera handed Den the bag containing his spare clothes and he started to get changed. The taxi driver said something, directing the words over his shoulder as he drove.

"He said you must be in some sort of rush if you can't wait till you get out of the cab to change your clothes." Gaga supplied a translation.

"Tell him I'm going to meet my Mum and I don't want to look scruffy. She thinks I'm a millionaire."

The driver said something else, before letting out a laugh at his own joke.

"He said she won't be fooled by that clobber." Gaga couldn't suppress a smirk at the louche clothing Den had chosen.

"I'd tell him to go fuck himself, but I wouldn't want you to have to translate it. Look, I want him to think we've boarded the scheduled service to Alpha Centauri. Can you and Beckham have a conversation that will make him think that?"

"Sure, no problem." Gaga made a grab for Beckham and started to shower him with kisses. Den was about to interrupt her to tell her to concentrate on the job in hand when she broke away and started talking. It was clear that Beckham was asking questions and Gaga was providing answers and Den was relieved when he heard the words 'Alpha Centauri' being used several times.

"I take it that's not where we're going." Ka Mera gave Den a worried look.

"No. We'll go to Sabik. I have a friend who's a bounty hunter and lots of bounty hunters hang out on Sabik. They like the bars there and the fact that they're unlikely to get shot at. I'll call in a few favours with my friend's name. Someone will be able to help two refugees."

"What about me?"

"I'm sure they'll help you as well. If not then someone will help you get a ride to the Flage system."

"And that's it then? I'm surplus to requirements now."

"Look, the deal was that in return for your help I'd give you a free ride out of here. You've kept your part of the bargain, for which I'm grateful and more than happy to keep my part, but after we get to Sabik you're on your own. I have to get back here to meet up with my friends again."

"And are your friends pretty?"

"Not right now." Den answered enigmatically. "But that's not the way things are between me and them. We have a job to do, so I can't hang around sorting out your life for you."

Ka Mera sat back and crossed her arms, clearly in a sulk. Den dismissed her from his mind for the moment as he considered the next part of the escape plan. The taxi drew to a halt outside the main entrance to the New London Spaceport. He paid the taxi the fare plus a generous tip. There was no chance they could have made it here without security cameras picking them up and when the taxi driver was traced he wanted him to remember them and the story that Gaga had been feeding him on the journey.

This was the final part of the escape and in its own way it was probably the most difficult. They were now going to have to come face to face with bureaucracy and security staff that had no sense of humour and who were as inflexible as steel bars. Over an hour had passed since he had released Beckham from his cell and still the alarm hadn't been raised. His luck just needed to hold out for a few more minutes and they would be free and clear.

Den flicked boarding pass codes across to their communicators. It would look odd that Beckham didn't have a communicator, but that couldn't be helped. Gaga would have to use hers to get Beckham through to the departures area. The boarding passes were supposed to get them on board the Alpha Centauri transport and maintain the fiction that it was their destination.

The official checking the passes co-operated with the plan more than Den could have hoped for. As was so common across the galaxy, and as they had discovered before, officials are more interested in who is entering their territory than who is leaving it. Den got the feeling he could have been carrying a dead body and it wouldn't have excited any curiosity.

They passed through to the security screening area. Den remembered his pulsar, but too late. There was no way of getting rid of it. He cursed himself for his stupidity until realisation dawned on him. The pulsar had been in the pocket of the green overalls, and they were now stuffed in the rubbish bin at the entrance to the spaceport. He let out a sigh of relief and stepped forward to allow himself to be scanned and then frisked.

Beckham started to hurry and Den was forced to slow him down. People looked at someone who was running, or even hurrying. It got you noticed. People who were walking casually and calmly didn't warrant a second look. Once in the departure lounge Den steered them away from the commercial gates and into a narrow side passage. It stretched away for what seemed like hundreds of li.

"This takes us to the gates for the privately owned space craft." Den told the three of them. "You and Beckham need to keep your heads down so that no one recognises you. If they connect you to the Adastra, it's going to cause me problems when I get back. Ka Mera and I will be OK, we'll change our faces to look like someone else, won't we?" Ka Mera was still sulking but nodded a grudging agreement.

They waited while Gaga explained the situation to Beckham, then they set off along the corridor, both of the humans with their shoulders hunched and their faces firmly downcast. Den had adopted the looks of the taxi driver that he had met a few nights previously while Ka Mera adopted the looks of her former flat mate.

They reached the dock where the Adastra was parked and Den punched in the access code, backed up by his palm print. He ushered

Ka Mera and the two humans into the small lounge then went forward to take his place behind the controls.

His hands worked quickly to bring the engines up to readiness for departure, then opened a communications channel.

"New Earth Traffic Control this is the Adastra. Request departure clearance."

"Adastra, clearance denied. You haven't filed a flight plan."

Damn. He forgot. Nowhere else in the galaxy were they interested in such things. Once a ship had undocked it could go anywhere and no one would be any the wiser, but here the boxes had all to be ticked before anything was permitted. He entered 'Towie' into the navi-com and it quickly calculated the course. Once completed Den transmitted it to Traffic Control.

"New Earth can I now have departure clearance?"

"Roger Adastra. You are cleared for departure." Den had no idea who 'Roger' was but the confirmation of his clearance was all Den needed.

He released the ship from the airlock and used the gas jets to push the ship away from the docking pier. The space station may be artificial but its huge size meant it had a gravitational system of its own. It wasn't as strong as most planets, or even as strong as that of the Earth's natural satellite, the Moon, but it was strong enough to keep the Adastra attached to it if he didn't give it a little nudge.

"Adastra, this is New Earth Traffic Control. Cancel departure. You are to return to your parking dock."

Damn and blast. So near and yet so far. The alarm must finally have been raised. On the viewing screen Den saw the ship bound for Alpha Centauri was also returning to its dock. So it was just a general recall, not one for him specifically.

"Sorry New Earth. What did you say? You're breaking up." Den fired the gas jets again, pushing the ship further from the dock. He needed just a few more li then he could turn the ship around and start the main engines.

"Adastra, you must return to your dock at once."

Or what? Thought Den. Out loud he said "Sorry New Earth, you signal is corrupted. I'm not hearing you properly. Hello New Earth, are you there? Hello? Hello?"

Den broke the communications link and turned the ship, firing up the main engines as he did so. The Meteor's main engines thrust it forward like a racing fiju out of the starting gate. By the time New Earth Traffic Control had re-established a communications channel the Adastra was already past Mars and approaching the speed needed to create it's wormhole. Den programmed a new destination into the navi-com, didn't transmit it to Traffic Control and blinked out of existence in that star system, all within a few heartbeats.

Den was very good at running away.

Glossary

Fiju - A horse like creature known for its strength.

Humdinger's Cat - Eminent physicist and cat hater Eli Humdinger described the paradox created by a thought experiment involving a cat sealed inside a box whose status could not be adequately determined. If the box contained a vial of poison which broke at some indeterminate time, then at any instant it wasn't possible to state definitively whether the cat was dead or alive. Further, it was possible to think of the cat as being both dead and alive (This is the lay-person's explanation. If you want to know more then you also need to get a life). By an almost unique coincidence Austrian physicist Erwin Schrödinger described the same paradox several centuries later on Earth, a planet which had yet to make contact with species from other star systems and which had therefore never heard of Eli Humdinger. They had, however, heard of cats.

Illuminati - A supposed secret society that rules the galaxy. The origins are real enough, starting out in Bavaria in Earth year 1771 as a secret society opposed to religion and superstition and also opposing the abuse of power. They were banned in their native

Bavaria and in other places and had died out by 1785. Augustin Barruel and John Robinson both wrote books in the 1790s that suggested that the Illuminati didn't die out and were behind the French Revolution, amongst other acts. Their theories crossed the Atlantic where they found popularity amongst the citizens of the fledgling American states. The Illuminati name reappeared in the period between the First and Second World Wars connected to Jewish conspiracy theories put around by fascist and neo-fascist groups. The llluminati also emerged once more in the Dan Brown novel Angels and Demons, though he places them in the 15th and 16th centuries, before they were actually founded, rather than the 18th. These ideas have been extended by some modern conspiracy theorists to suggest that the Illuminati have gained super powers and are operating in a dimension unknown to humanity in order to control the Earth. They may be right.

Navi-com - Navigational computer

Pulsar - A weapon that uses high energy pulses to destroy its target. Smaller versions are hand held and larger versions can be fitted to mounts for use on vehicles and space craft. Has an advantage over projectile weapons because it can be used under water with only minor loss of efficiency.

6 - A Step Back In Time

Opening the door to her hotel room, An Kholi stepped back in surprise as she saw the unexpected figure of her old friend and fellow bounty hunter Merkaloy standing on the threshold. That was until her brain did a quick analysis and concluded that it wasn't really Merkaloy. The height was wrong, just for a start. Merkaloy towered over her, but this Arthurid like figure was barely her size. He would be regarded as the runt of any Arthurid litter.

The clothes were also wrong. Well, they were right in terms of their style: superskin shirt and trousers, a broad belt on which a pulsar would normally be hung, if this wasn't New Earth of course, and all finished off with knee high boots. But when Merkaloy wore that sort of shirt his muscles threatened the manufacturer's 'no rip' warranty. This shirt seemed to almost hang on him, barely even qualifying for the definition of fitted.

"Oh, it's you isn't it…"

The new arrival pointed theatrically towards the ceiling lights, where listening devices might be hidden. He mimed drinking and An Kohli nodded her assent.

Thirty minutes later she was sitting in the noisy bar with Gala and the being that was supposed to be Merkaloy but was actually Den Gau, plus a fourth person as yet unidentified.

Since their last visit to the bar, just a few days earlier, the fashions had changed and yellow was now the thing, as all the young people demonstrated. Blue, clearly, was the colour of the past. Or maybe it was something to do with the day of the week. Who knew?

"Nice to see the swelling's almost gone." Den grinned mischievously at them. It was true that there was nothing to see on either female now but a little puffiness around the neck and jawline, which they were doing their best to hide with the use of rather old fashioned gauzy scarves.

"Yes. Once it started to reduce it went quite quickly. You don't look so good. As an Arthurid you look as though you've shrunk in the wash."

"Yeah. I'm afraid there isn't enough 'me' to make up a being the size of an Arthurid, so I've had to scale down a bit and hope these humans don't notice."

The so far unnamed fourth member of the party got up and wandered towards the back of the bar, where the toilets were situated.

An Kohli took the opportunity to quiz Den about the female. "So who's your friend? Is she a Sabik? She's pretty enough to be." An Kholi shouted as they sipped their drinks.

"She's a Gau like me, but we borrowed a Sabik identity for her. Her name is Ka Mera, but it's best if you call her Laurel while we're here."

"Can we trust her?"

"I trust her. She was really helpful and she didn't have to be. OK, the price was to help her get away from this place, but she's decided to come back. It must have been my magnetic personality. Look, if you'd rather she didn't …"

"No, it's OK. As a Gau like you she might be useful, but be very careful what you say in front of her. I don't want any references to the Magi, or the eggs or anything else. The less she knows the better. Once we've had a chance for her to prove herself, well, maybe we'll let her into the inner circle. Does Merkaloy know you're using his identity?"

"More than that, it was his idea. He leant us his ship as well, while he uses the Adastra." There was a hiss of disapproval from Gala but An Kholi shot her a warning glance. "Don't worry. I didn't even leave fingerprints on it. I'm sure Merkaloy will look after the Adastra."

"You didn't leave fingerprints because you're in the habit of wiping them." Gala snapped back "I'm more concerned about the dents that you probably left in her."

"So tell us the story." An Kholi broke in before localised warfare could erupt.

As Ka Mera, or Laurel, to use her alter ego, re-joined them, Den recounted the tale of the rescue of Beckham United and their escape to Sabik.

"I thought that air leak was your doing. It was too much of a coincidence. According to the local media, Space Force are blaming terrorists. They said it was caused by a bomb and it killed thirty innocent people."

"They're lying. I'm pretty sure no one died. The corridor would have been sealed before anyone went in there." Den hoped that was correct, but didn't want to have to deal with An Kholi's objections to an unnecessary death. "No doubt they're using it as an excuse to round up people they don't like."

"According to the media some arrests have been made, but they haven't said who or how many."

"Fairly typical of a totalitarian regime. I'm sorry we gave them an excuse. Have they mentioned Beckham United's escape?"

"Not a word. It would mean them having to say why they were holding him in the first place and that might be awkward."

"Anyway, when we got to Sabik I ran into Merkaloy. Well, I went looking for him, actually, and found him at the Three Moons; no surprise. He agreed to help Beckham and Gaga Sullivan. Then he suggested that we use his ship to come back here, just in case the police were looking for the Adastra. He also leant me his ID. Not his Guild one of course, just his general one and he arranged for the loan of a suitable ID for Ka Mera, or Laurel as she will be for the time being. The real Laurel is actually one of the waitresses at the Three Moons. I think she and Merkaloy have something going."

"Wouldn't surprise me. He's got a bit of a roving eye. Pleased to meet you, Laurel." An Kholi extended her hand for the Earth style greeting.

"And you. Den's told me all about you."

"And this is Gala." Den introduced her. Gala, too, shook hands though Den thought there was a little coolness in the greeting. Could she be a touch jealous? There had been that one time … Or was she, like An Kohli, suspicious of the new arrival?

"Well, now you're here we can make arrangements to go down there." An Kholi continued. "Our permits came through while you were away."

"What about Ka… I mean Laurel?"

"Sorry, she's going to have to stay up here. I don't want to hang about anymore while we wait for her to get a permit. She can use my hotel room and come down and join us later if we haven't returned."

"Why are you going down there?" Laurel shouted.

An Kholi shot Den an inquiring glance.

"I haven't told her anything about what we're doing. I thought I'd leave that to you."

An Kholi gave the matter some thought before she spoke, or rather shouted, again. "We're trying to recover some stolen property. It's very, very valuable and there's a large reward for it. We think some of it may be down there."

"Oh, OK. What sort of stolen property?"

"Some jewellery."

"Oh, I thought you said it was valuable." Jewellery had ceased to be considered valuable in the galaxy when solid diamond planets had been discovered.

Laurel excused herself once again and headed over to the jukebox to select some music. She seemed to be easily distracted.

"What arrangements have you made with regard to the bounty?" An Kholi decided it was best to discuss the subject while Laurel was absent.

"I haven't. I told her I got a share which represented the amount of effort I had put into whatever we did and also the amount of danger in which I was placed. To be honest I didn't think about whether you would want to count her in."

"Well, if she helps she's entitled to a share, but that means less for the rest of us." Gala commented, clearly not keen in reducing the size of her own share.

"I'll tell you what. Let's call it a trial arrangement. I'll pay Laurel out of my share this time. If it works out then we can think about a more permanent arrangement."

"Seems fair." Gala agreed.

"That's settled then." An Kholi announced just as Laurel returned.

"What's fair?"

Den answered, "We were just talking about how the bounty will be split if we find what we're looking for. If you get involved, I've agreed to split my share with you. If it works out then we'll sort out something more permanent."

"And if it doesn't work out?"

"That's in your hands." An Kholi told her. "This is dangerous work and not everyone's suited to it."

"Well, where Den goes, I go."

Den looked slightly discomfited by this news. "Look, I agreed to bring you along because you had nowhere else to go. It's a work arrangement, OK?"

"If you say so." Laurel replied a little huffily. An Kholi and Gala found it difficult to hide their smirks.

"So what's the plan?" Den continued, quickly trying to change the subject. "How do we go about searching?"

"The shuttle from New Earth will land at a commercial shuttle port, which means there won't be any convenient rock or cairn to guide us this time. Su Mali must have found some other way of hiding the stuff, instead of just burying it. We've done some checking. From New London Spaceport there are eleven shuttles a day to earth. One each goes New York, Los Angeles, Moscow, Beijing, and Johannesburg. They're all major population centres and from there you get a connecting service by what the humans call 'aeroplanes', to wherever it is you want to end up. However, because this spaceport is in New Britain there are six shuttles a day to destinations there. Four go to London, that's old London, one to Manchester and one to Edinburgh. Gala hacked the ticketing computer and found out that Su Mali took the first shuttle to London in the morning, then returned on the last shuttle in the evening a couple of days later."

"So, that should be easy enough. We go to London, take a look around and work out where she hid the stuff."

"No Den, you don't understand. London isn't like any city you've ever seen before. It's huge. Over a hundred million people live in it. It runs from the sea on this side of Britain," she held up her right hand, "to the sea on that," holding up her left hand. "That's over two hundred Earth miles; that's about sixty four thousand li. It also runs from the sea to the south to a place called Stafford in the middle of the country. In between it's so heavily populated that it's hard to find a tree or a flower or even a blade of grass in some places. Then there's a few thousand li of open land which they laughingly call a National Park, but according to the galacticnet is mainly used for dumping broken furniture and old domestic appliances. Then Manchester starts. That runs from the sea to the sea as well, and stops at a place called Kendal. Then there's another park until you get to the border with Scotland."

"What about that other place you mentioned; Edinburgh was it?"

"Believe me, you don't want to go there. It's the Capital of Scotland, which used to be part of Britain when it was still called the United Kingdom. For some reason it decided to break away, but it's economy wasn't good enough. Its major source of revenue was a fossil based fuel called 'oil' and when that ran out the economy collapsed. Those that could get out did so, but many couldn't. It was the biggest economic migration that Britain had ever seen. Anyway, Scotland is now a poverty stricken wasteland. The biggest employer is the government, well, the only employer really. The President, Nickel Surgeon, blames Britain of course. Says it's all a plot to keep the Scots poor, but no one except the Scots takes her seriously any more. The only reason the New Earth shuttle still goes to Edinburgh is a political gesture to make the Scots feel important."

"So, if London is so huge, how do we find where Su Mali stashed the goods?" Den gave a slight sideways glance towards Laurel, to see if she had noticed his terminology, but she was examining her finger nails as though she expected to find money under them.

"Well, the centre of the city is about twenty miles from the spaceport. That's about six thousand four hundred li. It takes about an hour to get there."

"An hour!" Laurel was suddenly attentive. Perhaps she had been paying more attention than Den had thought.

"Yes, and that's on a good day. Most days it takes longer. The city never invested in high speed local transport. It's quicker to get from London to Birmingham, which is about thirty nine thousand li away, than it is to get from the shuttle port to the centre of the old city. You have to go there first anyway, because all the other transport services start and terminate there."

"It doesn't sound very efficient for travellers." Laurel commented.

"It isn't, but something called the railways were founded first and no one thought to shift their termini to the shuttle port when space travel started up. You can't even go direct from the shuttle port to the places they call airports, where you catch the aeroplanes. What can I tell you? It's Earth. There are far worse inefficiencies down there than that."

"So, if Su Mali arrived and left the same day, how far could she have gone?"

"She was there for about sixty hours. Taking into account the security and immigration procedures at the shuttle port, she had no more than fifty five hours to play with. Deduct two for travelling to and from the centre of the old city and you've reduced that to fifty three hours. Like I said earlier, you can get to Birmingham quite quickly, or even Manchester and still be back in time for the evening shuttle, but I'm guessing she stayed in central London."

"Why?" Den was fascinated by the way An Kholi's mind worked. She seemed to be able to work a problem through with a logic that few other people possessed. She was also rarely wrong. It was the reason she was so successful as a bounty hunter; that and her single minded determination.

"I mentioned it earlier. She buried her loot the last two times, so I think it's a reasonable bet that she buried it again when she went to London. But there's more than one way to bury loot. There's the banking equivalent. The safe deposit box."

"What's one of those?" Laurel was taking more interest now that banks had been mentioned. Simultaneously Den and An Kholi started to wonder about her history. In truth Den knew very little about her.

"It's a secure place where you can store valuables that you don't need on a day to day basis. You hire the box to put your stuff in. It usually needs two keys to open it. The bank keeps one key and you keep the other. They then keep all the boxes in a vault, which will be virtually impenetrable."

"There's no such thing as impenetrable when it comes to security." Laurel's comment caused An Kholi and Den to start to worry a bit more about her.

"True. There have been break-ins in the past. But they take a lot of time and they risk detection, so safe deposit boxes are a safer bet than keeping the stuff under your mattress."

Laurel shrugged, clearly unconvinced. Den moved them along.

"So how do we find the place where Su Mali chose to have her box? If she actually did that of course."

"I'm guessing now, but she will have left herself some sort of reminder. She won't have wanted to record anything, like an address, so there will be the local equivalent of a rock or a cairn."

"So we wander around London until we spot it, do we? You said it's a big city."

"It is a big city, but its financial district is quite small. They used to call it the square mile, that's just over a hundred thousand square li. If we have to walk every sim of it then it will only take a few days."

"And then what? Do you have the key to the box? Do you have her ID to get past security?"

"I don't have the key, but I do have an ID in her name. I was going to ask you to morph into a female form to take on her identity if it's needed, but now we have Laurel. She'd be much better. Totally indistinguishable from the real thing, in fact. How about it Laurel?"

"Is it dangerous?"

"Not in the getting killed sense, but you could go to prison if you get caught."

"Prison I'll risk, if it's worth my while."

"That's great. We'll see what needs to be done when we get down there and find the right place."

"That means we do need to take Laurel with us then. You said we didn't."

"But she doesn't have to travel down the same day. It will take us time to find the right depository. By that time her permit should be through."

"OK. It's some sort of a plan I suppose, and we've worked with less. When do we go?"

"We have to book tickets for the shuttle, which we can do tonight. If there are seats available we go tomorrow."

* * *

Through the tiny windows in the shuttle, all An Kholi could see was the dirty brown smog that made up most of the atmosphere of Earth. The thought of breathing that muck didn't endear her to the planet, but the galacticnet had advised them to buy smog masks when they got to the shuttle port.

The shuttle itself was crowded with workers travelling home at the end of their contracts. Most had been in the spaceport bar before launch and the craft was loud with the sound of raucous laughter, and occasional voices raised in anger. Cabin staff rushed up and down the aisles in an effort to keep up with the demand for more drinks, working hard to follow the instructions from the shuttle company to separate the travellers from as much of their money as possible. More used to travelling in their own ship, An Kholi, Gala and Den were finding the journey quite stressful.

At last the shuttle settled onto its designated landing spot. Everyone stood up and started rummaging for their luggage before clogging the aisles with their bodies as they waited for the boarding ramp to be put in place. With the engines powered down the interior of the shuttle soon became hot and the air fetid. An Kholi would rather face a hoard of Meklon pirates than travel by BrianAir again, she decided.

At last they were released into the arrivals hall and were able to join the queue for non-human travellers, which was much shorter than the one they had stood in when they arrived on New Earth. Most sane alien beings avoided travelling down to the planet if they could conduct their business on the relatively uncrowded space station.

The unfeeling hand of bureaucracy guided them through two hours of ID checking, questions, more ID checking. They tolerated the intrusive search for contraband, though what they might be carrying that could possibly do any harm to the wreckage of this planet they couldn't fathom. Finally there were more questions before they were disgorged into the main concourse. They searched the overhead signs for clues as to where they could find the transport to the city and were rewarded with a picture of a box with lines under it to represent tracks of some sort.

An Kholi was never so glad to be travelling light as they trudged through what seemed like several thousand li of tunnels to find the railway terminal. They felt as though they were walking all the way to the city centre when they finally found a long, empty platform with vacant tracks lying next to it. A destination board displayed the time of the next train in English, which they couldn't read. Welcome to Planet Earth, stranger, it seemed to mock them. Hope you don't want to find your way around without being able to speak our language.

Fortunately their communicators still worked and Gala quickly found the train timetables and worked out how long they had to wait.

"I can see why it took Su Mali two days to do her business here." Gala commented. "The journey time is fifty Earth minutes, but the next train isn't for another thirty minutes. If the return journey is the same then it really ate into her time."

An announcement came across speakers, tinny and crackling. Of course it was made only in English. Gala got to work with her communicator once again and found an update.

"The train's been delayed by another twenty minutes. Wrong sort of smog as far as I can make out."

The three aliens settled themselves onto hard seats for the extended wait. No wonder the platform was empty. Any sane person would have used one of the many hover taxis that were plying for hire in the street above their head. Unfortunately one of An Kholi's lesser qualities was extreme parsimony. The train was cheaper, so they would wait.

All things come to an end eventually, even waiting, so the three of them found themselves on the train heading for the city centre. Only a handful of people boarded with them at the shuttle port, but as the train headed northwards it stopped regularly to pick up passengers and by the time they were halfway to their destination the vehicle was packed to danger point. Bodies crushed against each other, noses in sweaty armpits as arms were raised to hang on to the ceiling mounted hand rails.

As strangers, they attracted some stares and they suspected they were being discussed, but no one seemed actively hostile towards them. Although interstellar travel between Earth and other systems had existed for some time, aliens still didn't visit Earth very much. There was little to attract them and what little did attract them could be satisfied by visiting the space station. It occurred to An Kholi that Su Mali may have disguised herself as a human to reduce the amount of attention that she attracted.

With her nose pressed up against the carriage window, An Kholi was able to view what passed for scenery. What they passed was mile after mile of high rise dwellings, people crammed in like cattle. She would have used the term 'battery chickens' if she had ever heard of it. It wasn't an unusual sight; she had encountered similar living conditions before on other planets, but not on the scale of

London. If it wasn't a dwelling then it was some sort of factory or warehouse. Signs were mounted on the roofs to announce what was made or sold, but the words meant nothing to her. The same ones were repeated several times as their journey continued. Trashco, Basda, Baldey, Ludl, BSF, CSC and more. Idly she wondered what was inside, then decided that she didn't really need to know.

The train finally ground to a halt and disgorged its load of passengers onto a platform. Others started to board even before the train had been vacated, creating a log jam in the doorways. As some of the last beings off An Kholi, Den and Gala felt as though they were swimming against the tide. They found themselves at a place where several railway lines ended, side by side with just the platforms separating them. Trains stood at most of them, either just arrived, like them, or readying for departure. Hordes of people were coming and going, heads down, intent on their own journey, not wanting to get involved in the lives of others.

"I hate this place already." Gala raised her voice in order to be heard above the constant bustle and noise of trains, people and loudspeaker broadcasts.

"I hated it the moment we boarded the shuttle." Countered Den.

"Get used to it. We're going to be here a few days at least, maybe longer." An Kholi cautioned them. "Gala, can you call up a map to get us to our hotel. It shouldn't be too far."

Even inside the station, as it was called, the gritty foul taste of the smog was present, so they pulled their masks over their faces and headed in the direction set by Gala, out into the packed streets. They were narrow, built in a time before there were so many people. Hover taxis occupied the centres while the people traipsed down the sides, crammed in against the walls of the buildings. Larger vehicles, wheeled double story constructions, thundered by from time to time.

"Buses." Gala informed them. She had been the one to study London and its culture while she had waited for her swollen head to reduce in size. "There's also a train system that runs underground, called the Underground."

"Highly original." Den commented. They came to a standstill outside a building with a narrow glass door with a sign above it that proclaimed it to be the Travellers' Inn. At once Den new that An Kholi hadn't spared any expense. It had 'cheap' written all over it, along with a lot of other words spray painted in fanciful scripts across its outer walls.

They entered a small foyer and approached a desk. There was no one present, but to one side stood an automated check-in system, at least that was what it proclaimed itself to be. It had instructions displayed in a number of languages, and one of them, hooray, was Common Tongue. On it hung a sign, written only in English, that said 'out of order'.

An Kholi rapped on the counter, but there was no response. She tried again and again with the same result. After ten minutes of waiting a young man appeared from somewhere and seemed surprised to find them waiting.

"Can I help you?" he asked in English. Despite hers and Gala's lilac skin and Den's pale green imitation Arthurid the youth seemed to think that they would understand.

An Kholi asked "Can you help us?" In Common Tongue.

"I try." The youth tried.

"We have a reservation. An Kholi, Gala Sur, Merkaloy Triffid.

The young man processed the information slowly, as though chewing tough meat. "I check." He ran his fingers over a computer and he seemed surprised when it confirmed An Kholi's claim. "Room not ready." He announced. "Come back three o'clock."

"Three o'clock this afternoon or three o'clock tomorrow morning?"

This puzzled the young man even more, as though he didn't understand that there were two three o'clocks in a day. The Earth system of counting time confused the whole galaxy, but this youth should have understood it. Apparently he didn't. At last the penny dropped as he worked his way through the clauses of An Kholi's sentence in Common Tongue. "Yes, afternoon."

"That's five hours away." Den observed.

"Can we leave our bags?" An Kholi hefted hers to show what she meant.

"No. No leave bags. Take with you."

Welcome to London, thought An Kholi. They turned and left the shabby foyer.

"What now?" Den asked.

"We start our search. Any suggestion as to how we proceed?"

"There's a river here, seems to mark one edge of the city." Gala pointed to the map on her communicator. "Why not start there and head away from it. When we get to the far side we turn round and come back again."

For a want of a better plan, they agreed to do it that way and headed back the way they had come until they found the river, or what was visible of it under the buildings that had been built over it. They were tall, modern structures of towering steel and glass, standing on stilts sunk into the river bed. They sat at odds with the much older structures that fringed the river bank. To one side was what appeared to be a castle. It was certainly old. People milled about it, taking images on their communicators.

"What are they doing?" Den asked, pointing to a group that had their arms extended, their communicators on the end of thin poles.

"It's an Earth thing." Gala provided. "You don't just take an image of what you are seeing, you take a picture of yourself and the thing together. It proves you are really here, apparently."

"But you must be here, or how could you take the image?"

"Don't ask me, I'm a stranger here myself. That's just the way they do it."

Den felt he had stepped back into history; at least the history of Earth. He had seen movies depicting scenes like this. Ancient buildings and castles. He half expected to see mounted knights ride across the drawbridge of the old castle. It was far more impressive than the fakery of Genghis's efforts *(see Genghis Kant)*.

Beyond the castle was a gap between two of the towering buildings which allowed a passage across a bridge. At one end they could see a rectangular tower supporting the blue painted steel framework of the bridge, but the distant end was obscured by the newer buildings. "We may as well start there, where the road comes off the bridge. Let's see where it takes us."

They skirted round the castle to its far side and joined the road. Hover taxis flew across the bridge and one of the huge 'buses' thundered past, packed with sweating humanity. It belched black smoke into the air to add to the already thick smog.

An Kholi and Den followed Gala's lead and called up a street map on their communicators and discussed the route they would each take. After a few minutes of arguing Den headed west along Tower Hill the way they had come, An Kholi went straight ahead up the Minories and Gala angled off right to Mansell Street. They knew that back in the twentieth century the old city had spread eastwards into the abandoned docks areas, but they hoped that Su Mali had stuck with traditional banks who'd had their premises in the older part of the city for several centuries.

* * *

They were eventually allowed into their rooms at the hotel, though considerably later than the promised 3 o'clock. The rooms were spartan, just a bed and a cupboard, a door led to a tiny shower room. Against the wall opposite the bed was a table and chair with a media centre mounted on the wall above.

The media centre was basic, just allowing access to entertainment and news channels and a few selected commercial feeds. An Kholi found she could order something called a 'kebab' but couldn't find out what was in it without consulting the galacticnet by using her own communicator. When she did find out, she lost her appetite.

For two more days they pounded the streets of London, their clothes becoming grimy from the smog. Fortunately the Superskin ™ material was easily washed in a hotel hand basin and dried quickly. It was stiflingly hot, even though it was the coldest season of the year. It was a consequence of centuries of climate change, the galacticnet informed them.

Den found himself outside a pub. He checked the time and found he had been walking for three hours already. Time for some refreshment. The one thing they agreed on was that English pubs beat any other place of refreshment in the galaxy. At least the ones in central London did. They were usually old and comfortable, with low ceilings and dim lighting. Although music was played, it was at a volume conducive to conversation. But it was the beer that was the real attraction. There was so much choice and it tasted better than any other beer served in the galaxy. Even Gau beer, Den was forced, rather reluctantly, to concede. There were other drinks, of course. One pub boasted over fifty different types of whisky, though notably not Grovian. It wasn't the expense that prohibited stocking it, it was the latent xenophobia of the humans. They drank Scottish or Irish.

Den and the others had become used to the hostile glances of the local people. They weren't quite threatening, but it felt as though violence might break out at the smallest excuse. However, pubs provided a sanctuary. In most of them they were made welcome. Their money was as good as anyone else's.

Den was just about to enter when his eyes were drawn to the sign hanging above the door. His English still wasn't good but he had learnt to interpret the symbols and sound them out, even if he didn't know what they meant.

Den's pale green fake Arthurid face broke into a broad smile and he sent a triumphant three word message to An Kholi and Gala. "I've found it."

Glossary

Meklon - A collective noun for a group of people who live outside the law. They live a wide variety of criminal lifestyles but one of the most common is space piracy. The origin of the term is lost in the mists of time. Some say it is taken from Mik Lon, a legendary figure who robbed from the rich, there being very few sane reasons to rob from the poor. Legend has it that he then shared the proceeds of his robberies with the poor but that is just lunacy as that would make the poor richer and he'd then have to rob them as well. Another version is that a planet called Meklon, location unknown, was a safe haven for a group of these criminals. Neither version is verified by the galacticnet, but then again, very little is.

Superskin material - Many advances have been made in the manufacture of synthetic fibres that are warm, waterproof and breathable. The Superskin Company (a subsidiary of the Gragantua Corporation) produce some particularly attractive skin tight clothing that is thermally insulated and also water repellent, while being the thickness of a hair. Their clothes are also very hard wearing, which is why bounty hunters like them.

7 - Susikins

"How do you know this is the right place?" An Kholi challenged him as she sat down, placing a foaming glass of tawny beer on the table in front of her. She eyed it appreciatively, savouring the moment when she would take her first sip.

"You saw the sign, didn't you?"

"It isn't conclusive evidence."

"Perhaps not, but that is." Den pointed towards a picture frame hanging on a black painted wooden post which supported one of the ceiling beams. The frame enclosed a sheet of paper bearing a lot of words written in English. "It's a history of the pub. I got it translated through Moogle Translate. The pub is very old, it's been here at least five hundred years and has changed names several times. Three years ago it was on its uppers, just about to close down, when along came an investor and saved it. There was one condition placed on the investment. It had to change its name to what it is today. It used to be called O'Malley's Irish Pub. Now it's called O'Mali's Irish Pub. What do you want, a neon X to mark the spot?"

"OK, if this is the marker, where is the secure repository?"

"Across the road. It's one of the oldest banks in London. Smooge and Harley." *

"There are no others it could be?"

"Not as far as I can see."

Gala joined them. She had opted for a glass of white wine and a frosty dew was forming on the outside of the glass. Den brought her up to date. While he did that, An Kholi perused the bar menu. It was what the English called 'lunchtime' and the pub was starting to fill up with hungry workers.

The food in the majority of eating places was made from the kelp processed on New Earth or in one of the few areas where the sea wasn't so badly polluted that nothing would grow. Any other form of food, such as meat, fish, vegetables or fruit, were so hideously expensive that only the wealthy could afford it. Pubs such as this catered for the modestly paid workers of London and so anything they served would be the tasteless output from the kelp factories.

"Have they got any curry?" Den asked when he had finished bringing Gala up to date. He had found that any food with the word 'curry' in the name was covered in a sauce that was capable of numbing the taste buds, making even kelp edible, even if it did play havoc with their digestive systems.

They ordered three chickenkelp balti's and savoured their beers while they waited.

"So, what's the plan now?" Gala asked.

"Let's go and sit by the window, where we can see the bank. It might help." They stood and took the only vacant table near the window, a fraction of a second ahead of four smartly dressed young men. They raised their voices in protest but Gala gave them one of her brightest smiles and they shrugged, turning to take the table that the three aliens had just vacated.

They started conversing in loud voices, laughing uproariously at whatever was being said. A waiter arrived and tried to place food in front of them, which brought more protests. An Kholi realised that the food must be theirs and there was a brief hiatus as she left her seat to try to explain herself to the waiter in Common Tongue.

The waiter looked at her with a blank expression, clearly unable to understand her.

"Allow me." One of the smartly dressed young men interjected, before launching into a stream of rapid English. The waiter responded at once and placed the food in front of Den, Gala and An Kholi's vacant seat.

"Thank you." An Kholi rewarded the young man with a smile as the waiter hurried away.

"Don't mention it." He extended his hand, which An Kholi felt obliged to shake. "Bob Scratchit," he continued, "of Smooge and Harley. Here's my card." His communicator appeared in his hand with practised ease and he flicked the screen in her direction. An Kholi heard her own communicator give a soft ping to let her know that new data had arrived.

"You speak very good Common Tongue."

"I'm in Interstellar Banking. I wouldn't be much good at my job if I didn't speak several languages. Now, let me see if I can place you." He studied the three of them with a serious expression on his face. "Arthurid." He pointed at Den, who smiled and nodded his head in a lie of acknowledgement. "Not one of my languages."

He turned and addressed his friends in English. They responded with shakes of their head. "No, none of us speak Arthurid. Now, what about you two little ladies." He oozed at An Kholi and Gala. Den inwardly cringed. That was not the language to use when chatting up one of the best bounty hunters in the galaxy and her more than capable friend.

"No. I can't place you. Tell you what, why don't you come over to my place tonight. We can open a bottle of Grovian while we get to know each other and you can teach me your language."

At the mention of Grovian whisky Den was about to accept the invitation when it occurred to him that he probably wasn't included. An Kholi gave the young man the sort of smile that would have had Merkaloy, the genuine one, running away in terror. It seemed to have no effect on the young man.

"Sorry, but we have a prior engagement." An Kohli's voice could have been used to cut diamonds, but the young man appeared not to sense the hard edge, or chose to ignore it.

"Oh well, suit yourself, but if you change your mind you have my card." He turned away from them and re-joined his friends, apparently dismissing them.

With their normal linguistic security blanket having been removed, An Kholi, Gala and Den ate their meal in silence. However, they weren't idle. An Kholi and Gala studied the front of the bank, looking for any clue as to how they might gain entry. Meanwhile Den studied the barmaid, with similar intentions in mind.

The four young men didn't order food, but managed to down three drinks each in quick succession. They stood to leave. Bob Scratchit turned to speak to An Kholi again. "Ah well, back to the coal face. Got to earn another gigantic bonus by bankrupting another star system. Hope it isn't yours." He grinned at them before taking his leave.

The three of them laughed dutifully, but An Kholi would have felt an awful lot more comfortable if she had been able to believe he wasn't just joking.

"I've been watching the bank's customers come and go." Gala opened, once the men were out of earshot. "The place is bristling with security cameras, which you would expect, but the front door is operated by a security lock. The customer submits to a retina scan and then enters a personal number into the key pad. It's a different number for each customer, so it must be linked to the retina data. However, it's an eight digit keypad number, which means it's a Clubbe lock..."

"And you know how to bypass one of those." Den completed the sentence for her, getting a trifle bored with her cleverness.

"Yes." Gala chose to ignore the interruption. "Now, Den, when a Gau morphs, do they take on the retinae of the person they are replicating?"

"Not normally, but it can be done. All it needs is a copy of the scan."

"And we have all the contents of Su Mali's data banks stored in the Adastra's computers. I'm prepared to bet that there's a copy of her retina scan amongst the files."

"What you have forgotten, Clever Clogs," Den sneered, "Is that the Adastra is in orbit around Sabik. It may not even be there anymore, if Merkaloy has gone chasing a bounty."

Gala was visibly deflated. "We could contact him and get him to send it to us." She attempted a recovery.

"With the greatest respect to Merkaloy," An Kholi broke in before Den could say something sarcastic, "He isn't one of nature's best when it comes to computers. Unless we can direct him straight to the relevant file it's unlikely he would find it, at least not quickly. In the meantime there's a lot of very sensitive information amongst that data and I'd rather Merkaloy wasn't given free rein to read it. It would place him in danger just to know where it is." She paused.

"The way I see it, we need to get someone inside the bank. The easiest way to do that is to pose as a prospective customer. If one of us were to go in and ask to rent a safe deposit box it would be quite legitimate to ask to see what sort of security they operate. That would give us the lay of the land."

"They wouldn't show you everything, they'd only tell you things in general terms."

"That's all we would need for starters. Once Gala knows what we're dealing with she can start to plan a way in."

"There is an alternative." Den said slyly. "That Bob Crotchet fellow seemed quite keen on you. We could set a honey trap, well you could anyway, An Kholi."

"We'll call that Plan B, shall we?" An Kholi gave Den a frosty smile.

"Whoever goes in, needs to look the part. The sort of person who has something valuable enough to need it to be kept in a safe deposit box. I suggest I go shopping." Gala started to rise from her seat.

"If anyone's going shopping it's going to be me." An Kholi forestalled her departure.

Den rose, "While you two argue it out I need to take a leak, if you'll excuse me a minute." He headed towards the back of the pub. He was only halfway there when he suddenly stopped and examined a picture hanging on the wall. He took a closer look at it then turned and hurried back to the table.

"You'd better take a look at this." He beckoned to the two females and they followed him across the crowded room.

"Wow. Well spotted Den."

In the picture were two females. One was unfamiliar to An Kholi and Gala, but they all recognised Su Mali. The two females had their arms draped around each other's shoulders, their heads angled inwards until they were touching. It was obvious that they were very close companions.

"Who's the other one?"

Den nodded towards the bar. Standing behind it, pulling hard on a beer pump, was the other woman from the image. "I think this warrants some further investigation." Den whispered.

They turned back to their table but it had already been claimed by two new arrivals. Den shrugged and led them towards the bar, where they ordered more drinks for themselves.

*To find out more about Smooge and Harley visit **http://selfishgenie.com/free-stuff.html** and download a free copy of the short story "An Alternative Christmas Carol".*

* * *

The woman recognised An Kholi and her friends as being from off-planet and was keen to talk to them, especially when they told her that they knew Su Mali, but with the pub busy with lunchtime customers she had to put them off. It was nearly three p.m. before she was able to pour herself a glass of wine and join them at their table. By this time Den was face down and snoring gently, but An Kholi and Gala were still able to speak coherently.

"Dorothea Maserati." The woman extended her hand as she introduced herself. "But call me Dotty, everyone does except for my dear old Ma." An Kholi wasn't sure how to judge the ages of humans, but this woman appeared to be in the first half of her life, good looking by Earth standards. She spoke with a difficult to understand accent, as though she had a mouth full of pebbles. The young man they had spoken to earlier had a similar accent.

An Kholi and Gala introduced themselves, shaking hands as they did so. When the woman laughed it reminded An Kholi of a fiju snorting.

"So how do you know Su Mali?" The woman asked.

"We could ask the same question. In fact we probably will." An Kholi laughed to suggest she was joking, which she wasn't. "Our paths crossed in a professional capacity."

"So you're in property investment as well, are you?"

That was clearly the cover story Su Mali had used, no doubt as an excuse to put money into the pub.

"Not in the same way as Su Mali. We're more in the line of public security, but our paths crossed."

"Ah, of course. Susikins suggested she had a lot of business rivals she had to look out for."

Susikins? An Kholi could hardly imagine Su Mali allowing herself to be called by that name. "You speak excellent Common Tongue."

"Yes, I had to learn it as part of my job. Not this one, the one I had before."

"What was that?"

"I was in banking. I managed the New London branch of Smooge and Harley. Up there." Dotty pointed towards the sky. "That's how I met Susikins. One day she came into my branch to make inquiries about getting a safe deposit box down here and 'bingo'. We just clicked at once."

"So you're in a relationship."

"We would be, if she wasn't dashing around the galaxy like a mad thing. It's been three years since I last saw her. Do you know where she is right now?"

"She could be in any number of places." An Kholi wasn't quite lying. She had no idea which prison it was to which Su Mali had been sent. "It must be eighteen months since we last saw her. So how come you ended up working here? It must have meant quite a salary reduction to leave the bank."

"Well, yes and no. Susikins can be quite persuasive. She wanted to invest, but only if she had a good manager to run the place for her. She offered me the job and threw in a partnership as a sweetener for the deal. I always wanted to be my own boss, so I took a chance. It's worked out really well. Three years ago you could have played football in here without the risk of spilling any beer, but I've really turned it round now."

"We noticed. It's pretty busy."

"It will be like that again, from about five thirty through to around eight, then the place empties out. Most of the customers work around here but live elsewhere. I normally close up around nine, except on a Friday. Friday nights are busy. I don't open at all at weekends. It's not worth it. The city is empty at the weekend except for tourists, and we aren't near any of the major tourist attractions."

They exchanged a little more small talk, but Dotty's curiosity about her visitors wasn't yet satisfied. "So what brings you into my little pub?"

"We're actually going to Smooge and Harley to open a safe deposit box, just like Su Mali, really."

"What a coincidence. Did Su Mali recommend them?"

"In a way. Are they any good?"

"For safe deposit boxes they're as good as anyone else. I wouldn't trust them for any other banking business. They're a very old company and they know all the tricks in the book and some of them are borderline illegal... What am I talking about, they're as crooked as a corkscrew, but that isn't anything unusual in the banking world." She paused as she took an elegant snip of her wine. "It's a very exclusive bank, you can't just walk in, you'll have to make an appointment. I'll sort that out for you if you like. I still have contacts there. In the banking world it isn't what you know, it's who you know that counts."

"So what are Mr. Smooge and Mr. Harley like. They are 'Misters', aren't they?"

"At the moment it is Mr. Smooge. There hasn't been a Mr. Harley since the nineteenth century, when the business was founded. He died without any legitimate heirs. The original Smooge had a soft spot for him so he kept the name. The present Mr. Smooge isn't down here anymore. He lives on Khan Epsilon and runs the bank from there."

That was an interesting coincidence. Khan Epsilon was the planet where Genghis had lived until An Kholi had involuntarily relocated him to Sadr Gamma *(see Genghis Kant)*. They would have been sort of neighbours. It was one of the many places where the mega rich lived if they weren't quite rich enough to own their own planet.

"So who manages the bank down here?"

"That would be Bob Scratchit. The Scratchits have been with Smooge and Harley from the beginning. There's always one of the family working at the bank, sometimes several."

"He was in here at lunchtime."

Dotty looked a little puzzled. "I don't think so. He would never be seen in a pub. Ah, I think you mean Bob junior. He's the current manager's grandson. Yes, he's a regular in here. A right little shit, pardon my French."

An Kholi didn't recognise French so the last comment puzzled her a little, but she let it go.

"Traditionally the youngest Scratchit is always called Tim, so I guess there must be at least one more at home, God help us."

"You believe in a God?"

"Just a turn of phrase."

As the conversation descended once again into small talk, Den drifted off to the bar to get another drink and try to flirt with the barmaid.

"You don't see many droids working behind bars down here." He opened.

"What makes you think I'm a droid?"

"Only something manmade could be as beautiful as you." he leered.

The barmaid pretended to be dismissive of the weak chat-up line but couldn't quite cover up her smile. "Well, we don't liked droids much down here. Have you ever seen Terminator?"

"But that's just make-believe. Surely humans aren't afraid of machines?"

"Maybe, just a little bit. But it's more than that. Every droid that is used in the workplace is one less job for a human to do. That means that the human has to be paid to do nothing, or else they'll starve. On a small scale that doesn't matter too much, the system can cope, but if you follow that to its logical conclusion then you have droids doing most of the jobs and most of the humans not earning anything. That means that the few humans left actually working have to pay all the taxes to keep the rest of the population alive. It isn't sustainable."

"Well, surely, it means that all the companies are more profitable, so they can pay all the taxes instead."

"You're new around here, aren't you?" the woman said sarcastically. "Businesses on Earth fight like demons to hang onto their profits. They pay as little tax as possible. Half of them, maybe more, are registered in uninhabited star systems for tax purposes. It's become even worse since the Fell arrived." She dropped her voice to a whisper as she mentioned their name. "There have been so many changes in tax law to benefit business that everyone is getting mighty suspicious. Anyway, that's one of the reasons people don't like droids. Besides, going into a pub and being served by a machine isn't much fun. You wouldn't want to come over here and try to chat-up a machine, would you?" she asked as she set Den's drink down in front of him.

"No, I must admit it's much more fun chatting to you."

"There you go. And if I were a bloke we might talk about football while I pour your drinks. Blokes are passionate about football. All a droid would do is quote loads of statistics at you. There's no passion in that; no emotional engagement. So there's no fun."

Den nodded his agreement as he sipped his drink, though he personally didn't care much for football.

"A pub chain opened up a few years ago." The woman continued. "You went to the bar and placed your order at a terminal. You could even use your communicator to order your drinks in advance so that they were ready when you arrived. You just came in and sat down and the communications system recognised your location and a droid was sent over with your drinks. They went bust within six months. They were certainly efficient; you always got served quickly and with the right drinks, but everyone hated them."

"Does anyone use droids down here?"

"They're used in dangerous places, where humans might get injured or sick. It was trendy to have a domestic droid for a while, a century or so back, but people got fed up with them. They turned out to be too efficient. If you left the table to go to the toilet while you were eating a meal you'd come back and find your food in the bin and the plate in the dish washer. One woman was woken up by her droid trying to make the bed while she was still in it because it had sensed that it was messy. There are still a few of those droids around, and every now and then a new company will come along and try to convince people that their droids are better than the old ones, but people just don't trust them really. Even the best are just too… well, different."

"So, in the meantime, what are you doing tonight?"

"I'm studying. I only work here to earn the money to pay my university tuition fees. See, if I didn't have this job, I couldn't afford to get an education. In fact with more droids doing more jobs there wouldn't even be any point in getting an education."

"What are you studying?"

"Robotics… Ironic I know." She laughed. "Here, I'll give you my number." She pulled out her communicator and flicked her card across to Den. "Maybe give me a call at the weekend."

8 - Peeling The Onion

The clothes didn't feel comfortable on An Kholi and she was starting to wish that she had allowed Gala to go on the shopping spree. Earth styles were loose and flowing, 'to allow the air to circulate around Modom's skin and keep you cool' the overbearing assistant in Jarrods had told her. Firstly the less of the air of Earth that flowed around An Kholi's body, the better she would like it, and, secondly, she felt as though the clothes were hanging on her.

But needs must, as they say, and An Kholi had a need to look more like a wealthy fashionista with lots of valuables that needed safe keeping, which meant wearing these ridiculous Earth clothes rather than her own Superskin ™ Second Skin suit that made her look like a million dollars but in which no rich Earthling would be seen dead. With their kelp diet there were few, if any, Earth women who could carry off such a look

She stepped out of the hover taxi and up the short flight of steps to the imposing front door of Smooge and Harley's. The door swung open before she had time to press the doorbell. Inside a very small man was waiting, slowly moving his hands around each other in a washing motion.

"Ah, you must be the famed An Kholi." The tiny figure gushed. "May I welcome you on behalf of Smooge and Harley's Bank. My name is Tim Scratchit, manager of the Safe Deposit Department." The tiny figure extended a minuscule hand to be shaken.

Why are these humans so besotted with pawing each other? She wondered. The air outside was heavily polluted and no doubt loaded with bacteria, yet these people seemed to be set on sharing every little microbe with each other every time they met. She stifled a shudder and extended her own hand. At least on this occasion she would be the bacteria donor and this tiny man the recipient.

The man granted her a mirthless smile and turned on his heel. "Please follow me to my office, where we can talk in private." He held a walking aid in his hand, which An Kholi believed was called a crutch. It appeared to be gold plated. Scratchit saw her looking at it.

"Purely ceremonial." He assured her. "One of my family's ancestors started the custom, my namesake to be precise, though I believe he had a more practical need of it."

Dotty Maserati had been as good as her word and news of An Kholi's appointment for the next day had been passed to them when they returned to their hotel after leaving the pub.

The man who had introduced himself as Tim Scratchit ushered her into a wood panelled room and took a seat behind a desk that was so large it dwarfed him. The chair too was far larger than was necessary for a man of his stature. An Kholi feared he might disappear completely as he sank into the padding. She settled herself into a chair that seemed to envelop her. "Refreshments?" he inquired brightly.

"Coffee please." Smooge made a selection on a keypad and a droid entered the room bearing a tray of coffee.

"A service droid. I do believe that's the first I've seen since I arrived here." An Kholi commented.

"Here at Smooge and Harley we pride ourselves on embracing all things modern. Not everyone on Earth is a Luddite. Sorry, you are probably not familiar with the term. I mean that we don't all despise modern technology. It would be hard for me to convince you of the satisfactory nature of our security precautions if I had a kettle in the corner of the room and started to boil water for your coffee."

An Kholi allowed herself a small smile of acknowledgement. "On the subject of security." She broke in, wishing to get to the heart of the matter. "I have some valuables that I would like to keep in a safe place and your bank has been recommended to me by a friend. You may be acquainted with her? Su Mali?"

"I do indeed recall the lady. Is that the correct term for someone of her species? No matter. Yes, we made our facilities available to her, for our usual fee of course." He smiled ingratiatingly again. It made An Kholi feel nauseous.

"Of course. Everything comes with a price tag. What I wish to satisfy myself of is that your security systems are adequate for the task."

"But of course. Let me take you on a guided tour."

An Kholi started to stand up but the diminutive figure waved her back into her seat. "As I said, Madam" The word grated on An Kholi's ears. She was nobody's madam. "We at Smooge and Harley pride ourselves on our use of technology. We will do the tour from here, and in real time. He used his keypad again and section of wall slid open to reveal a viewing screen; an image of the front of the bank appeared on it. She could see passers-by toing and froing.

"What you are seeing is the image from one of our many CCTV cameras. Are you familiar with an earth vegetable called an onion? Good. Well, onions consist of layers of material, each surrounding the other. On the outside, the layers are thick, to provide a strong structure, while towards the middle the material is thinner, but very much still present. That is how our security systems are constructed, in layers just like an onion." He paused to take a sip of his coffee. The cup, small in An Kholi's hand, looked large in his.

"So, first we have CCTV cameras that allow us to see who is approaching the bank." He switched view. "Even on the roof. They are motion sensor controlled, so if any movement is detected a camera will automatically zoom in and lock onto it. The other cameras, however, will increase their scan rate in case the movement is just a diversion. On the roof we also have pressure sensors. Anything larger than one of our native species of bird will trigger them. A camera will then zero in on that location. Next are the walls of the bank. While they look normal from the outside, they are reinforced concrete and steel. Not fool proof against all forms of attack, but the noise of the blast needed to get through them would alert the police several counties away. Of course within the walls are vibration sensors and heat sensors, so any attempt to drill or burn a way in would also be detected. The door looks like wood but is in fact titanium and the windows are fake. They serve only to meet planning requirements that this building looks like a commercial premises and not a fortress. The entry system requires a personal identification number and retina scan. If you present the wrong number with the right retina, or vice versa, the lock won't let you in. It's an eight digit number, very hard to decode without specialist equipment."

Not nearly as hard as you think, An Kholi thought but didn't say. The image on the screen changed and An Kholi found she was looking at the bank's interior and some sort of scanning archway.

"Of course we have to respect the privacy of our clients, so we can't ask them to reveal what they have brought into the bank for safe keeping, but we can make sure that they aren't smuggling in explosives or weapons. Our up-to-the-minute security scanners will reveal all such threats, without compromising our client's possessions."

"What if they wanted to store weapons in the safe deposit boxes?" An Kholi thought she had spotted a flaw in the system.

"Then we would have to decline their custom." Scratchit seemed saddened by the thought. "No one on Earth is allowed to hold a privately owned gun. We would also be obliged to report the matter to the police. The Americans weren't happy about that law being passed, I can assure you. Caused no end of trouble, I can tell you." And many deaths, he didn't add.

"Of course there are also procedural systems," he continued, "passwords and more identification numbers etcetera. Then we get into the vault itself." An image appeared of rows of rectangles, each of which was the front of a safe deposit box. On the lower rows the rectangles were larger, extending higher than the top of one of An Kholi's boots, if she had been wearing the ones she normally wore. The next few rows were smaller, about the height of her forearm, while the one on the upper rows she could have spanned with her hand.

"Each box requires two keys. We at the bank hold one key while the owner of the box holds the second. A bank employee inserts our key and turns it, then they leave while the box owner opens the box and either places their property inside or removes it, as is their purpose. Of course each box has an individual alarm, so that if someone attempts to open a box that hasn't had the alarm deactivated then the alarm goes off."

"Then what happens? Surely they could just make a run for it."

Scratchit's face broke into a satisfied smile, as though he had just made a rabbit appear from a hat. "No, that wouldn't be allowed. He tapped his keypad and a camera zoomed in on the top of the door that led into the vault. A thick strip of metal was revealed.

"That is the bottom of a secure steel door. As soon as the alarm sounds, that door drops into place securing the vault. Anything underneath it will be crushed, I'm afraid. It takes just nought point five of a second to close. Just in case the would-be thief has any confederates there are two more doors just like it. One by the security scanners and the second at the main entrance. They aren't opened again until the police have the whole building surrounded. The police have the only set of command codes to open them."

"Keys seem terribly old fashioned. Most locks are electronic these days, with all sorts of scanners and identification systems built in."

"We work on the principle that if it's not broken, why fix it? We have already scanned people every way that technology allows before they get to here. A mechanical key of the right design is extremely difficult to copy; far more difficult than an electronic key."

An Kholi knew this already, having read everything there was to read about bank security available on the galacticnet. But it was a question she would be expected to ask. "What about the walls and floor of the vault?"

"The same construction as the exterior walls, with the same types of sensors. When the bank is closed there are also motion sensors, thermal sensors and pressure pads. A mouse will trip all types of sensor. We have a pest control contract in place to make sure we have no mice to cause false alarms."

"It all sounds very formidable" Although An Kholi made her voice sound admiring she actually felt quite daunted by the thought of having to overcome such tight security. "I'm a little surprised, however, that you don't use high energy force fields as part of security precautions. All the other banks make a big thing out of them."

Scratchit gave a small chuckle, not quite derisory, but very close. "The reason is in the name: high energy. If you want to get high energy out then you must first put high energy in, and that requires stand-by power generation facilities in case the primary power fails or is sabotaged. That means that they, too, have to be protected because if they can be turned off then the energy fields collapse and security fails. That in turn means that the security systems protecting the stand-by power generators have to be protected and so on and so forth. You have to try to protect everything and end up protecting nothing, so we just protect the things it is absolutely vital to protect, which are your valuables.

"So how do you protect against power failure? Your systems run on electricity, just like all the others?"

"A good question. We use batteries. A little old fashioned, to be sure, but they will run the system for up to forty eight hours, more than long enough for us to be notified of a power failure and to take appropriate action. The batteries are within our security perimeter and therefore protect themselves by keeping our sensors activated. That is not something that can be easily done with stand-by generators. We aren't complacent, however. We are aware that anything designed by man can be overcome by man... or alien of course. But this repository has been in existence for three hundred years and we have never had a loss; unlike some of our competitors who use high energy force fields."

Well, that record is about to be broken, An Kholi thought to herself. In watching the presentation and listening to Scratchit's commentary she'd had the glimmering of an idea. She would have to test it out on Gala and Den of course. They would spot any weaknesses, but they would also bring some fresh thinking to it. Especially Den. When it came to not getting caught, Den was the master.

* * *

Gala sat despondently with her communicator in her hand. On it were displayed the schematics of the bank, or at least the only version she had been able to access. The up-to-date plans, showing the bank's modern security systems, weren't available. The ones she had dated from 1862 when the Smooge and Harley Bank had first bought the building.

"When the original Mr. Smooge's nephew took over the running of the bank from his uncle he had big plans. The bank was a small but very profitable regional one, based in Kent, wherever that is. It was he that decided to open the London branch that we see today. He bought the building and commissioned the work needed to turn it into a proper bank building, including the installation of a vault that is at the core of the building. It's even better protected than the safe deposit box vault. Those are the last plans that we have available. Presumably the more modern schematics are locked away in the vault so that people like us can't get our hands on them."

Den sat opposite her, a glass of beer standing in front of him They seemed to be no nearer to a plan than they had been when An Kholi had left for her meeting at the bank. "Perhaps An Kholi will find some loophole in the system."

"Well, it had better be a good one and it had better come with its own set of schematics, because these are useless." She cleared the screen, obliterating four hundred years of history with a swipe of her thumb.

An Kholi swept across the almost empty pub, a broad smile on her face.

"You look happy." Den said moving, across one seat so that she could sit down opposite Gala.

"I am very happy. Tim Scratchit, that's who I saw, told me exactly how to get hold of the egg. Well, not in so many words, of course, but he told me what I needed to know."

"You're bursting to tell us, I know."

"First things first. We need the key to Su Mali's safe deposit box. It will be amongst her possessions on board the Pradua, I'm sure of it. We need to get Merkaloy to find it and get a 3D scan done, which he can send to us. Then we get a 3D print at this end. I'm sure there must be somewhere around here that can do it."

"I saw a shop just along the road that offers 3D printing." Gala suggested.

"Good. That's the easy part. The next bit is a little bit harder, but it isn't the hardest part of all."

9 - The Bank Robber

The woman that showed An Kholi through to the vault was one of those terribly well bred, very cool, English women that seemed to be able to look down their nose at you even if they're shorter than you. Most females were shorter than An Kholi, except perhaps for the Verticalli, but then they were taller than everyone, and they didn't have noses they could look down. In fact they didn't have noses.

The woman operated a key pad, entering a lengthy number. She then stood back, ostentatiously turning away as An Kholi entered her own number, reading it from the screen of her communicator as she hadn't yet had the time, or the inclination, to learn it off by heart.

The door to the vault swung obediently open and the cool woman led the way inside. She confirmed the box number with An Kholi and inserted her key into the lock, turning it fully to the right and then back to the left before turning it back to the centre once again. She stood back and once again looked down her nose at An Kholi, though she had to raise her face to look up as she did it.

"When Modom is finished, please lock your box and then press the button by the door. I will then let Modom out."

She swept out of the vault leaving only a trace of very expensive perfume behind her and the vault door swing shut once again. It was locked, An Kholi knew, but it wasn't the most secure of the barriers between her and the outside world. She inserted her key into the lock and performed the intricate manoeuvres necessary to release the door of the box. A final click told her she had succeeded. She opened the door and drew out the long metal container that made up the interior. When it was half way out she stopped and opened the lid to give her access to the contents. After removing them she locked the box again, withdrew her own key and then that of the female bank employee.

With the object and both keys in her hands An Kholi stepped along the line of boxes until she identified the one that she now knew to be Su Mali's, the number being engraved on the key which had been produced by the 3D printer. It was almost, but not quite, identical to her own key.

She inserted the bank's key into the lock of Su Mali's safe deposit box. A metallic voice startled her.

"Security violation. You are not authorised to open that box. If you continue a full security lockdown will be initiated."

An Kholi ignored the warning as she reached inside her handbag and withdrew a small canister. It fitted neatly into the palm of her hand. She used her fingernail to flip back a safety tab then pulled the arming pin. The canister immediately started to spew out clouds of smoke. She dropped it at her feet, allowing the smoke to swirl up around her, screening her from the view of the ever present CCTV cameras. Of course they would still be able to see her using the infrared spectrum, but the poorer quality images would hide certain details. A new announcement was made, this time by a more obviously human voice.

"Cease and desist. You are ordered to stand where you can be seen. Security lockdown will commence in ten seconds."

An Kholi wondered why they would allow her ten seconds of grace, but then realised that they wouldn't want to upset genuine customers by initiating a lockdown prematurely just because someone had made a mistake. She carried on unlocking Su Mali's safe deposit box.

As soon as she made the final turn of the key an alarm shrieked out and she heard the solid titanium security door slam down, locking her in the vault until the police arrived. She had just one more thing to do before she went to sit in the corner and wait for her inevitable capture. The smoke continued to billow around the room, helping to conceal what she was doing.

* * *

An Kholi placed her eye against the aperture of the scanner and allowed her retina to be examined. She then tapped her identification number into the keypad. The solid front door of the Smooge and Harley Bank swung open and she stepped through, walking straight towards a receptionist. The young female's jaw dropped as she recognised the tall female alien that was approaching her.

"But…but…" she stammered. Her hand started to move towards what An Kholi assumed would be a concealed panic button.

"But nothing. I'd like to see Mr. Scratchit please, Mr. Tim Scratchit."

"I'm not sure…."

"Don't worry, Agrathea." A voice broke in. An Kholi turned to see the obsequious smile of Tim Scratchit approaching her, appearing to dominate all of his other features. It made him look like a smile on legs. "I'll take care of this." He concluded.

"Well. You appear not to be in prison after all." He turned his full attention to An Kholi, his professional smile unable to hide the curiosity in his eyes.

"I never was in prison. The female that was captured in your vault was an imposter."

"And how can I be sure that you aren't the imposter."

"Did you compare the criminal's DNA with the sample you took from me?"

Scratchit's smile slipped a little. It was clear that he hadn't. "Er…."

"I suggest you send a copy of the DNA code to the police and ask them to check it against the sample they will have taken from your would-be thief. It won't match. I'll wait while that is done."

"But she had your key….."

"The trouble with mechanical keys is that they can be stolen. I'll explain once you have satisfied yourself of my identity. By the way, just to avoid mistakes, you had better take a fresh sample of DNA from me and compare it to the original. Or maybe you were just about to do that?"

Scratchit was struggling to retake the initiative from this very self-assured woman. No, she wasn't a woman, was she? She was from an alien species and she referred to herself as a female. He had to get that right. People… beings, were so touchy about such things.

"Of course… yes… of course." He flustered. "Perhaps you'd like to wait in my office."

An Kholi allowed herself to be escorted across the bank's impressive reception area and into the luxury of Scratchit's office.

"Refreshments? I seem to recall that you favour coffee."

"Yes please." An Kholi settled herself into the chair she had used on her previous visit, trying very hard to conceal the smile that was trying to break out onto her face. She had to keep reminding herself that she was the victim of an attempted robbery. She forced a stern expression back into place.

Scratchit bustled about, using his computer to send a copy of her DNA code to the police then taking a fresh sample from An Kholi and sending it for analysis in their in-house facilities. The results were back within minutes.

"Well, An Kholi, it seems that we have been the victims of an elaborate attempt to impersonate you. I'm sure that the police will confirm this as soon as they have compared your DNA to that of the perpetrator."

"I'm sure that they will. As soon as I saw the media item on the attempted robbery I knew that something had gone wrong with your security systems."

"Yes, but I'm not quite sure…"

"What went wrong." An Kholi completed the sentence for him. "Quite. Well, I may be able to enlighten you. Are you familiar with a species called the Gau?"

"Of course. Their ability to assume the identity of other beings is a major threat to security and we have to…. Oh."

"Oh indeed. I don't hold the bank responsible, of course." An Kholi's voice made it clear that she really did. "It was a simple ruse and I have to admit I fell for it myself. Perhaps I had better tell you the whole story." She took a sip of her very excellent coffee and then started her pre-prepared explanation.

"On my last visit I made reference to Su Mali." Scratchit nodded his head in acknowledgement. "Did you know that Su Mali is a Gau?" Scratchit's jaw dropping open told her that he didn't.

"Well, as you may or may not know, she was a very successful criminal. As you definitely know, because I told you, I am a bounty hunter. I was the bounty hunter who captured Su Mali. Since then I have been trying to capture Su Mali's accomplices. We tracked one of them, a female, to New Earth where she had assumed a human identity. This is where things get a little bit messy." An Kholi took another sip of her coffee. "I now think that she was here to try to reclaim whatever is in Su Mali's safe deposit box. I don't know if Su Mali has asked her to do that or maybe the accomplice, I don't actually know her name, is double crossing Su Mali.

Anyway, I had a Gau in my employ, who I was using to identify other Gau for me. They have a telepathic link with each other, in case you don't know." Scratchit was still doing cod fish impressions so An Kholi carried on speaking regardless of whether Scratchit was keeping up with her.

"It turns out that my employee did identify the female Gau, but rather than tell me about her he chose to reveal himself to her and he then double crossed me and went off with her. I think they planned this bank robbery between them. Somehow they got hold of my safe deposit box key, then the female Gau disguised herself as me. She had to do that because male Gau can't adopt female sexual organs and if she was arrested the police would find out very quickly if a male was impersonating me. With my key, and also Su Mali's key, in her possession she bluffed her way into your bank and the rest you know."

"But how did she think she would get away with it?"

"She didn't know about all the security systems you have in place, especially the security lockdown doors. She thought she could just get into Su Mali's safe deposit box and then walk out as me, just as she had walked in as me."

"But with Su Mali's key she didn't have to disguise herself as you. She could have walked in disguised as Su Mali and we would have been none the wiser."

"I'm guessing here." An Kholi lied, "but I don't think this Gau had access to Su Mali's retina scan, so she wouldn't have been able to get past your front door. However, my scan data was with my box key, so she was able to copy it and complete her disguise."

"Ah, yes. I see. I think I said the last time we met, that any system that can be designed by a person can be overcome by a person."

"You did indeed say that, Mr. Scratchit." An Kholi was finding it increasingly difficult to conceal her triumphant smile. "Which is why I hold myself at least partly responsible for the attempted robbery. I should never have kept my retina scan data with my safe deposit box key. It was very remiss of me. I take it that the contents of Su Mali's box have been secured once again?"

"They have."

"Good. I wouldn't expect you to reveal the contents of my safe deposit box, so I won't insult you by asking you what was in Su Mali's. I will contact my employers and I'm sure that now they know for certain that Su Mali has a security box here they will arrange a court order to have it opened and the contents handed over to the relevant authorities."

Realisation dawned on the face of the banker. "So that was what this was all about, was it? You just wanted to confirm that Su Mali had a safe deposit box here."

"You see right through me, Mr. Scratchit. We had a suspicion, no more. Your minor indiscretion when we last met was all the confirmation I needed, but I had to proceed with the charade of opening an account with you, just in case you became suspicious and tried to notify Su Mali that we had found her hiding place."

"But we would never…" An Kholi raised her hand to stem his protests. "Unfortunately not all banks are as honest as Smooge and Harley." She had to fight to keep any trace of scorn from her voice. "We couldn't take that chance. Which brings me to my final item of business. Time to retrieve the meaningless items I put into my safe deposit box and close my account, if you would be so good as to make the arrangements."

"But your key is with the police; it's evidence against the thief."

"That is your problem, Mr. Scratchit, not mine. I have an urgent appointment on the other side of the galaxy and I won't be returning this way for the foreseeable future. I would like to get my property back before I leave."

"You said it was meaningless…."

"Meaningless to anyone else. It is of very great sentimental value to me. My grandmother's…" she let a sob creep into her voice, making her unable to continue.

Scratchit did what most men do when faced with the tears of a female. He capitulated. "Of course. I'll have a word with the police. I'm sure that under the circumstances they will be understanding. If you would wait here while I make the arrangements." He stood, his head hardly higher than the enormous desk, and left the office.

It was nearly an hour later when the cool looking woman looked down her nose at An Kholi. "When Modom has finished please lock your box and then press the button." She pointed at the small green button positioned next to the door. She gave An Kholi a look that said 'I'm watching you,' clearly more suspicious of this tall alien than her boss, before she left the vault and the door swung shut behind her.

An Kholi completed the unlocking of the box, withdrew the metal container within it and opened it up. There, lying inside, was the bag that contained the egg, just where Ka Mera had left it after taking it from Su Mali's box, after the alarm had gone off and the security door had slammed down, locking her into the vault. Her movements had been disguised by the smoke and the infra-red of the CCTV images told police little about what she had been doing after the alarm sounded, other than hurrying back to An Kholi's own box once again. They assumed she was trying to conceal her attempt on Su Mali's box.

Replacing the egg in Su Mali's box was a PMD storing a mass of encrypted data files. If anyone ever got around to decrypting them they would find themselves reading nothing more interesting than the entire contents of the Encyclopaedia Galactica. Very educational, of course, but of no intrinsic value. Gala had smiled as she encrypted each volume in turn. However, until they were decrypted they gave the impression of being a highly valuable artefact which Su Mali might go to the trouble of locking away in a safe deposit box. After all, for all anyone knew, the data might contain the secret of where the Magi were hidden.

An Kholi concealed the prize within her handbag, secured her safe deposit box for the final time and pressed the button beside the vault door. Five minutes later she was standing in the street as the door of the Smooge and Harley Bank closed behind her one last time.

It might be assumed that the recovery of the Magi egg was the hardest part of the plan, but it wasn't.

Glossary

PMD - Portable Memory Device. They come in a range of shapes and sizes and use a variety of different technologies to store information, but they all perform the same basic function. They are all fully compatible with each other except for those produced by the Banana Computing Corporation, which don't even work with the equipment they are supposed to work with.

10 - The Solicitor

As An Kholi left Smooge and Harley's Bank a well-dressed solicitor presented himself at the entrance to New Holloway Prison. He looked up at the grey stone walls, first constructed on a site first used ten years before the original Mr. Smooge's nephew purchased the premises being visited by An Kholi.

Rain turned the grey limestone shiny and the headlights of passing hover taxis and buses reflected off, giving the stone an almost festive appearance until the lights disappeared to leave only a blank forbidding surface behind.

A prison warder examined the solicitor's credentials. Solicitors were a common enough visitor to the prison, there were normally two or three inside at any time during normal office hours. The warder decided that Mr. Grabbit of Sioux, Grabbit and Rhun was OK to enter and passed him through a Judas door which pierced the forbidding gates of the prison, for the next step of the procedure. A sign above a door told him where to go for the reception, where he was subject to more entrance procedures.

Mr. Grabbit (the junior, his father being too important do such mundane things as prison visits), allowed himself to be patted down by another warder while a second searched his brief case. His umbrella was removed, the warden tapping the blunt tip of the ferrule to indicate that it could be used as a weapon.

"You can 'ave that back when you leave." The warder stated, placing the umbrella behind the counter.

"The contents of that device are confidential, between myself and my client." The solicitor warned, as a communicator was lifted from the case. The warder gave him a look that would make an oak tree wither and replaced the device. That, the warder said to himself, would cost the solicitor a lengthy wait before he was allowed to see his client. Who the hell does he think he is? Grumpole of the fucking Bailey? Jumped up little shit.

"Why are you talking sprag?" The warder asked, his tone surly but also using Common Tongue.

"If you mean Common Tongue, as you are I'm sure well aware my client isn't from Earth. She speaks no English. Under the Galactic Legal Convention Volume Six, Chapter Four, Clause D, Sub Clause Three she is entitled to have all her business conducted either in her own language or in Common Tongue. As I don't speak her language, whatever it may be, Common Tongue will suffice. 'All her business' includes any dealings I have with prison authorities. Smithzoid versus The Government of Arcturis refers."

"Didn't bother the last brief to visit her." The warder muttered. But faced with the barrage of legalese he returned to his work, more determined than ever to extract some petty revenge.

After what seemed like an age sitting in a waiting room, Grabbit was shown to an interview room where his client was waiting. He was surprised to see that she no longer resembled the leggy brunette that went by the name of An Kholi. She was smaller, though still slender, and her hair was a sort of dull red. Her skin was also a sort of nondescript grey colour rather than An Kholi's pale lilac. Her forehead bulged to accommodate the additional brain capacity required of a shape shifter. She looked as though she had been in prison for years rather than just a few days.

The female could see that her solicitor was taken by surprise by her appearance. "They've found out that I'm not the real An Kholi, so there didn't seem to be much point in trying to maintain the pretence." She stood up and offered her hand to the solicitor. It was a different one this time. It was always a different one, she had noticed. No wonder the prisons on this planet were so full, she thought. "I'm Ka Mera, by the way. In case you don't know. Call…" She stopped, surprise of her own registering on her face for a fleeting moment. She looked at the warder, still standing by the door, then continued. "…me by that name. I'm from a species called the Gau. We have the ability to change our shape."

"I've heard of the Gau, but never met one of your species. Is that the correct term?"

The warder swung the door shut, leaving them to conduct their legal chat in the privacy that was required by law. She wouldn't be far away, Ka Mera knew. They were never far away.

"Den, is that you?" she hissed.

Den winked at her and made a big show of introducing himself, raising his voice so that if the warder was positioned as close to the door as he suspected she would be then she was bound to overhear.

"My Gaudar must be weakening." She whispered across at him. "I didn't feel you until we were nearly touching.

"I think it's all this stone." Den indicated the walls. "I had the same problem." More loudly he said "If it has become known that you aren't really who you said you are, then it will weaken our defence."

"I'm innocent. It was all just a huge misunderstanding." Ka Mera almost shouted back.

"Of course it is. Now, do I call you Ka, Mera, or Ka Mera?"

"Ka will do." She replied. She leaned forward and dropped her voice to a whisper. "OK, what's the plan?"

"Just as we discussed. Pity they've already discovered you're a Gau, we should have been out of here before An Kholi revealed that deception, but they kept me waiting so long. But they haven't put in any of the normal precautions, like using more than one guard to watch and make sure you don't assume another identity and bluff your way out."

"Which is what we're going to do, right?"

"Right. There's no DNA or retina scans. The whole security set up is so antiquated that I'm surprised there aren't more breakouts."

"The cells are old, but pretty solid, which is probably why. Supervision is tight when you're moving around as well, so there aren't many opportunities to make a run for it. Too many locked doors between the inside and the outside."

"But not from here. I only came through two in the corridor, plus the reception area and main gate, of course. If we hold our nerve we'll make it."

"And if we don't?"

"Then you and I are both going to be spending a lot of time in here."

"Not you, at least not here. This is females only. There's another place down the road for men, or so the other women have been telling me."

Den tried to push that gloomy thought from his mind and made himself sound positive, for his own sake as much as for Ka Mera's.

"You're going to have to do all the talking. Is your English up to impersonating that guard?"

"Should be. English isn't her native language either, so she has an accent. If I get the change right the vocal equipment will do the rest."

"We'll keep up with this lawyer - client mongo shit for a few more minutes and then I'll get the warder to open the door. You kick up a bit of a fuss, which will make the warder come further inside. I'll grab her and then we'll have to find some way of gagging her and tying her up. We'll use the clothes you're wearing for that; you won't need them again. Then you change into her, dress in her uniform and we head for the great outdoors."

It was the plan they had agreed days before when Ka Mera had arrived from New Earth to join them. She hadn't been happy with it, perhaps because she hadn't trusted An Kholi not to abandon her once she had what she wanted, but Den had given her his solemn word that he would come and get her, and she trusted Den. Why she trusted him she wasn't sure, because she now knew enough about him to know that he was probably the most untrustworthy Gau in the galaxy. Perhaps she was just fooling herself, she thought. But if she wanted to be allowed to stay with this group, she had to make herself useful, even if it meant risking her own freedom.

"How have the other women been?" Den asked, as a way of filling in time.

"Not too bad. A couple of them thought they might have a go but I changed into a Gelvik when the warders weren't looking and that seemed to put them off the idea."

"Yes, that would do it." Gelvik were twice the size of Ka Mera and armed with a pretty ferocious looking set of teeth. Of course Ka Mera wouldn't have had the physical strength to go with her adopted size but the human women wouldn't have known that. The humans were a pretty ignorant bunch when it came to their knowledge of the rest of the galaxy. Come to that they were pretty ignorant about everything except pop stars and footballers.

They chattered away about inconsequential matters for a few more minutes: The food, the bathing facilities, the cells and so on, then Den looked at the time on his communicator and signalled that they should get ready to leave. He stood up and raised his voice.

"OK, Miss Ka Mera, I think I have enough to be getting on with. I'll find a barrister to represent you, but I'm afraid it is going to be a difficult case to defend."

"Well, do your best won't you."

Den walked the few paces to the interview room door and rapped on it. "Of course you must prepare yourself to spend some time in prison."

"No. you can't let that happen." Ka Mera raised her voice to a shout as the door swung open. "I can't stay in here. You've got to get me bail" She started screaming hysterically, pulling at her hair.

"Calm down, Ka Mera." The warder said from her place in the corridor.

"Bail is out of the question for a Gau." Den added, making it appear that he was stoking the flames of Ka Mera's desperation.

The Gau continued to scream and sob, throwing herself on to the ground and rolling about, thrashing her arms and legs and in danger of doing herself and injury. The warder eyed her suspiciously. She was an older woman, no doubt very experienced at her job. She had seen it all before. She crossed her arms but made no move to enter the room.

"My client seems very distressed." Den said, trying to encourage the woman to intervene.

"Your client's play acting." Was her cynical reply. Den noted the thickness of her words, as if she was struggling to get them past her teeth.

"How dare you suggest such a thing." Den did his best to look affronted by such a suggestion. "She looks to be in severe distress. If she hurts herself…" Before he had finished the sentence the warder gave a heavy sigh and stepped forward. She had no wish to be on the wrong end of a lawsuit because the Gau thrashing about on the floor had chipped her nail varnish. She might be cynical, but she wasn't stupid.

But then again she was stupid, because as she stepped past Den he grabbed her, placing a hand over her mouth before she had a chance to cry out. She was a bulky woman and strong, so her spirited resistance was testing Den's ability to hold her. Her right hand grabbed at her chest and Den realised, almost too late, that she had a panic alarm pinned to the crest of her large bosom. He adjusted his grip to grab her wrist and try to stop her reaching it, but she simply switched hands and stretched towards the button with her left.

Ka Mera intervened by planting a fist firmly into the woman's stomach, driving the air from her lungs and making her double over in agony. As the warder struggled to suck in more air, Den grabbed at her neck in what he fondly hoped was the Vulcan Death Pinch, as demonstrated in old TV sci-fi shows. Ka Mera gave him a disgusted look and swing a right hook to connect with the woman's jaw. The punch didn't knock the woman out but it did make her sufficiently groggy for Den to force her to the ground.

Ka Mera stripped off the loose blouse she had been wearing in her disguise as An Kholi and started to tear the thin material into strips. As she succeeded in producing a length she passed it to Den who used them to bind the warder's hands and feet. The warder let out a loud groan and Ka Mera stuffed a whole sleeve of her garment into the warder's mouth while Den tied it into place. The woman started to regain her full faculties and started to thrash about once again, trying to free herself from her bonds but it was obvious to the three of them that she had no chance of escaping them.

It was at that point that Den realised that trying to remove the clothes from a woman who was bound hand and foot was going to be something of a challenge. Den was no stranger to dealing with women in restraints, but they had normally removed their clothes before allowing themselves to be tied up. With Ka Mera's upper body now being covered by only a rather flimsy bra there was no way she could leave the cell.

Having reached the same conclusion the woman glared at the two Gau with a triumphant look in her eyes.

"OK, Den, You're going to have to hold her while I get her clothes off her." She turned her attention to the woman, now half sitting, half lying on the floor. "We can do this the easy way or the painful way." She announced bending over until her face was only sim away from that of the warder. The warder glared at her but with the memory of her recent rough handling still fresh in her mind, she made no attempt to struggle

Den went to the door and pushed it until it was almost shut. It could only be opened from the outside, so he daren't fully close it.

He turned back to find Ka Mera stripping the heavy shoes and thick socks off the warder, before attacking the broad belt that secured her over-stretched trousers. She dragged them down to knee level before removing the strips of rags that secured the warder's ankles. The warder immediately started kicking out, but a sharp warning slap across her bare thighs told her what would happen if she didn't calm down.

Removing the warder's anti-stab vest and shirt proved a more complex operation, with Den having to work hard to prevent the woman from striking out. Physically she was stronger than both Den and Ka Mera and a lucky blow to the head of either one of them might render them senseless.

At last the warder was reduced to her functional and appropriately robust underwear and once again securely trussed up. Den turned away while Ka Mera undressed then morphed into the form of the larger woman. Her bra, designed for Ka Mera's more slender form, gave up the unequal struggle and flew across the room, propelled by the sudden expansion of Ka Mera's new breasts. The Gau seemed to take on an almost translucent appearance as her body's cells were forced further apart to accommodate the larger form, allowing light to pass through. She quickly dressed herself in the warder's uniform and announced that she was ready.

Den turned back just as Ka Mera was securing the belt, from which was suspended the heavy bunch of keys that were so vital to their escape plan. Again Den said a silent word of thanks to the prison authorities who were so distrusting of new technology that they had refused to install electronic locks controlled by retina data, DNA, fingerprints or even digital combinations.

"You go first." Ka Mera instructed. "The warders always follow behind."

They left the interview room, not even glancing back to take a last look at the firmly bound and gagged warder. Ka Mera pulled the door of the room shut and the lock slipped into place with a satisfyingly loud click. Den turned left and led the way along the narrow corridor towards the visitors' exit. He noticed the CCTV cameras and wondered if they had been able to capture any of the goings on inside the room, but the lack of any alarm or warders arriving to rescue their colleague suggested that they hadn't.

They were nearing a corner which Den was sure was the last one before the first gate when Den almost stopped dead in his tracks, causing Ka Mera to bump into him. He realised that he had absolutely no idea what would happen when they reached the gate. Was there a warder in attendance, and if so would he expect some sort of coded exchange to take place, just in case his own guardian was acting under duress? Would they just unlock it and walk through?

"Do you know what happens when we leave?" Den hissed over his shoulder, now reluctant to run the risk of exposure by turning the corner.

"Not a clue." Ka Mera hissed back. "I can tell you what happens when you arrive, if that's any help?" She added beneath her breath, the memories of the indignities she was subjected to still at the forefront of her mind.

They could delay no more. Den turned, blocking the narrow corridor. The outer one couldn't be opened if the inner one was still insecure, Den had noted as he had come into the building, which meant that prisoners couldn't rush the gates and get through. Other than that, the corridor was empty. Den's eyes swept the ceilings, picking out the four cameras that kept the barrier under surveillance.

"Look at the cameras and smile." Den muttered, doing his best to keep his lips from moving, just in case any of the unseen observers might have lip reading skills.

They approached the first gate and Ka Mera did as she was told and beamed at the nearest camera.

"You're very cheerful today Grebula." A metallic voice addressed them from a grill mounted high on the wall.

"Nearly start of my holidays." The fake Grebula answered.

A chuckle came from the wall and there was a clunk as an electronic bolt slid open. Den remembered this from the entrance procedures and pushed on the gate. It didn't move. He pushed again, harder. His heart leapt into his mouth as he started to panic. Perhaps the bolt sliding into place was to lock the gate, not to unlock it.

"Perhaps Sir would like to try pulling the gate." The metallic voice prompted. Ka Mera muttered the instruction in Common Tongue before Den's lack of action could give them away

Den's shoulders almost visibly sagged with relief as he realised his foolishness. He pulled and the gate swung open with a well-oiled smoothness. They stepped through and Ka Mera pulled it closed behind them, another electronic buzz-clunk telling them they were now trapped between the two gates.

The second gate had to be opened with one of the keys that was on the bunch hanging from Ka Mera's belt. The problem was, which key was it? The real warder would know at a glance.

"Try the biggest one." Den suggested. Ka Mera did but the key was obviously too big for the lock.

"You 'aven't forgotten again 'ave you, you dozy mare." The voice mocked from the grill.

"Oh shut up, smartarse." Fake Grebula snapped back. It would have been more authentic to have tagged the voice's name to the end of the retort, but that couldn't be helped. She had started trying the keys at random when Den spotted a dot of green paint just above the door lock. "Is there a key with green paint on it?" he whispered into Ka Mera's ear. She examined them, selected one and slid it smoothly into the lock, gave it a twist and the gate swung open under the weight of her hand.

"Thank you." Ka Mera flung over her shoulder towards the grill, now behind them.

"Thank you Petrov." The voice replied.

"Thank you Petrov," Ka Mera responded obediently.

"Thank you Petrov Darling" The voice added.

"Fuck off Petrov Darling" Ka Mera improvised.

There was a loud laugh from the hidden watcher. "That's better."

The metal grill fell silent as they turned another corner and found themselves in the visitors' waiting area.

The row of hard plastic seats, the only furnishings in the room, were empty. The walls were bare and austere, painted in that sickly shade of green beloved of institutions across the galaxy. Opposite the chairs was a single door. With a start of alarm, Den realised there was no handle on their side of it. The ubiquitous CCTV cameras covered all four corners of the room, with an extra one positioned to observe the door, just for good measure.

Ka Mera had more presence of mind than Den, and spotted the intercom on the wall adjacent to the door. She stepped forward and pressed the button. There was a sound of buzzing in the distance.

"Yes" snapped a voice. Even with the electronic distortion Den recognised the voice of the surly warder that had taken against him when he had entered the prison.

"One to leave." Ka Mera stated flatly, using the terminology she had heard the warders using since her arrival. Den had to admit she was doing a good job with the voice.

"Is it that stuck up solicitor?"

Ka Mera smirked, knowing that Den wouldn't be able to understand the English. "Yes it is."

"I've a good mind to keep him waiting."

"Not good idea." Ka Mera replied. "He already threaten to report for not notify identity of prisoner."

"Wanker." The disembodied voice replied, but there was a buzz and the sound of a lock opening.

Ka Mera pushed the door and it swung outwards. She stepped backwards and allowed Den to pass through ahead of her, as a warder would do.

"Where do you think you're going" The warder snapped from his position behind the counter. As he spoke in English Den assumed he was talking to the disguised Ka Mera. There was no sign of the second guard.

Ah, problem, thought Den, but he didn't know what the man had said.

"I go for fresh air." Ka Mera improvised, realising that interior guards probably didn't use this exit to leave the prison. There would be a staff entrance somewhere.

The male warder visibly relaxed. "It's raining out there. You'll get wet."

"You call what you get rain? You go to my country, there you see rain."

The warder laughed but turned his attention back to his computer screen and started tapping away. Den led the way to the exterior door. "Goodbye" he called at the man, assuming it would be normal. The warder grunted a reply but didn't look up from whatever was absorbing him.

The exterior door wasn't locked and they stepped through into the small courtyard that lay between the reception and the main gate. The stout, castle like construction loomed over them. The two huge gates were firmly shut, but Den assumed that they were used only to allow vehicles in and out. When he had entered the prison the gate guard had opened a Judas to let him through. It now stood slightly ajar, allowing a tantalising glimpse of freedom to creep through it.

"Oi!" A shout came from behind them. The two stopped in their tracks. Slowly Ka Mera turned back to face the reception entrance. Den followed suit.

The warder stood in the doorway, brandishing an umbrella. "You forgot this."

It was clear what the warder was saying, so Den was able to respond, careful not to let the relief show in his face.

"Thank you." he muttered in English, one of the few things he could say, other than 'more beer please' and 'is the curry any good?'.

The warder didn't bother to reply, he just turned and went back into the dry of the reception area, closing the door firmly behind him.

Ka Mera pulled the Judas open and stepped through, followed immediately by Den. The guard in the small gate lodge gave them a cursory glance, waving a greeting to Ka Mera, which she returned.

"Just going to get ..." her voice tailed off as she realised that the guard wasn't listening. "I have no idea what I was going to get." She muttered to Den.

"Doesn't matter. Walk slowly to the corner of the street. There's a pub not far from there, it's called The Bank and Fraudster. I've hidden your Sabik clothes in the ladies toilets. When you've changed head straight for the shuttle port. The others will meet us there." Den turned and headed in the opposite direction. Best for them not to be seen together until Ka Mera was less recognisable and he himself had changed his identity once again.

Glossary

Sprag - Derogatory. Earth slang for the language known as Common Tongue. Habitual speakers of Common Tongue are Spraggers.

11 - The Kelp Workers

Tiny Blur grimaced as the face of Alison Fakescottsman appeared on his viewer for their regular conference. He really would have preferred to use someone else as his 'fixer' but Fakescottsman was the only one he could trust; the only one who had as much to lose as he himself had.

"Bad news, I'm afraid." Fakescottsman didn't waste any time on preamble. "The polls are telling us that less than 20% of those eligible to vote will actually do it. The abstention campaign is really starting to hurt us."

"Polls get it wrong, sometimes." Blur observed, trying to sound sanguine.

"Only sometimes and usually only in terms of the winning margin. Even if this poll is a little bit out it means we won't be able to claim the election result as being legitimate."

"I remember the days when a turnout of 20% was regarded as being perfectly legitimate. At least the vote organisers claimed it was."

"In those days you just had to have a vote, you didn't have to actually persuade people to take part in it. Times have changed and what once applied on Earth doesn't hold good across the galaxy. If you want your government to be accepted as legitimate then you're going to have to persuade more people to get out and vote. We may be able to fix the result, but we can't fix the turnout."

"Could we round up the organisers of the abstention campaign and just lock them up?"

"Might work on Earth, but we'd have trouble elsewhere. A lot of the planets are still very old school about that sort of thing. They still believe in democracy and all that twaddle."

"OK, we go for discrediting them then. Get something on the organisers, maybe fake some evidence, you know what to do."

"OK, I'll get on it, but I can't promise anything."

"Well, remember, your job is on the line just as much as mine. Now, what's going on with An Kholi?"

"Looks like you were right. It's almost certain one of the eggs is in the bank vault. Someone impersonated An Kholi and tried to steal it, but they got caught. Turned out it was a Gau impersonating An Kholi, my sources tell me, but they didn't know that individual safe deposit boxes were fitted with alarms, so she got caught."

"So where is An Kholi now?"

Fakescottsman turned very red and wouldn't look directly into the camera. He muttered something unintelligible.

"What was that?" demanded Blur.

"I said we lost her. Look, it wasn't my fault. We were using police and military drones to track her. As soon as An Kholi, or the Gau we thought was An Kholi, was arrested they were re-tasked. By the time we found out that she was a fake we had lost track of the real An Kohli. We weren't the only ones to be fooled." Fakescottsman hurried to excuse himself. "The bank and the police were both taken in. These Gau are a menace. You need to do something about them when you get into power."

"If I get into power. That's looking doubtful at the moment. OK. Get someone inside the prison to talk to this Gau; find out what's going on."

Fakescottsman shuffled and muttered again, forcing Blur to make another snappy demand for him to repeat himself.

"She escaped this morning. A fake solicitor smuggled her out disguised as a warder. We think he was a Gau as well."

Blur let out an exaggerated sigh of frustration. "An Kholi is known to travel with a Gau. Did no one anticipate this?"

"But there seem to be two of them now. How could we know that?"

Blur had to admit that the arrival of a second Gau, a female one at that, had changed things, but he wasn't going to admit that to Fakescottsman.

"OK. Get the police and Space Force onto it. I want them stopped before they leave the planet. Is that clear? I want to know what's going on and it seems that they are the only ones with any answers. I also want whatever is in Su Mali's safe deposit box. Make it happen."

Blur didn't allow Fakescottsman any time to answer as he abruptly cut the conference connection.

* * *

While Den was busting Ka Mera out of prison, An Kholi had left Smooge and Harley's Bank and now stood before the sales counter of an electronic supplies warehouse. Eventually a bored looking sales assistant came up and grunted something at her, which An Kholi took to be a greeting.

"Do you sell memory eggs?" An Kholi asked before boredom led to the girl's early demise.

The girl gave an exaggerated sigh at being addressed in Common Tongue, but had obviously understood the question. "Not much demand for them these days. People prefer PMDs." The girl answered. Her use of the inter-galactic language was good, so An Kholi was at a loss to understand why she had been reluctant to use it, but then remembered she was on Earth and in England in particular.

"But do you sell them?"

"Oh yes. What size?"

"Twenty zettabyte"

"Oh, the small ones. Yeah, we've got them. How many do you want?"

"How many come in a box?"

"We normally sell them one at a time, but if you want a box there would be twenty in it."

"OK, I'll take a box. Can you ship them anywhere I want?"

"That will cost extra."

"Not a problem."

The girl wandered off, presumably to locate the eggs, though she hadn't said as much. For all An Kohli knew it might be the last time she ever saw her.

One of the problems with stealing the Magus egg was how to get it off the planet without taking it through the security procedures that were required before they could board the shuttle back to New Earth. If any of the Fell were to discover that they were now in possession of the egg they might well use their influence over the authorities to try to recover it. The shuttle port was the ideal place to intercept it. So how to conceal the egg had been a major stumbling block.

It had been Ka Mera who'd made the suggestion. "Where do you hide a tree?" she asked. When they all looked puzzled she had answered her own question. "In a forest." So An Kholi had travelled half way across London to buy a forest.

The girl sauntered back carrying a sturdy looking box. She laid it on the sales counter and opened it up for An Kholi to inspect the contents. Inside lay twenty memory eggs, identical to the one concealed in An Kholi's bag. She was relieved to see that each egg was sitting in a cushioned recess, protected against shock or vibration. There wasn't a postal service in the galaxy that wasn't capable of damaging an anvil, she knew, let alone something as fragile as a memory egg.

"Oh, and do you have an interface cable for them please?" An Kholi asked with a sweet smile.

The girl gave a scowl to indicate her displeasure at being asked to do more work, then stomped off to find the requested item. An Kholi dipped into her bag and pulled out the stolen egg. Lifting one of the new eggs out of the box, she concealed it in her bag and placed the Magus egg in its place in the box. It was done so quickly that even an attentive sales assistant might have missed it. It was several more minutes before the girl returned with the requested, if redundant, cable.

In her hand she also held a communication device, which she handed to An Kholi. "Enter your name and the shipping address." She commanded, folding her arms to indicate that nothing more would happen if she wasn't obeyed.

An Kholi did as she was asked then presented her communicator to make payment. The two communicators exchanged data and the girl examined hers suspiciously. The data was from off-planet, which in her mind immediately made it suspect. Her eyes widened as she saw the credit limit displayed. Her attitude of boredom disappeared at once and she actually managed to produce a smile.

After having her funds stolen by Genghis *(see Genghis Kant),* An Kholi had been concerned in case it should happen again. Nzite, the Valon telepath, had presented her with a new credit account from Gib Dander. An Kholi was reluctant to take something that would allow the businessman to track her every move through her purchases, but the amount of credit the account offered her was too much to resist. Nzite didn't even seem to be too worried about how she would repay any bills she ran up. Besides, Nzite seemed to turn up at the most unexpected moments, which suggested he had others ways to track An Kholi than using such a clumsy method as her shopping transactions.

With her business completed, An Kholi went back to her waiting hover taxi and directed the driver to her meeting with Gala. With the egg now protected by authentic documentation from a supplier of impeccable reputation, it was time to turn her attention to getting herself and Gala off the planet undetected. She had no doubts about the probability that people, very nasty people, would now be searching for her, Gala, Den and Ka Mera.

Ka Mera and Den had the ability to adopt any disguise they wished and providing they had the identity documents to back that up they would pass unnoticed through the myriad channels of Earth bureaucracy. They would simply re-adopt their disguises as Merkaloy the Arthurid and Laurel the Sabik. An Kholi and Gala had to gain such an advantage for themselves.

As a bounty hunter An Kholi had gone undercover several times to track her quarry. She therefore had to learn to use prosthetics, wigs and theatrical make-up to change her appearance. That was half the battle and a theatrical supplier in the heart of Soho had been most helpful. However, that still left the documentation.

Ka Mera had once again proved to be of value. To their surprise, not least that of Den, she turned out to be quite an accomplished burglar. It was a skill they had employed to steal the Justice Department identity card held by Mr. Grabbitt Junior of Sioux, Grabbit and Rhun. While prowling their offices in the dead of night Ka Mera had taken the opportunity to hack their computer system to locate the case files of criminals with particular talents. That information had led them to Franky the Faker, a master forger. He in turn had, for an exorbitantly large sum of money in untraceable galactic credits, provided them with identity documents that he personally guaranteed would pass the closest inspection.

"They're real people." Franky the Faker assured them. "If the Feds do any background checks they'll check out right down to last dot and comma, so long as they don't take your finger prints, DNA, or retina scans. I could replace the originals of those of course, but it will cost more."

An Kholi had politely declined. There was stealing an identity and there was wiping out the existence of innocent people from all known records, which she couldn't countenance.

It would soon be time to see just how good the fake IDs were.

The problem with a convincing disguise, of course, was getting the right skin colour. Her's and Gala's pale lilac skin tones would stand out a mile from the beige that seemed to be the norm for humans, but they had noted that there were plenty of people with darker skin tones around. An Kholi had discovered years before that it was easier to go darker than lighter. So it was that An Kholi and Gala Sur checked into a flea pit hotel in Bermondsey and two hours later Rani Gopal and Sunita Patel, two kelp workers from Muswell Hill, left by a back door, never to return.

* * *

If they were being hunted by the authorities then they would surely be looking for a group of four beings rather than two groups of two. So it was that An Kholi and Gala watched Den Gau and Ka Mera make their way through the security procedures. Their genuine identity cards were accepted by the machines and none of the lounging security staff paid them any attention. As they headed for the X-ray and body scanning machines they were lost to sight.

An Kholi joined the back of the queue and shuffled towards the identity checking machines. No matter how many machines were installed. it always seemed that it was too few for the number of people travelling. Or perhaps it was the fact that half of them seemed to be out of order, or working at half speed, or maybe the people using them just seemed unable to insert their card the right way, no matter how often they attempted it.

At last An Kholi reached the front of her queue. Gala was still two places back in the queue for a neighbouring machine. At least if An Kholi's ID failed her Gala would still have time to retreat and rethink the plan.

An Kholi slid the card into the slot. On top were two lights, one red and one green. If the red one lit, she knew, the turnstile would remain locked and an alarm would sound, summoning an official.

The slot spat the card out and an error message appeared on the display above it. Just for once the message was in Common Tongue as well as English. "Card Reader Failure - Please Try Again".

An Kholi did as she was instructed. Again the card was spat back at her. She noticed that one of the security guards was watching her attempts. Would he intervene, even without the red light illuminating? She tried for a third time with the same result.

The guard detached himself from the wall he was supporting and sauntered over. Wordlessly he held out his hand. An Kholi obediently passed the card over to him. He glanced casually at the card then rubbed it briskly against the fabric of his uniform before handing it back.

"Try it now." He instructed, though An Kholi couldn't understand his English. However, the message was clear enough from his previous actions.

She inserted the card once more. This time it stayed in place. She panicked as the red light glowed, but forced herself to remain still. The red light went out and was replaced by the green one. There was a clunk as the locking mechanism released the turnstile. She pushed her way through.

"That happens sometimes." The security official smiled at her. "The readers get bunged up with dirt so they get confused, but they're programmed to re-read the card three times before they sound the alarm."

It was all gibberish to An Kholi but she smiled back and said the only two words of English she knew. "Thank you." and walked on.

Gala's shoulders sagged with relief. Feet shuffled and there were impatient mutterings behind her as the people in the queue became frustrated by her reluctance to have her ID checked. Gala gave them a reassuring smile and inserted her card into the slot. When it was spat back at her she rubbed the surface of the card as she had seen the security guard do and tried again. No red light for her though. The green light was reassuringly fast in appearing and Gala hurt her thighs as she rushed to get through the turnstile before the locking mechanism had time to release itself. She backed off and waited, then walked through more calmly to join An Kholi in the queue for the scanners.

They had checked and then double checked to make sure that neither they nor their hand luggage carried any items that would trigger the alarms on the X-ray and body scanning machines. It was a wise precaution as they saw people being taken to one side and subjected to a more detailed search. Neither of them could have afforded to have their make-up accidently smudged by a clumsy or overly enthusiastic official. One pale patch, let alone a hint of lilac, and their disguises would be exposed.

Finally they found themselves passing through the Duty-Free shop, crowded with kelp workers and others looking for cheap booze and gadgets to take up to the space station with them. An Kholi spotted Den Gau loading up with bottles of alcohol while Ka Mera was spraying herself with perfume samples, different brands being aimed at different parts of her anatomy as she tried to decide which fragrance she preferred. She wafted a wrist under Den's nose and he recoiled with a grimace. Obviously not his favourite scent.

An Kholi hurried past them, taking care to avoid eye contact. She scanned the departure board to see when their shuttle was due to depart. Her heart sank as she saw that there was expected to be a sixty minute delay.

The shuttle was capable of carrying three hundred passengers and it seemed that they had all gathered in front of the board. Conversations speculated about the cause of the delay, with some travellers appearing nervous, other pretending to be unconcerned and someone announcing that the last time this had happened the shuttle had crashed on take-off killing everyone on board. People started to move away from him, creating a space that no one wanted to enter, despite the crowded conditions.

An Kholi headed for the bar, Gala close behind her. There she joined the queue of thirsty kelp workers who were making the most of the delay.

An Kholi felt a sharp nudge in her ribs. She turned to see who had inflicted the pain and Gala nodded her head towards the entrance to the bar. Two Space Force officers stood scanning the crowd. They were clearly looking for someone.

"Keep calm and keep looking towards the bar, just as though you are impatient to get your hands on a drink." An Kohli muttered.

"I think my wig's slipping" Gala hissed back at her.

An Kholi made a pretence of brushing some imaginary dust off Gala's shoulders as she examined her hairline for faults.

"No, you're OK. No sign of any blonde."

"Are you sure? It feels all wrong."

"Trust me. You're imagining it. I've had that problem in the past. Just keep calm. If you're worried then head off to the ladies. You don't have to pass the two goons to get there."

Gala relaxed and did her best to keep her eyes off the two Space Force officers. They had now come inside the bar and were weaving between the crowd of drinkers. Their course would take them around the back of the queue, leaving several people between them and An Kholi and Gala. The queue moved forward several feet as a party of passengers picked up their drinks and relinquished their places at the service points.

An Kholi checked again and saw that the Space Force officers had become surrounded by a group of people who were clearly the worse for drink. They tried to force their way through but the drinkers were in no mood to be bullied and pushed back. Some more jostling occurred and one of the Space Force officers drew out an object, giving it a shake. It turned out to be a pepper spray, which he discharged right into the face of a belligerent drinker. Mayhem erupted at this use of force and punches were thrown.

"Let's put some distance between us and the trouble." An Kholi said. She had to shout as the noise levels suddenly grew as the crowd shouted encouragement at the combatants. There was clearly no sympathy for the two Space Force officers, who were being given some rough handling.

As An Kholi and Gala left the bar they were shoved to one side as reinforcements arrived. Half a dozen Space Force personnel barged past and into the crowded bar. They had short wooden clubs in their hands, and started wielding them as soon as they were through the doors.

They reached the relative calm of the area beneath the departure board just in time to see the status of their shuttle change from "wait in lounge" to "Boarding Gate 4." Without pausing they headed along the corridor to the departure gates, followed by a growing surge of fellow passengers.

Glossary

Zettabyte - 1000 to the power of 7 bytes of information, or 1×10^{21}. In numerical terms it is a 1 followed by 21 zeros. In order of magnitude it fits between an exabyte (1×10^{18}) and a yottabyte (1×10^{24}).

12 - Bomb Disposal

The mood in the pub was sombre. Gone were the young people with their coloured hair, to be replaced by two apparent kelp workers, an Arthurid and a Sabik. At that time of day the pub did little business. Even young people have somewhere else to be in the late afternoon before the working and school days end.

"How do you know those documents won't allow you to leave New Earth?" Den asked.

"Oh, they'll allow us to leave, but only to go back down there. I should have told Frankie the Faker what I needed them for. It's my own fault." An Kholi sighed and took a long drink from her beer glass.

"It was on the display when we scanned the documents in Arrivals." Gala added. "'Only valid for return to Earth' they said. It's not something that can be confused."

"Well, now you're up here you could use those documents to apply to leave; to go somewhere else. We'll just say you're hitching a ride with us, just like the original plan."

"I looked up the procedures for that." Gala's tone said that she wasn't as stupid as Den was trying to suggest.

"Don't tell me. You have to apply in person and you can only do it from down on the planet."

"Almost right." Gala replied. "You can apply up here using a government galacticnet site, but you have to collect the documents in person to avoid identity fraud. They do an on-the-spot DNA test."

"So, you see, unless we contact Frankie the Faker and accept his offer to replace the DNA samples with our own, we're stymied."

"Hey, have you seen this?" Bored with the debate Ka Mera had been watching the news on the media screen mounted above the bar. They all turned to see what she was looking at.

On the screen was a rubble strewn hole in the ground, smoke still drifting from some of the more combustible components. Firefighting droids were spraying foam over the area. The camera panned to show the crowd that had assembled to watch. Police were holding them back behind strips of blue and white tape. Below the images a 'ticker' rolled stating that they were being broadcast live from outside the remains of Smooge and Harley's Bank in London.

"Holy shit." Breathed An Kholi. "No prizes for guessing what someone was after. They all pulled out their communicators and searched for the live video stream with an audio feed in Common Tongue. Den turned up the volume on his so that they could all hear the commentary.

"It is suspected that there is another bomb inside the cellar of the bank, possibly in the area of the secure vault that houses the safe deposit boxes. The police have said that they have had a coded communication warning of other devices being in the area" The voice burbled at them. "The police are now waiting for the arrival of a bomb disposal team to check out the area before they will allow crime scene investigators inside to try to establish what happened here." The camera cut to a second scene, this time with a reporter standing with three men. He had to stand back to get all three figures into shot as two were about average size but the third was quite small. Two of them were immediately recognisable but the third, the oldest, wasn't familiar.

"I'm standing here with Mr. Bob Scratchit Senior, Mr. Bob Scratchit Junior and Mr. Tim Scratchit, who are part of the team that manage Smooge and Harley's Bank. Gentlemen, what do you think happened here?" The reporter pushed his hand under the nose of the oldest of the three men so that the microphone in his wristband could pick up the older man's voice.

The older man scowled at the camera. "Well, it would appear to be a break-in that has gone terribly wrong. We were given a warning that the bomb had been planted so we were able to get out through the emergency exists. When it went off instead of blowing the doors open it did, in fact, destroy the whole building."

"So you think it was only supposed to blow the doors off?" Asked the reporter.

"Yes. It was only supposed to blow the bloody doors off." Snapped the older man.

"Our apologies for Mr. Smooge's language there, viewers. Now, it appears that the bomb disposal team have arrived so let's go over and see what they're up to."

* * *

A man in military style uniform strode self-importantly over to stand at the edge of the crater. He placed something the size of a water melon on the ground and then took out a communicator and started to speak into it. The microphone was too far away to hear what was being said and viewers could see the arm of a police officer trying to hold the camera operator back out of the danger zone.

As the man in the eye of the camera spoke, the object on the ground started to make mechanical jerking movements. Legs unfolded and it raised itself up, looking for all the world like a spider, but one the size of a manhole cover. The legs flexed briefly and then the spider like drone started to scramble over the rubble as the operator guided it towards the stairs down to the vaults. As it descended from sight the soldier kept his eyes glued to the monitor on his communicator.

"We have been able to tap into the images being sent by the drone." The reporter whispered, as though the slightest sound might scare the spider away. "This is what the operator will now be seeing."

The image switched to jerky footage of a dark, dusty environment, the camera descending steps. Doors hung off their hinges and scanning equipment was barely recognisable other than as a tangle of twisted metal, broken plastic and tangled cables. An Kholi recognised the entrance door to the safe deposit vault. The steel security door lay across the opening, almost blocking it. The spider found a way under the obstruction and into the vault itself.

"The operator has called someone over. He seems to think that there might be something in there."

The images switched to a split screen with one half showing the view from the drone's camera and the other showing the operator deep in consultation with a man dressed in what appeared to be a green space suit. The reporter explained that it was padded body armour designed to protect the bomb disposal technician when he tried to defuse bombs.

"Why don't they use a droid to do that?" Den mused.

"Hands are more touch sensitive." Gala supplied. "There's no droid in the galaxy with better touch sensitivity than most living creatures. That's very important if you're trying to defuse a bomb."

"You make it sound like you've done it." Den smirked.

"I have." Gala replied enigmatically, causing Den to look up in surprise.

"Sshh" An Kholi hissed at them. "I think we're just about to witness a robbery."

"How do you know."

"Because as far as I can see there's nothing in there that needs the attention of a bomb disposal technician."

An Kholi's words were hardly out of her mouth when the heavily padded figure started to follow the path previously taken by the drone. He too had a camera attached and the broadcast images changed once again to show a split screen of what both the engineer and the drone were seeing.

The reporter's voice rose to a fever pitch of whispering as he described the struggle the man had with the steel door, as though the viewing public couldn't work it out for themselves from the images. Then both halves of the image broke up into a mass of coloured pixels that swirled across the screen.

"We have to apologise to viewers." The reporter apologised. "It appears that the camera images have now been encrypted. Ah, I'm being told that this is so that terrorists can't observe the procedures that the bomb disposal officer will use to defuse the device."

The screen cleared to show a long shot of the whole bank, or what was left of it, followed by a close up of the top of the stairs that led to the cellar. There was a long anxious wait which was ended by a loud report, as though a gun had been fired.

"I'm told by our experts in the studio that the engineer has fired a controlled explosion to neutralise the device's trigger and so make it safe."

"Bollocks." Muttered Gala. "He wouldn't use a controlled explosion with him still inside. It might not work. It might trigger the bomb, blowing the whole place up and bringing the roof down on him. You're right, An Kholi. Looks like they're breaking in to one of the boxes."

It was a further ten minutes before the bomb disposal technician returned above ground and headed straight for his vehicle, parked some distance away, carrying an object that, to An Kholi at least, looked like the interior compartment of a safe deposit box. The drone operator recovered his mechanical creature and followed.

"The bomb disposal team will now return to their headquarters with the bomb in order to examine it and try to find any clues that might lead police to the perpetrators of this outrage." The reporter announced self-importantly, the imparter of great knowledge, though most of what he was saying was being fed from the studio into his earpiece. He realised that the story was pretty much dead as far as action was concerned. "So it's back to Nigel in the studio."

"Good luck to them with that." Gala laughed. "I don't think anyone will ever see those two again."

She was right. It was another two hours before the genuine bomb disposal team were discovered bound and gagged inside their own abandoned vehicle.

"How long before they're able to decrypt that PMD and find out they've been fooled? An Kholi asked.

"Depends on how good they are, how powerful their computers are and how good their decryption programmes are and a whole host of other things. I double encrypted it and used an obscure programme developed on Andromeda Beta as the outer layer of encryption. I'd say two days maximum if they're crap at it and maybe six hours if they're any good.

* * *

"How long will it take to decrypt the contents of the PMD?" Tiny Blur asked Alison Fakescotsman.

"Difficult to say. The encryption programme is out of this world, quite literally. We've got to track down where it's from just to be able to work out what the symbols mean. Then they have to find a way into the encryption algorithm. Then they have to do it all over again if they've used more than one level of encryption."

"Is that likely?"

"This is Su Mali we're talking about. She wouldn't trust her left hand to know what her right hand was doing. Yes, I think we can safely assume it will be double encrypted."

"So, in answer to my original question...."

"Two days minimum, but anything up to a week unless we get a lucky break."

"OK. Let me know as soon as you find out what's stored on it."

"What do you think it is?"

"I can't be sure. I was half expecting to find a Magus egg in that box. But a PMD can hold anything. But it was locked up in a bank vault, so it must be valuable. At a guess it's details of where Su Mali has hidden all her loot. Bank account details, that sort of thing. The timing of her coming here also ties in with the Magi eggs going missing, so I'm thinking it also contains the locations where she has hidden them."

"Wow, so we could be rich men soon."

"Yes. I..." he paused to let the use of the personal pronoun sink in, "could be a rich man soon and the Magi will be gone forever."

* * *

As An Kholi and her colleagues had watched the robbery from the bank vault they had been vaguely aware of an increasingly loud noise building up outside the pub. This gradually resolved itself into human voices, chanting something unintelligible. Only the odd word was recognisable above the general hubbub. Den's curiosity finally got the better of him and he went to the door of the pub to see what was happening. After a few moments he signalled his friends to come across and take a look.

"It's an election boycott demonstration." He explained. "Look, plain clothes Space Force officers." He pointed to a man who seemed to be paying more attention to the crowd than to the speaker who was haranguing them over a public address system.

"How can you be sure?" Asked Ka Mera.

"Instinct first, but look, he's wearing spectacles. Practically no one wears spectacles any more. But they're excellent for concealing a camera to record who's present. I think they must be looking for someone in particular. Look, they're using drones as well."

Above the crowd, drones were buzzing around, though their cameras were clearly visible. Many of the protesters had taken the precaution of covering their faces.

"Won't make any difference." Ka Mera, their resident expert on hiding, advised them. "With the sort of facial recognition technology available now they can be identified with a 97% accuracy rate on just the eyes, ears or nose."

"Oh no. What's she doing here?" Den groaned. "I nearly got myself killed trying to get her off this giant flat pack planetoid."

An Kholi peered past him, trying to identify the person he was talking about. He pointed to a pretty young woman trying to edge her way down the side of the crowd towards the platform on which the speakers were standing.

"That!" He spat with some venom. "Is Gaga Sullivan."

13 - The Golden Garter

"After all the trouble I took to get you and your boyfriend out of here, what in the galaxy are you doing back." Den almost shouted into the face of Gaga Sullivan.

The girl scowled at Den sulkily, having been almost dragged off the street and into the pub. "It's none of your business." She snapped.

"It's my business if you go and get yourself arrested."

"No it isn't. But anyway, we had to come back. The movement needs us. Earth is the heart of the abstention campaign and it needs all the organisers it can get, so Beckham is needed. Where he goes, I go."

"So he's out there as well?"

"Yes. I was trying to find him when you dragged me in here."

"You know the square is filled with plain clothes Space Force, don't you?" Den exaggerated.

"We know. He's in disguise."

"How did you get back anyway." Ka Mera interrupted.

"That pal of yours, Merkaloy, he got us a lift to Alpha Centauri. There's an Earth colony on the gamma planet, a bit wild, but there's a daily passenger service back to New Earth. We got hold of some stolen identity documents and that got us back here. Now we have to try to get back down to the planet again. That's where we really need to be. But it's harder here. Our documents may get us through the electronic checks, but Space Force here would recognise Beckham in a moment."

An Kohli had been silent during this exchange, not wanting to risk giving away her disguise by revealing that she was able to speak Common Tongue. She tapped Den on the shoulder and nodded towards the rear of the pub before walking in that direction.

"Sorry, Gaga. My friend needs to show me something." Den threw over his shoulder as he hurried after An Kohli. "Don't go away. We aren't finished."

In the narrow corridor that led to the toilets An Kohli stopped and waited for Den to catch up. "This could be our way off New Earth." She said without preamble. "She has documents that will allow Gala and me to go to Alpha Centauri. It will mean one of us having to disguise ourselves as a man, but I think I can pull it off. They obviously don't examine the IDs too closely or your pal would have been caught. So, we give her the ID cards that we have, help them with make-up and what have you and they can get back down to the planet. We then go to Alpha Centauri and you and Ka Mera meet us there."

"Sounds like it might work. We had better see the stolen IDs first though. Space Force will be looking for you trying to leave and if the ID doesn't give you a fighting chance then you may as well hand yourself over right now."

"Good point. I still have quite a lot of make-up and foam rubber left though. I can probably adjust my appearance a little bit."

"There's also the chance that the documents have been reported missing as well. If that's the case they'll be flagged on the database and they'll trip the alarms when you use them."

"Only one way to find out, isn't there? Have you got any other ideas?"

Den shrugged his shoulders. "Fresh out right now."

"OK, that's what I thought, so we'll run with this until it's proven to be a non-starter.

They returned to their table where Ka Mera and Gaga were deep in conversation.

"Gaga is concerned about Beckham." Ka Mera supplied. "She really wants to find him to make sure that Space Force haven't picked him up again."

"Can you hang on for a minute, Gaga." Den pleaded. "We think we have a solution for your problem." He looked at An Kohli, who nodded her assent. "These two women." He indicated An Kohli and Gala, "Aren't humans. They're not kelp workers either. They're my friends An Kohli and Gala Sur; the bounty hunters I work with."

"I thought they were from the other side of the galaxy? Ah, I get it. Disguises. They're good. They fooled me."

"Good, because the idea is that you and Beckham adopt these disguises and use them to go down to the planet, while An Kohli and Gala use your stolen IDs to get them where they're going." Den decided not to mention Alpha Centauri. What Gaga didn't know she couldn't reveal if caught, though it wouldn't take a lot to work out. There were only a handful of potential destinations available from New Earth's spaceports. "Can we see your ID?"

Gaga drew the thin plastic strip from her pocket and passed it over. An Kohli passed it over her communicator and the stored image revealed itself on its screen. "That will have to be you, Gala. I'm too tall. What do you think?"

"We'll have a bit of trouble with the skin colour, but I think a bit of hair dye and plenty of make-up will cover up a lot."

"So we just need to see Beckham's ID."

"I think you'll like that." Gaga gave a mischievous grin. "The IDs were stolen from a couple of… let's call them friendly ladies. Beckham had to disguise himself as a woman to use it. Nobody batted an eyelid either."

"Well, that will help when we trade identities then. But we still need to see the ID card. If I can't get close to what the woman looked like then I'm not going to risk it. I'd rather stay here till I die than risk going to prison."

"Didn't seem to bother you when it was me that was going to prison." Ka Mera muttered, but not loud enough for An Kohli to hear. Den shot her a warning glance.

"Fair enough. In that case I'm going to have to go and find Beckham. Where shall we meet?"

"We'll stay here."

"Maybe not such a good idea." Ka Mera voiced her opinion. "A whole lot of uniformed Space Force have turned up; full riot gear. I think they're going to try to break up the demonstration, which means there will be a lot of panic and people will get hurt. I suggest we get away from here right now."

Den trusted Ka Mera's instincts. She was a Gau and as such she had a keen sense of self preservation. "Gaga, you remember the café where you and I met up when I was working for you? The one opposite the Sutran nightclub. We'll meet there."

"Will you be alright?" An Kohli looked worried and Den wondered if it was for Gaga's safety or for her chances of getting hold of the IDs that might get her off New Earth.

"I'll be OK. I know where Beckham will go if things get nasty. He'll help to get the speakers away at the first sniff of trouble and then we have a place where we'll meet."

"I'm more concerned about you." An Kohli said. "I don't think those goons will be too fussy about whose heads they'll break."

"It's OK. I've been at this sort of thing before. I'll keep to the fringes. Space Force always dive straight into the middle of the crowd where there are more people to lash out at. That's good for us, because it means it leaves plenty of escape routes."

They agreed a meeting time and then went their separate ways.

* * *

"I don't think they're coming." Gala said for the fourth time. Den scowled at her, also for the fourth time.

"They'll be here. I'm sure of it. Even if Beckham has got himself arrested again she'll come and tell us. She'll probably try to get us to help her again."

"Well, she can think again on that one." An Kohli snapped. "I'll do what I need to do to get off this space borne prison, but I'm not going to stick my head in a noose for her and her idealistic boyfriend."

"No one is asking you to." Den fought to keep his temper under control. "All I'm saying is…"

"Sorry we're late." Gaga puffed, clearly out of breath from rushing. Behind her stood Beckham, sporting a black eye.

"Wow. Someone's been in the wars." Ka Mera said in English, bringing a rueful smile to Beckham's face.

"You should see other guy," he said in heavily accented Common Tongue.

"The other guy was encased from head to toe in body armour and probably wouldn't feel anything less than an anvil falling on his head." Gaga gave Beckham a disapproving look, but they could all see that she wasn't seriously displeased with her boyfriend.

Den introduced Gala and An Kohli and then asked to see the young man's stolen ID, which An Kohli examined closely.

"Yes. I think I can get away with that. She's a lot older than me and tries to hide it with lots of make-up, which helps. The hair colour is no problem. I can get some hair dye to cover my natural colour."

"What about compatibility?" Den asked. "Remember what happened with that spa treatment."

"Don't remind me." An Kohli grimaced. "It's OK. I've seen a brand in the shops here that's made by Glossy Locks. They're a Gargantua Corporation subsidiary and I know all their products are compatible with our physiology.

"So, are we agreed then? An Kohli will help you to make yourselves up to look like them, and you take their IDs in exchange for yours." Den put the proposition to Gaga and Beckham.

"I woman again?" Beckham didn't seem too happy about the prospect.

"Yes, darling. You must." Gaga soothed him. "Just think of it as being like that time when…" she leaned in and whispered in his ear. He went bright red and suddenly didn't seem to know where to look.

Den came to the young man's rescue. "OK. That's agreed then. First thing we need to do is to book passage for the four of you to where you're each going. Once we have done that we can work out a timetable for getting together to sort out the disguises. We'll need a secure base for that."

"We can help there. We have the use of a back room behind a hover taxi repair workshop. The owner is sympathetic towards the abstention movement."

"Sounds ideal, thank you Gaga. Can he also provide us with some discreet transport to the space port?"

"Yes. He should be able to help there as well."

"OK. Well, if we swap the ID cards over now we can each make the bookings we need to make. Then we'll take it from there.

* * *

The two women who stepped from the hover taxi attracted the attention of most of the men outside the space port, and more than a few of the women. They were the sort who would catch the eye and, in a professional sense, it was their purpose. A wolf whistle screeched out, followed by another, and then more.

"If we play our cards right we could make some money here." An Kohli said from the corner of her mouth.

"Don't even joke about it." Gala snarled in reply. "It gives me the creeps thinking about what's going through the minds of those men right now."

An Kohli chuckled at her friend's discomfort, but Gala had a point. With their clothes, hair and make-up there could be no doubt about their assumed profession. An Kohli's hair was an explosion of crimson around her head, fighting with her emerald green eye make-up and her purple lips. A casual observer might assume that her cosmetics had been applied with a spatula. It was so thick, her natural skin could have been any colour. She wore thigh length boots with heels so high they defied the laws of physics to keep her tall frame upright.

An Kohli was used to wearing skin tight Superskin outfits, but they were usually opaque, unlike the one she was wearing now. The only parts of An Kohli that were properly concealed were the bits screened by her luggage. The containers for her body make-up alone had filled a waste disposal bag.

For her part Gala had been dressed, much against her will, in similar fashion but she had insisted on some strategically arranged faux leopard skin accessories. "I don't care; I'm not showing off my bits to the world!" She had stated with some menace. An Kohli was more sanguine about the whole issue. Having once worked undercover as a striptease dancer she knew that after a while men ceased to see all the flesh; they only saw the fantasy of what the flesh represented. She herself wore only three small pieces of material to cover her modesty.

The departure lounge was busy with mine workers heading for Alpha Centauri Gamma, or New Klondike as it was known colloquially. Muscles and tattoos were in abundance, augmented by more than a few scars. Haircuts all tended to be of the same skin revealing type and polished domes were much in evidence, which went with the multitude of broken noses and cauliflower ears.

The men were no better looking. The favoured form of dress was a tight tee shirt, designed to emphasise the muscles but which also emphasised the beer bellies. The floor of the space port rang with the sound of heavy work boots striking it.

An Kohli was relieved to see that they weren't the only women dressed in the style they had adopted and assumed, correctly, that there was a considerable demand for her simulated profession on the remote mining planet. Gaga Sullivan had described it as the modern day Wild West, with little law enforcement and even less morality. The company security staff maintained order within the mining camps but not in the towns that had sprouted up around them. 'Towns' was a somewhat grand title for the sprawl of bars, gambling dens, and brothels that comprised most of the establishments. There were only a few overstretched police officers to try to maintain some semblance of order and the Space Force had yet to take up residence. Political activism wasn't a major pastime on Alpha Centauri Gamma so there was no need for their dubious talents.

An Kohli steered Gala away from a group of women who were passing a bottle of gin from hand to hand. If anyone tried to engage them in conversation in English, their disguises would be revealed instantly. Humans departing from the New London spaceport that couldn't speak English would attract attention.

An Kohli presented her fake ID to the scanning machine while Gala hung back, just in case it failed them. It would allow her time to leave the area and return to Den and Ka Mera to report the failure. A sigh of relief escaped from An Kohli's lips as the green light came on at once. The official overseeing the bank of security gates glanced in her direction, but only to leer at her. She paused and waited for Gala to join her.

While An Kohli had applied Gala's make-up she and Den had discussed the idea that they could try to reach Merkaloy's ship, but he had dismissed the idea. Two hookers heading for the private spacecraft docks would attract attention. It wasn't impossible that someone wealthy enough to own a private spacecraft might employ a couple of ladies of their profession, but it was unlikely that they would be allowed to dress so indiscreetly and risk the reputation of their employer. They had to go to Alpha Centauri and meet up with Den and Ka Mera there. Den and Ka Mera were waiting back at the hover taxi repair shop to make sure that An Kohli and Gala made good their escape. If not it was back to the drawing board and that meant Merkaloy's ship still being available, so Den couldn't depart before he knew An Kohli was safe.

They had timed things with precision and were pleased to note that the departures board displayed their gate number and the legend 'Final Call'. They had noticed a man leave the toilets still adjusting his clothing, soon followed by a woman dressed in similar fashion to themselves, so there was no doubt that business was being transacted within the spaceport confines. They had no desire to be approached by potentially lustful customers with all the complications that might ensue.

They boarded the spacecraft and received a professional smile from the cabin attendant. The smile didn't reach his eyes and barely reached his lips; they were being judged. Well, at least it meant their disguise was being accepted and that was the purpose of a disguise. An idle thought crossed An Kohli's mind as she wondered how Beckham United had dealt with the situation while wearing a similar disguise. She hoped it would encourage him to think differently about women in the future.

An Kohli settled herself into the seat nearest the outside skin of the ship and Gala settled into the centre seat. There was only the briefest interlude until a female mine worker dropped heavily into the aisle seat, strapped herself in and rested her head on the chair back. Within seconds the woman started to snore and didn't wake until they were roused for food service, several hours into the journey. In the four days they shared the row of seats the woman made no attempt to engage An Kohli and Gala in conversation and her bulky presence meant that no one else could try.

* * *

When Gaga Sullivan had described New Klondike as being similar to the Wild West, An Kohli had no idea what she really meant. She had never seen a human western movie so Gaga had to describe it to her. She had failed to do the planet justice.

As Gala eased herself out of the back of a hover taxi she was thrown back inside to land in An Kohli's lap as two burly men barrelled through the doors of a building to slam into the vehicle. They now grappled together on the ground, so evenly matched that neither could gain an advantage, but too drunk to realise that they were doing little harm to each other and might as well put an end to their combat.

The females decided to leave the taxi on the far side and squelched through thick mud to reach the building entrance, stepping over and around the two fighters as they continued their fruitless struggle. Above the doorway an illuminated sign buzzed and flickered to announce that the establishment was called the Golden Garter and was 'a leisure establishment for the discerning gentleman.' The noise coming through the doors suggested that the discerning gentleman was an enthusiast of skunk rock and the smell suggested that he avoided taking a shower.

A muscled bouncer barred their way, though he seemed more interested in the fight that was still going on behind them. "Good morning ladies." He leered suggestively. "Can I help you?" though his words meant nothing to An Kohli or Gala.

An Kohli drew her communicator out of her bag, called up a communication and handed it to the bouncer to read. He furrowed his brow and his lips moved as he sounded out the characters to himself to try to make sense of the message that Gaga Sullivan had composed. At last he grunted and stood aside, indicating that they could enter. An Kohli threw a last glance at the two fighters. One was now lying supine, gasping for breath, as the other vomited into the mud. She wrinkled her nose in distaste and then followed Gala through the door into the Golden Garter.

The small bar was packed with humans. Each had a drink in his or her hand and some had drinks in both hands. An Kohli felt that the place was one ill-advised word away from a full scale riot.

At one end of the room drinks were being dispensed by two sweating females. It was easy to see they were sweating because they were naked to the waste.

At the other end of the room there was a small stage with a shining metal pole in its centre. A naked woman was entwined around it, writhing in simulated ecstasy in time to the raucous music, but no one seemed to be paying her much attention. A barely visible force field stretched across the front of the stage to intercept the occasional bottle that was thrown in its general direction. The bottles may have been polyviol but they could still inflict injury, especially if they were still full. Every so often the field sparked as another missile was vaporised.

It was early morning, by the human clock, but that didn't diminish the enthusiasm of the clientele as they attempted to drink themselves into oblivion before they had to return to work on their next shift. An Kohli wondered when they found time to sleep.

She and Gala pushed their way towards the bar. They felt the occasional hand on various personal parts of their bodies but the place was so crowded it was impossible to identify whose hand it was, nor was it possible to try to hit the offending hand away. However, it did encourage the two females not to linger and eventually they forced their way into a gap just as it was created by a man carrying armfuls of beer bottles back to his friends.

One of the female bar workers crossed to them and shouted "What can I get you?" into An Kohli's ear.

"Micah Jelly." An Kohli shouted back. The woman held up a finger, indicating that An Kohli should wait. She went to a door at the rear of the small serving area, opened it and shouted something through. She turned back to An Kohli and mimed that someone was coming and went off to serve someone else.

Gala felt a hand on her behind and turned and smashed her fist into the face of the man nearest to her. He fell backwards into the men and women around him. There was an uproar, equal measures of laughter and protest. Punches started to be thrown by those who'd protested.

An Kohli prepared herself for the worst, scanning the sweaty faces around her to identify the man or woman who she would probably have to hit first. She had just settled on a target when a strong hand grabbed her arm and pulled her away. Behind, Gala was being dragged along too. The pair found themselves being propelled through the door behind the bar. As they turned to protest, the door was slammed shut, blocking out the noise of the brawl that was developing. Standing in front of the door, seemingly occupying the whole frame, was a giant of a man.

"This had better be good, or I'm going to throw you back out there." The man addressed them, jerking his thumb over his shoulder at the same time to emphasis where 'out there' might be, just in case there should be any doubt.

It took a moment before An Kohli registered that the man had spoken in Common Tongue.

"Sorry. We were given your name by Gaga Sullivan. She told us to remind you of Swindon."

The man seemed to relax. "Ah yes. Swindon." He replied enigmatically, extending his hand. "I'm Micah Jelly. And you are?"

An Kohli provided introductions. "Gaga told us you might help us with somewhere to stay until our friends arrive. We'll pay of course."

The man waved a dismissive hand at the thought of payment. He shuffled round the small room to where there was a chair in front of a desk that was squeezed into a corner. He lowered himself into it. An Kohli was surprised that it didn't collapse under the weight of the man's bulk. "I saw Gaga just a while back; I helped her to get back to New Earth. You don't happen to have those IDs I got her, do you? I know two girls who will be glad to find out they've not been stolen after all."

"Can we hang onto them until we're on board our own ship? We'll need them to get us off this planet.

Micah signalled that they could. "Just send them back when you're finished with them."

"You spoke in Common Tongue. How did you know we weren't English?"

Micah's face broke into a smile. "Your make-up has become a little bit smudged." He pointed at An Kohli's chest. "Your true skin colour is showing through."

An Kohli looked down to see that the hair thin transparent material covering her breast had indeed smeared away some of the make-up, exposing a streak of lilac beneath. No doubt it had happened as they fought their way across the crowded bar. She wondered what other parts of her body might no longer be disguised. Judging by the stabs of pain where she had been pinched there might be several.

"You spotted it in that crush?" An Kohli's voice sounded incredulous.

"Small things, and that is by no means small, sometimes make the difference between life and death "

As a bounty hunter, An Kohli had to agree with that. More than once she had avoided death or injury by spotting a small tell-tale sign. An Kohli decided to take the reference to the size of her breasts as a compliment.

"There are some rooms upstairs where the girls take the punters. You can have the use of one of those. It will be a bit noisy, I'm afraid. This place wasn't designed for long stay guests. I'll have food and drink sent up from the bar. I'll make sure no-one disturbs you."

"Thanks. That will be great. Our friends shouldn't be long. They were leaving New Earth the same day as we did."

"Stay as long as you want. Pay for the food and drink but you can have the room for free as a favour to Gaga."

"Aren't you going to ask why we need a place?"

"If you are friends of Gaga then I already have a good idea. What I don't know I can't tell."

"Sorry to ask so many questions." An Kohli said, preparing to ask another question, "but what's with this thing about Swindon?"

"What happens in Swindon stays in Swindon." Micah grinned. "Come with me, I'll show you your room. Don't expect too much."

Micah took them back into the bar, where the fight seemed to have run its course. The place had emptied out considerably and An Kohli commented on it.

"Shift change." Micah said. "We've got about an hour to clean this place up before the off coming shift gets here." An Kohli noticed that there were women, dressed in functional overalls, rushing around the room gathering up empty beer bottles and picking up litter. One was wielding a mop as though her life depended on it. The dancer had vacated the stage and Micah took them through a door at the side of it and into the backstage area. The dancer was now dressed in a thin robe, sitting in front of a mirror with a bottle of beer in one hand and a make-up brush in the other.

"Good night tonight, Jezebel?" Micah asked as he passed.

"So so. Made a few nuks in tips."

"Good, good." He hurried on. "Jezebel isn't her real name," he commented over his shoulder. "It's Tinkerbell Froo Froo, but no one with any sense would use that as a stage name."

They went through a door into a back yard, then climbed a flight of metal stairs before re-entering the building on the upper floor. A long corridor stretched away from them. Micah led them though the first door they came to, into a small bedroom.

"The punters come up the stairs at the far end of the corridor, so they have no need to come this far along, but there's a bouncer stationed down there and I'll make sure no one gets curious, not even the other girls."

Gala had been agitated for some time and now was clearly about to burst unless she said something.

"I don't mean to sound judgemental, or anything." She said, sounding extremely judgemental. "But don't you feel ashamed exploiting these women for profit?"

Micah looked puzzled for a moment, then burst out laughing.

"You think… ha ha. You think I own this place?" Micah let out another wry chuckle. "The Golden Garter is owned by the Camp Eleven Working Girls' Co-operative. Jezebel, who you saw downstairs, is one of the founding members. Those women working so hard cleaning up are also shareholders. Don't be fooled by the overalls. Underneath they're all glammed up and shortly the overalls will come off as the off coming shift arrives. Jezebel and three others came here five years ago and set up the Golden Garter and all the rest of the girls have bought shares since then. Almost all the girly bars on New Klondike are owned that way."

"Maybe there's men behind them, bankrolling them." Gala persisted, still sure that someone must be exploiting the women.

"Well, if there is, the girls aren't doing too badly out of it. Jezebel says she's going to quit at the end of next year and she's already bought herself a beach house on some far flung planet or other. I forget where. The other girls are all saying much the same. It's not a matter of if, it's only a matter of when. There's a queue of girls back on Earth and New Earth waiting to buy the shares in the Golden Garter when the current shareholders retire."

"So what's your role?" An Kohli asked as Gala mulled over this information.

"The girls employ me to manage front of house. I hire and fire the bouncers, kick out the drunks, the brawlers, and the drug dealers… and make sure that the girls come to no harm. But I don't hold any shares. When my contract expires I have to re-apply for my job or

I'm on the next transport back to New Earth. Or worse, I have to get a job at the mine"

There was the sound of feet on stairs and a girly giggling underscored by a male voice. A door slammed.

"Sounds like business is starting to pick up again. I'd better get back downstairs. Any preference for food?"

"Do you serve curry?" asked An Kohli.

"Ah, you've learnt that trick, have you? Well, we serve the best curry in this township. That may not be saying much, by the way."

An Kohli and Gala agreed to try the curry and opted for a beer accompaniment. Micah left them to their own devices.

The room was basic, small but clean. The bed was covered in a washable fabric of some sort and smelt of disinfectant. In one corner stood a tiny shower cubicle. On the wall above the bed hung some erotic pictures and opposite the bed was a viewing screen. Gala switched it on and tried a variety of channels before concluding that the clientele had little interest in anything other than pornography. Gala lay back on the bed and gave a gasp.

"What's up?" An Kohli asked, concerned by her friends reaction.

"Up there." Gala pointed.

The ceiling above the bed was made entirely of mirrors. Gala had never seen that before. An Kohli, in her employment as a strip tease dancer, had. "Better keep our clothes on, I think. It may not be just a mirror."

"In these clothes, do you think it really matters?" Gala burst into a fit of giggles.

14 - Coddled Eggs

Den nosed the Meteor class ship between two gigantic mining vessels and out of New Klondike orbit. Just as he completed the manoeuvre, Ka Mera, Gala, and An Kohli entered the cramped command deck from the shuttle dock. Thanks to Ka Mera's arrival with their luggage, An Kohli and Gala were now more modestly dressed; An Kohli in her skin tight opaque Superskin outfit, though she'd held onto the thigh length boots just in case. Gala wore her comfortable, functional, and unglamorous flight suit.

An Kohli scowled at Den sitting in the Captain's chair. Den gave her a broad smile. "It's Merkaloy's ship and he has entrusted it to me. That makes me Captain." He smirked, pleased to be able to put one over on his employer.

An Kohli conceded ungraciously, then dropped into the co-pilot's seat a hair's breadth ahead of Gala, who gave a yelp of protest.

"How was it down there?" Den asked.

"You're familiar with Towie?" An Kohli said by way of reply. *(see The Magi)* "Well, it's like that but ten times worse. You'd love it."

"I'll give it a go sometime. Now, I haven't set a course yet so where do you want to go?"

"I addressed the box of eggs to Merkaloy on Sabik, so I guess that's where we go. Besides, I'd like to get the Adastra and the Pradua back and I'm sure that Merkaloy is pining for his own ship."

Den started programming the navi-com. "What shall we do about sleeping arrangements? We have three beds and four people. Of course I'll be taking the Captain's cabin." He hurried to stake his claim.

"Well, I'll take the co-pilot's cabin, so Gala… you and Ka Mera will have to fight it out for the Navigator's bunk."

"Surely Ka Mera will be sharing with Den?" Gala suggested with the sweetest possible smile.

Den shot her a glance that said 'why the heck did you suggest that?'

"Or Ka Mera can hot-bed with you." he fired back.

"What's hot-bed?" asked Ka Mera.

"You sleep when Gala is up and vice versa."

"No, no offence Gala, but I'd much rather share with you, Den." Ka Mera gave her fellow Gau a meaningful look. Den tried his best to respond with a smile, but he didn't really pull it off. "I'll move my things in." She squeezed past Gala to leave the command deck.

"Why did you say that?" Den shot at Gala in a hoarse whisper.

"Why? Don't you fancy her? After all, she has got a pulse."

"Keep your voice down, she's only next door. She might hear you. I don't know. There's just … something …"

"Not quite right about her." An Kohli completed the sentence for him.

"You felt it too?"

"Yes. I don't know what it is. We hardly know anything about her though. What we do know is that she managed to get in and out of that solicitor's office without detection and that required a quite specific skill set. Ka Mera is no stranger to crime. I think you're right to be cautious Den."

"Well, she's going to be sharing your bed for the next few days, so you may as well make the most of it." Gala smirked. "Try not to keep us awake."

Den gave her a scowl and muttered something under his breath. He passed his hand over the ship's controls and the craft started to accelerate up to the speed required to create its worm hole.

* * *

Merkaloy gave An Kohli a great big bear hug, practically squeezing the breath out of her. Forewarned, Gala managed to keep him at arms' length and planted a kiss on both his cheeks. Den got a hearty slap on the back and Ka Mera a more cautious pat on the shoulder. Merkaloy signalled a female who, thanks to Ka Mera's former disguise, they all recognised as Laurel. She came across with a tray of drinks.

"Yours I think." Ka Mera handed over Laurel's ID documents.

"I hope they're still clean." Laurel said suspiciously. "I don't want to be triggering alarms the next time I go through spaceport security."

"Yes, they're clean." Den pacified the attractive Sabik. "Speaking of which, Merkaloy, here are yours." He handed the Arthurid his documents.

"Did my parcel arrive?" An Kohli asked.

"Oh yes. Safe and sound, under lock and key in my apartment."

"You have an apartment here now?" An Kohli sounded surprised.

"Yes. Laurel and I are getting married." He smiled at the retreating form of his fiancée as she returned to the bar.

Den headed towards one of the gambling machines, while Gala had spotted an old friend and went over for a chat. Ka Mera made an excuse and headed towards the toilets. Merkaloy took the opportunity to beckon An Kohli towards him, so they could whisper. "I've been a bit suspicious about that one." he advised conspiratorially.

"You and me both."

"Well, I did some digging while you were away. She's no stranger to the inside of a prison. Nothing recent, but the Guild database shows three fulfilled warrants for her over the years."

"Well, that means she's going straight now." An Kohli was prepared to be forgiving.

"Yes, but on her last trip inside she shared a cell with Mia Crie. You remember her, she's the wife of Safo Bit, the Gau who set you up on that genocide charge. They were released at about the same time." *(See Genghis Kant)*.

"It's a coincidence, I'll grant you, but it doesn't mean anything."

"Not as such, not until you add in the fact that my sources tell me that Su Mali is now cell mates with Mia Crie. It could be that Su Mali let slip that she had been to New Earth not long before she was arrested, or maybe even told Mia Crie outright so that she could pass on the information to Ka Mera."

"Doing a bit of time with Mia Crie doesn't mean she is suspect."

"Not until you look further back in her record and find that she was a known associate of Mia Crie from way back."

"You think that Mia Crie deliberately put Ka Mera onto us in the hope of getting…..what? Revenge?"

"Not revenge. I don't think so. It was them who were paid to set you up. They know they caused their own downfall. No; the contents of the package you sent me are worth a fortune. You know that and I know that; the whole galaxy knows that. I think Mia Crie may just have put Ka Mera onto you so she could make a bit of money. She could make Mia Crie's life a lot more comfortable inside prison by spreading some of that money around the right people. She might even be able to finance a jail break."

"It's a bit of a long shot."

"You think so? Everyone knows what you're after. Mia Crie just had to remind Ka Mera who you're travelling with; Den Gau. He's her way in. She monitors the GSTC galacticnet site to keep track of the Adastra and when you arrive at New Earth she turns up and latches on to Den. It's not multi-dimensional flame theory."

An Kohli mulled over the idea. There was a logical consistency to it. The Magi eggs were worth a lot of money to the right people and Ka Mera had proved that she was willing to take risks if it was worth her while and, of course, her criminal record said she wasn't averse to a bit of theft. She hadn't even made any secret of her criminal skills.

"Is there any proof they were communicating?" An Kohli asked, unwilling to condemn the Gau on such circumstantial evidence.

"You know what prisons are like. There are a dozen ways to get messages in and out without the prison authorities knowing."

"OK. Look, she's been useful and we couldn't have got the… you know what, without her help. I owe her a bit of leeway for that. I'll give her the benefit of the doubt, but I'll keep an eye on her. No mistake!" An Kohli turned towards the bar to signal Laurel to bring more drinks and noticed Ka Mera and Merkaloy's beloved in deep conversation. The two females laughed, which appeared to signal the end of whatever they were talking about. Ka Mera returned to the table.

"I've ordered more drinks and Laurel's going to send a service droid over with them." Den staggered back to the table under the weight of a bucket full of coins, a beaming smile spread across his face. Of course the machine didn't have to pay out in cash. Its programming was more than capable of crediting Den's bank account, but for some reason gamblers loved the feel of hard cash in their hands. Bar and casino owners were only too happy to oblige, sure in the knowledge that most of the winnings would either find their way across their bar or back into the gambling machines.

An Kohli had little doubt that Den would now attempt to drink his way through his winnings and was glad she wouldn't have to share his hangover the next day.

* * *

"And you let them slip away." The voice of the Fell member known as Tiger hissed over the galactic net. It was the weekly virtual conference of the Fell and it wasn't going well for Warrior.

He had already had to address the issue of the success of the abstention movement's campaign and what he intended to do about it. The best he could come up with was to suggest that a version of Space Force be established on the most rebellious planets to try to disrupt the activities of the activists, but that had gained little support.

"And who will pay for this force?" Although it was Shogun who asked the question, it had been on all their lips.

"Once we have won the election we will levy taxes to pay for it." Was the best that Warrior could do.

"And until then?"

"Well, you may have to pay for it from your own fortunes."

The stony silence that greeted this was so deep that it couldn't be measured by any conventional means. Warrior could feel the resulting waves of cold fury. The Fell had seized control of the galaxy in order to benefit their own bank accounts. None of them had signed up to paying for anything, not even the security of their own positions.

Warrior now had to explain the mistakes that had led to An Kohli slipping away from New Earth undetected.

"We were fooled. That's all I can really say. She tricked us. She had a female Gau working for her that we knew nothing about. That meant that when the being we thought was An Kohli was arrested we thought she was safely under lock and key and all we had to do was recover the contents of Su Mali's safe deposit box. It wasn't until much later we discovered that the egg had been switched and we were left with a worthless memory device."

"I'm not sure that someone who could so easily be fooled deserves a place in the Fell." Shogun's pronouncement, while delivered in a calm voice, filled the air with menace.

"We still have a chance of recovering the Magus. A tracker was planted in An Kohli's ship. That was something else that confused us. The ship has been in orbit around Sabik for weeks, even though we knew that An Kohli was still on Earth or New Earth. She still has to deliver the Magus to the Galactic Counsel in Exile. When she does that we can track her ship and intercept her."

"Perhaps you should let someone else take on that task." Shogun suggested. It was phrased as a suggestion but was meant as an assertion.

"And I suppose that you will do the job." Mocked Warrior. Shogun was known for avoiding responsibility for anything and everything.

"I can't possibly make a worse job of it than you have. Yes, I'll do it."

Surprise echoed over the galacticnet. This was a new departure for Shogun. But it was accompanied by a sense of relief. If Shogun took on the job then it meant that none of the other Fell members had to. The thought of going head to head with An Kohli was not a pleasant one. Three former members, now presumed dead, could vouch for that.

"What if Shogun fails? So what if the Magi are recovered? We hold the reins of power now." Drac pointed out.

"No we don't." Reminded Warrior. "We rule by fear and many star systems don't fear us, or at least they don't fear us enough. They need only a leader to rally behind and they will attack us and bring us down. We have no force capable of quelling any but the most minor of revolts. That is why we need to form a legitimatised government, one that can raise taxes. With tax revenue we can build a proper space force that will maintain and strengthen our rule. Without it we have to rely on mercenaries and pirates, and they are unreliable to say the least."

"So we have to win this election then, don't we. Which is where we came in. Don't fail us, Warrior. The stakes are too high." With that threat hanging in the ether, Tiger's avatar faded from their viewing screens. Wordlessly the remainder also disappeared one by one.

* * *

Den was woken by a banging. He couldn't be sure if came from the door to his hotel room or if it was inside his head. The addition of a voice clarified the situation.

"Den, wake up. I need to talk to you."

"Fuck off An Kohli. It's too early in the day."

"It's almost mid-afternoon. I need to speak to you, so let me in."

"No."

"I'll keep banging on this door until you do." To back up her threat the banging started up with fresh vigour.

"OK, OK. But somebody better be dying." And I don't mean me, he groaned to himself. Den used a remote control to release the door lock and An Kohli pushed the door open and stepped into the room."

"Where's Ka Mera?"

"No idea. She was with me when I got back here last night. She must have gone out."

An Kohli found the remains of some take-away food lying on the floor. To avoid standing on it she picked up the torn packaging and offered it to Den, hoping he would dispose of it. Instead Den put his hand in front of his mouth and launched himself from his bed and through the door to the bathroom. There followed ten minutes of repulsive noises before An Kohli eventually heard the shower start to run. Another ten minutes passed and Den returned to the room, wrapped only in a towel.

"So, what was the big rush? What was worth all that banging?"

"I need to talk to you about Ka Mera." She repeated what Merkaloy had told her the previous evening.

Den sat in silence until she had finished. "That all works until the very last bit. Ka Mera had clearly been on New Earth for some time. She had a job; she shared an apartment. That isn't the sort of thing you can sort out within a few days of arriving if she had followed us there."

An Kohli nodded her understanding and chewed on the inside of her cheek for a moment.

"OK, but what if she knew that we would turn up on New Earth eventually. If not when we did, then sometime in the future. After all, we couldn't get the egg out of Smooge and Harley's Bank without going there first. So she goes there, she establishes herself, hides away in her disguise, but monitors GSTC waiting for us to arrive. When we do she's there at the spaceport to identify us and follow us. All she has to do is stay far enough back to avoid you picking up her brain waves until she was ready to make contact. The location, opposite where she worked, was just a coincidence, but maybe she thought that you were on to her; that you had picked up on her and were trying to find out what she was doing there. So she breaks cover and finds that you were doing something else entirely. But that gives her a way in and she used it. Now she's on the inside and knows pretty much all our plans."

With Den's suspicions having already been aroused, he was open to persuasion.

"We can't prove any of that, of course, but then again we don't have to. The thing is, when will she make her move? Once you leave to take the egg to the Galactic Counsel in Exile she loses her chance."

"And she'll know that. You know her best. What do you think she'll do?"

"What any good thief would do. She'll find the weakest point in our security and then use it against us."

"OK, role play. You're Ka Mera. You've spent the last few weeks studying our set up. What is our weak point? Oh Damn." An Kohli responded to the bleeping of her communicator. She identified the caller.

"What do you want, Merkaloy? I'm kind of busy."

"It's the eggs. They've gone."

"Wh…. Wh…."

"My apartment has been broken into. The whole package has been stolen."

"OK, look, thanks. Meet us at the Three Moons in fifteen." She broke the communications link and turned to Den. "No need for role play. I think we've just found out where our weakest point is."

"Oh My Galaxy. Ka Mera knows the access codes to the Adastra."

"Are you sure?"

"Not absolutely, but she was there when we went on board when we left New Earth to get Gaga and Beckham out. It could be that Gala isn't the only one who's good at memorising codes."

"Shit." She used the voice activation on her communicator to open up the GSTC galacticnet page. She scrolled own until she found what she wanted. "The Adastra left orbit ten minutes ago."

Glossary

GSTC - Galactic Space Traffic Control. Each inhabited star system with space travel capability, and some uninhabited systems, has a traffic control system to prevent collisions between space craft and between spacecraft and orbiting satellites and to monitor space activity within its system. These individual systems are linked together through the galacticnet to provide galaxy wide traffic control information.

Multi-Dimensional Flame Theory - When rocket science became run of the mill and younglings started assembling toy rockets capable of inter-stellar travel, a new metaphor for something difficult and/or complex was required, so Multi-Dimensional Flame Theory was used to fill the gap. Don't ask me what it means, it's far too difficult for me to understand.

15 - The Hideaway

Laurel was sobbing into Merkaloy's shoulder when An Kohli, Gala and Den arrived at the Three Moons Bar. She took one look at An Kohli's thunderous expression and fled to the safety of the staff rooms.

"Poor kid blames herself for what happened" Merkaloy explained. "She and Ka Mera had quite a chat last night and she wheedled the address of my apartment out of Laurel. Honestly, An Kohli, Laurel had no idea what Ka Mera was like. I hadn't even hinted at it. Laurel didn't even know I had the eggs."

"It's OK, Merkaloy. I know Laurel isn't to blame. We all took her at face value, me included. I'll talk to Laurel later and set her mind at rest, if she'll speak to me. But we have more pressing matters to address: to try and work out where Ka Mera has gone." They took seats around a table and a service droid brought them drinks in response to the order Merkaloy sent via his communicator. The bar was almost empty at that time of the day and the handful of other customers were so engrossed in their own business they paid the small group little attention.

"She must have been watching my apartment. Laurel and I left at the same time. She came to work and I went to the gym." Merkaloy's muscles seemed to ripple in reaction to the mention of the gym, but that could have been An Kohli's imagination. "When I got back the door was busted open and the eggs were missing. Nothing else had been taken."

"We can't be sure it was Ka Mera." Den made one last attempt to save the reputation of his fellow Gau.

"So who else do you think might have stolen the Adastra just a short while after Merkaloy's apartment was burgled?" Gala asked scornfully. Den looked at the floor rather than having to look her in the eye. There could be no passing the theft of the Adastra off as a coincidence.

"Where might she go, do you think?" An Kohli addressed herself to Den. "Will she head for Camoo?"

"No. The reason Gau like myself and Ka Mera hardly ever go home is because we're not really welcome there anymore. I'm not saying we would be pelted with rotten eggs, but it's better not to take the risk. No, she'll have a destination in mind where she can conceal the eggs while she does a deal with whoever is willing to buy them. That could be us. With Gib Dander's credit we could buy a small planet if we wanted to."

"True, but I have no intention of buying them back, except as a last resort. She stole them and for that she deserves to go back to jail. If I can arrange that I will, but only after we recover the egg."

"She's taking a big risk." Merkaloy chipped in. "The Fell will take a similar view. They'll buy the egg if they have to, but if they can get it by just taking it off Ka Mera, dead or alive, then that's what they'll do."

"The tracker!" Gala blurted, causing them all to look in her direction. She even managed to attract the attention of some of the Three Moons' other customers.

"Of course. Someone planted a tracker on the Adastra." An Kohli explained to Merkaloy. "We think it was Warrior, he's a Fell member and we think he may have been on New Earth. That means the Fell can get to her. Gala, could you hack into the tracker signal?"

"Well, I have the part number and serial number, because I recorded them when I found it. Give me a bit of time and I should be able to hack into the manufacturer's galacticnet site and intercept its signal when it communicates back to its owner."

"It won't be able to start sending until she gets to her destination and comes out of its worm hole. That gives us a bit of time, but then it's a race between us and the Fell to see who gets to her first."

"For Ka Mera's sake I hope it's us." Den said, his voice only just audible.

"Don't be too sure." An Kohli muttered back. "The mood I'm in right now, she better be good at begging or I may just kill her myself."

* * *

The mood on the command deck of Merkaloy's ship, which he had just renamed The Laurel, was sombre to say the least. An Kohli occupied the Captain's chair with Gala as the co-pilot. Den was on board the Pradua, just waiting for the co-ordinates of the Adastra so that both ships could give chase to Ka Mera. Merkaloy had offered to come but An Kohli declined.

"Laurel needs you right now. She needs bucking up a bit. Pamper her a little. Send me the bill. I really don't hold her responsible for what happened." An Kohli advised him. "I have told her as much, but I'm not sure she believed me. She was still in floods of tears when I left her."

They had been waiting for two days to receive the tracker signal and the nerves of all three of them were on edge.

"Do want another cup of coffee?" Gala asked.

"No." An Kohli replied, a little more abruptly than she had meant. "Sorry. No, thank you. There's only so much coffee a being can take. You're sure the tracker information will be received?" An Kohli quickly responded to Gala's look of annoyance. "Sorry again. Of course you're sure. Don't pay me any attention. You know how impatient I am."

"Why don't you go and lie down. Take a nap."

"You mean stop getting on your nerves." An Kohli interpreted. Gala's wry smile told her she was right. "I can't sleep. I'd just end up pacing up and down my cabin and there's not a lot of room for that. It would just make matters worse."

A quiet ping announced that a computer had just reacted to some new information. Gala picked out the correct image from the array on her screen and maximised it. It was the one that showed the location data being transmitted from the tracker on board the Adastra. The ship was no longer in a wormhole and the tracker had quickly identified the nearest location beacons to allow it to work out where it was, accurate down to five sim.

"Where is that?" An Kohli asked. "It seems familiar for some reason."

Gala was working feverishly at the navi-com, trying to answer An Kohli's question before she had even asked it. "Becrux Delta. Oh dear."

"That's putting it mildly. The worst criminal hell hole in the galaxy. How in Naron's name are we supposed to find her if she's down there."

An Kohli knew that as a bounty hunter she would be about as welcome as a dose of fleas at a dog show. Unlike dog owners, however, An Kohli could expect more by way of a welcome than a spray of pesticide.

"Ideas are your department." Gala commented. "I'm engineering. According to the navi-com you have forty three standard hours in which to come up with one. I'll transfer the co-ordinates across to Den."

"OK. Thanks. Then get us moving."

* * *

Ka Mera paused in her walk along the dusty street of one of the few towns that had been established. Well, it called itself a town. It had a couple of bars, a single shop, a couple of down at heel boarding houses, a grandly named town hall that was more of a shack, and a diner that sold the sort of food that would make a buzzard barf.

Becrux Delta, or The Hideaway as it was known by its inhabitants, was the kind of place where no one bothered with niceties such as funerals anymore or, for that matter, any sort of investigation into the cause of death. Murder was the default cause and there was no police force to investigate a death.

Someone finding a body reported it to a hotline number and a service droid was sent along to collect it. An underpaid and overworked junior official did his best to identify the victim from the contents of his pockets or communicator data, if he still had either, then recorded the death on a database before sending the body for an automated cremation.

The planet had never formally been colonised. It had once been used by a criminal to hide away from law and order, hence its name, then the location was passed from ear to ear and others started using it. Some entrepreneurs with big muscles started businesses to keep the criminals in home comforts, which provided the basis for a rudimentary economy which then supported a sort of government, but the idea of establishing a police force had been discouraged by people with even bigger muscles than the entrepreneurs. As a planet, it lurched from chaos to farce and back again and no one who valued their life went there unless there was no other place in the galaxy for them to go. Which was why Ka Mera was there.

Ka Mera's problem was that she had a prize worth millions of nuks, once she could convert it, but she had almost no money. She had fled Sabik before An Kohli could claim the bounty for the return of the Magus egg and the small advance that she had been given against her eventual share would last about thirty standard seconds in a place like The Hideaway.

Her cheapest option for accommodation would be to stay on board the Adastra, but that would be the first place An Kohli would look for her, so she had to go down to the planet and rent somewhere. She also had to earn some more money to keep herself alive until she could make a deal for the egg. That might take some time.

There was work she could get, of course. As a Gau she could make herself look like any female of almost any species, which was appealing to many of the male and some of the females who used The Hideaway, but she didn't relish the thought. Unlike the Gau's Sutran kin, the idea of selling her body was not one she relished. There was stripping, of course, but that was only marginally more attractive. Besides, to make any real money from the latter she would have to also be amenable to the former. There was bar work, which she had done before, but the pay wouldn't cover the cost of a room in the worst flop house, let alone food on top. She was fast running out of options.

She found herself outside a bar and dared to take a peek inside. The one blessing of The Hideaway was that it wasn't as crowded as some of the planets she could have chosen. The increasing lawlessness of the galaxy meant that planets like The Hideaway were not so much in demand. Some criminals came only out of habit, while others came only because there was nowhere else for them to go, even if they weren't wanted for a crime. Compared to New Klondike, for example, it was practically deserted. But that actually caused her more problems. Less people meant less money was being spent, which meant less demand for her limited talents.

Through the gap of the half door Ka Mera could see half a dozen beings sat around, drinking. One man had a female on his lap and another two or three females were standing at the bar trying to look alluring. They were failing. Music drowned out all sounds of conversation, but no one seemed to be talking much anyway. It was a place for the damned and the damnable. Ka Mera moved along, even more discouraged than before.

She was thinking of giving up and returning to the Adastra when she spotted someone coming out of another bar and crossing the street. She couldn't be sure, but he looked familiar. She called out.

He stopped in response to her call, his hand edging towards the pulsar hanging from his belt. On just about any other planet it would seem like a threat, but here it was almost part of the greeting ritual.

"Who wants me?" The being called.

"It's me, Ka Mera." She increased her pace, making her way towards him.

A look of recognition spread across his face. "Well I never. Ka Mera. What brings you to this hell hole? No, don't bother explaining. If you're here, I already know the answer. You can fill me in on the details over a drink."

"Thanks Basi, I'll take you up on that if you're paying."

He laughed uproariously. "Same old Ka Mera. Never two victels to rub together."

"Actually, I need more than just a drink. I need a place to stay and a job to pay for it."

"The place to stay is easy. You can crash on my couch. But the job could be a bit more difficult. What are you prepared to do?"

"It's more like what I'm not prepared to do, if you get my drift."

"Yeah. Pity, as a Gau I could get you plenty of work, but never mind. We all have lines we won't cross. Now let me think. Actually the owner of the Lucky Victel owes me a favour. Maybe I can get you some bar work. It won't be much, but it will pay for your food and you won't need to pay me rent, at least not in the short term."

"That sounds good. Can we go there now?"

"Actually I was just on my way there. They play an honest hand of cards there and I was about to try and get a game. When I say 'honest' I mean you won't actually get shot and the chances are there are no more than two aces up someone else's sleeve, but it's the most honest game in town, for what that's worth."

Ka Mera gave a knowing chuckle. "Maybe I can help out. You know how bar staff often see hands when they're bringing drinks over to the table."

A broad grin spread across Basi's face. "See, you're earning your keep already."

* * *

"I thought you were coming here to play cards." Ka Mera raised her beer bottle to her face and took a suspicious sniff. Her nose wrinkled in disgust.

"It says it's Gau Beer on the label," Basi provided, "But it's most likely to be Blash."

Ka Mera took an experimental sip and just about managed to prevent herself from spitting the liquid back out. She swallowed and took another sip. With her taste buds now numbed this one tasted slightly less offensive.

"So, why aren't you playing cards?"

"I never rush in. I watch the tables, see who's playing, who's winning and who's losing. I look for the tells and the shows."

"Is it possible to do that from this distance?" They were seated at a table several met from the three tables of card players.

"Actually it's easier. See the guy on the nearest table, the one with his back to us?" Ka Mera nodded her recognition. "Well, his foot is shaking like it's being driven by a motor. He's almost certainly been dealt a good hand. Now, if you were sat at the table you might not notice that. So if I go onto that table I make sure I'm sat next to him and keep my foot close to his so I can feel the movement. It will give me an edge."

"Anyone else?"

"Well, no obvious tells, but you see the big guy on the next table. The one who looks like he fell out of an ugly tree and hit ever branch on the way down?"

"Yeah. I see him."

"Well, he's a really honest player. Never cheats, never accuses anyone else of cheating. He often loses. But when that happens the person who has won seems to turn up dead the next day, with all his winnings missing. So I won't be playing that table." Basi changed the subject abruptly. "So, what have you been up to since we last met?"

"Well, after we pulled that scam on Towie, I bumped into an old pal, Mia Crie. We set up a used spaceship business, if you get my meaning."

"As in the owners didn't know they were selling their ships?"

"That's about the size of it. Unfortunately a clever dick of a bounty hunter set up a sting operation. When we tried to sell this really cool Andromeda class ship we found ourselves locked in. We spent some jail time for that."

"And what brings you to The Hideaway with no money?"

"Asset rich, cash poor as they say. I pulled a job on Earth but I need to convert the proceeds to cash so I'm hanging out here until I can find a buyer."

"Anything to do with that smoking hole in the ground that was on the media a while back?"

Ka Mera said nothing and just took a sip from her bottle. Basi took that as a yes. "So, what sort of buyer are you looking for? Maybe I can help."

"You can. Keep your ears open for anyone who says they're from the Fell. They're my target market. They probably won't actually announce their Fell connections, of course, but there will be giveaways. They won't be your run-of-the-mill crook."

Basi let out a low whistle. "You play with some seriously bad people."

"I know, but they're the people with the money and they're also the sort of people who would want what I have to sell. Don't say you know me, though. It could put you in danger. Just let me know and I'll do the rest. There's a drink in it for you."

"I could do with a little bit of cash, I must admit. Ah, here's Malkie. He's the owner of this dump. He's the one I need to talk to about getting you fixed up with some work. If you see someone with a good hand just say 'Who wants snacks?' when you serve the drinks. I'll know what you mean. If you can see a bluffer then say 'Will there be anything else?' Got it?"

* * *

Shogun, real name Elloway Fargon, stared at the image on his screen and tried to work out his next move. The image was of the Adastra but the oval shaped recess visible in its hull told him that its shuttle was elsewhere, which probably meant that his target was also elsewhere. Was the co-pilot still on board? Or her Gau sidekicks? Would she be back soon, or was she staying down on the planet? He discounted the latter option. From what he knew of An Kohli there would be nowhere on The Hideaway that would suit her style.

He tried again to scan the ship for signs of life but the Meteor class was thick skinned and wouldn't give up its secrets so easily. He made up his mind and pressed the button on the intercom that connected him to the passenger lounge. "Get suited up. We're going down to the planet."

A short while later he strode down the ramp of his shuttlecraft, followed by his four personal security guards. They were impressive; tall, clad head to toe in body armour topped with visored helmets and each carrying a long pulsar, fired from the shoulder for greater accuracy, with a smaller one carried in a holster at the hip. The idea was to present an image that said 'don't mess with me' and the image worked. Even on The Hideaway, Shogun would be given a wide berth.

The armour itself was useless against a pulsar. If such simple devices were effective it would put pulsar manufacturers out of business, but all that shiny armour did have a certain macho appeal and was resistant to punches, kicks and sharp objects.

Shogun spotted the Adastra's shuttle parked on the opposite side of the shuttle pad. A shifty looking character was hanging around outside the rundown terminal building, no doubt looking for unwary visitors to rob. Shogun sent one of his bodyguards over to ask him some questions. Their conversation was short.

"It was a Gau female that arrived in the shuttle." Reported the bodyguard. "She arrived alone, this morning and went off into town on foot. He hasn't seen her since."

"OK. Go and tell him that there's money in it for him if he comes and finds me if the Gau returns. Then you and Shelby go and see if you can find her. Alanwood and Hickor will stay here with me." He dismissed the bodyguard and went back inside his shuttle to wait for news while the two selected bodyguards headed off into town.

The appearance of armoured personnel in a place like The Hideaway was bound to attract attention and news of the two bodyguards in shining black was soon speeding around the small town. Ka Mera heard it shortly after she started her first stint behind the bar of the Lucky Victel.

Their arrival was unlikely to be a coincidence and she guessed that they were probably something to do with the Fell. No law enforcement officer would risk his life on The Hideaway, at least not in such low numbers as a pair and bounty hunters tended to maintain a lower profile so as not to alert their quarry. On The Hideaway just about the whole population was likely to be regarded as quarry by a bounty hunter.

She realised that she'd made a mistake by not assuming a disguise when she had arrived on the planet. In her natural state she stood out as a Gau and if the two armoured men were looking for a Gau it wouldn't take them long to find her. She pushed her way through the door into the back office, where Malkie was sitting at a battered desk, his raised feet perched on one corner.

"Sorry, I need to look like someone different for a while." Ka Mera apologised as she shape shifted into a simile of one of the bar girls she had seen earlier in the day. Malkie shrugged, not bothered by such odd behaviour. If someone on The Hideaway needed to disguise themselves then they were bound to have a good reason and it was nothing to do with him.

Ka Mera pulled the neck of her garment down to enhance her disguise then stepped back into the bar and caught sight of herself in one of the large mirrors. She could have done with more make up to look totally convincing and her clothes were totally wrong, they revealed far too little, but she wouldn't recognise herself so neither would the two mystery men. The ordering system pinged and she busied herself loading drinks onto a tray to take over to the card tables.

She was just returning behind the bar when the exterior doors slid open and the two men stamped their way in. They cast a look around the room, clearly looking for someone. Not seeing anyone they recognised they walked across the wooden floor, their heavily booted feet loud in the sudden silence. No one was going to play cards until they found out the meaning of this intrusion. Surreptitious fingers curled around the butts of pulsars, ready to draw and fire should there be any sudden threat.

"We're looking for a Gau." The left hand of the pair said, as the right hand one kept a wary eye on the card players.

"No Gau around here." Ka Mera denied her own presence.

"Are you sure." There was an underlying threat evident in the bodyguard's voice. "They can look like just about anyone."

"Sure I'm sure. What do you want her for anyway." Ka Mera instantly regretted asking the question. The bodyguard hadn't specified a gender for the Gau he was looking for. The bodyguard's mouth curled into a sneer below his visor.

"So you haven't seen a *female* Gau then? As it happens the Gau we're looking for could be male or female. There could even be two of them, one of each."

Ka Mera quickly concluded that they were probably looking for either Den or her, but were unsure if they were alone or together.

"Beings turn up here all the time. If you tell me why you're looking for him or her I can let them know if I see them."

"You know, you look familiar. I've just seen someone who looks just like you, down the road in that other bar."

"My twin sister." Ka Mera improvised.

The guard sneered again. "Yeah, and I'm an agravarg's uncle."

"That's nice for you. So why do you want these Gau?"

"Have you heard of a bounty hunter by the name of An Kohli?"

"Who hasn't?"

"Well, it's her we're really looking for. The Gau we want is probably travelling with her."

Victels started to drop into place. They knew about the Adastra, but not that she was its sole occupant.

"People don't usually go looking for bounty hunters. It's usually the other way round."

"Well, she has something that my boss wants and he plans to get it. He's not too bothered if An Kohli hands it over peaceably or not."

The last victel dropped into place. It was the egg they wanted. The egg she had hidden only that morning.

"You're boss, he wouldn't happen to be…. How shall I put this? He wouldn't happen to be well connected to certain beings in the galaxy, would he?"

"Who our boss is connected to is none of your concern."

"Even if I could point him in the right direction to find what he's looking for?" She could tell she had captured the bodyguard's attention.

"What would you know about that?"

"News travels fast in the galaxy these days, especially if it involves stolen property. Let's say I know someone who knows someone who might know where to find what you're looking for. If the price is right, maybe they might sell."

"Is it theirs to sell?"

"No more than it is anyone else's to sell, but no less so either."

The bodyguard thought for a moment. Ka Mera guessed that he wasn't authorised to negotiate and so was wondering how to proceed.

"I'll tell my boss what you've said. He'll probably want to speak to you. In the meantime if you see those Gau, or An Kohli, you tell me first. We're at the shuttle port. I'll be back in an hour, maybe less." He turned and he and his companion headed for the door. The card players relaxed and recommenced their game, speculating about what might be going on as fresh hands were dealt and chips were tossed into the centre of the tables.

Ka Mera delivered a tray of drinks, asking if there would be anything else while standing behind one of the players. Basi smiled and placed a bet.

Glossary

Agravarg - A large domesticated animal bred for food products. Not known for its aerodynamic qualities.

Blash - An extremely poor quality beer. Originally thought to be American in origin it turned out not to be so, however its actual origin is still unknown, though it is brewed under licence by Gargantua Enterprises.

Naron - An evil character who appears in a number of children's stories throughout the galaxy. His name is often invoked in the same way as Earthlings use that of God or the Devil, but unlike either of those, nobody actually worships Naron.

Victel - A unit of currency worth $1/100^{th}$ of a nuk. A one victel coin is effectively valueless

16 - The High Price Of Eggs

The Laurel took its place in orbit around The Hideaway. It was so close to the Adastra that the smallest navigation error would have seen the two ships hurtle towards the planet in a terminal embrace, but Gala was too good a co-pilot to allow that to happen. The message, however, was clear: I'm on your case.

"There's another ship in orbit. It's too high class to belong to most of the people down there." An Kohli observed.

"Bringing it up on screen now."

It was quite a distance away, but the elegant lines of the Starcruiser announced its pedigree to the galaxy. "Can you trace the registration?" An Kohli asked.

"Already on it. Oh, that's odd. There's no record of that registration number on the manufacturer's database."

"Which means that someone doesn't want to let anyone else know who the owner is. Now that is odd. Most beings that own a Starcruiser want to shout their ownership to the universe. Which means…"

"That it probably belongs to a member of the Fell." Den supplied as he entered the bridge, making it even more overcrowded than it had already been.

"I was just about to say that." An Kohli snapped.

"Sorry. You were just taking your time getting there."

"OK, well, there're no prizes for guessing why the Fell might turn up here. They're either after me or they're after the egg. My guess is that it's both."

"They've got a head start." Commented Gala.

"Yes, but you've a got a Gau." Added Den.

"And you set a Gau to catch a Gau." An Kohli provided the cliché. "Thank you Den. Get dressed, we're going down there."

Den was dressed in his normal space cruising outfit of boxer shorts and tee shirt, a habit which neither An Kohli nor Gala's threats had been able to break, despite several attempts. He headed off to his room, the Navigator's cabin, to put on some clothes.

"How will you be able to identify the Fell member?" Gala asked.

"Oh, I think they'll stand out. Either the locals will have spotted them or they'll be the ones asking the questions no one wants to answer."

"Well, be careful. It's not just the Fell who are the danger. You've probably locked up half the beings on that planet at one time or another, so they'll hardly be rolling out the Green Carpet."

"That thought had crossed my mind. Perhaps a disguise would be in order." An Kohli activated the intercom. "Den, don't go looking like a Gau. Try to find something that will fit in." She turned to Gala. "Any suggestions?"

"You do 'cheap hooker' quite well." She grinned mischievously.

"Any other suggestions?" An Kohli's patience was starting to wear thin and it was betrayed by her tone of voice.

"Try crook on the run. Well-worn travelling clothes, serious kicking boots, plenty of weaponry and a couple of well-placed scars."

"OK. I'll give it a go and see what I can come up with."

"Nothing skin tight. Your figure is almost as recognisable as your face."

An Kohli pouted. She hated concealing her figure. But she had to admit that Gala's suggestion made sense. "I suppose I had better change my hair as well."

"It would help. Criminals don't usually go in for 'drop dead gorgeous' when it comes to hairstyles. Try 'hacked about with an out of control hedge trimmer'."

* * *

The emergence of a couple of thuggish looking characters from the newly arrived shuttlecraft caused the two bodyguards to take a better grip on their weapons, holding the butts of their weapons tighter against their shoulders and moving their fingers a little closer to the firing buttons. It was something of a coincidence that it was the shuttle for another Meteor class ship, but coincidences happen. Meteors were common enough craft. The shuttle they were interested in was clearly marked as being from the Adastra, while this new one was from a ship they had never heard of, The Laurel. They decided it need not concern them unless the unsavoury looking occupants decided to take a closer look at their own shuttle.

"Don't look now," An Kohli cautioned, barely moving her lips, "but those two couldn't look more like hired muscle if they tried. The only thing that's missing is a sign round their necks saying 'henchmen'."

"I think we can assume that shuttle belongs to our Fell member then. That's assuming that he or she is a Fell member."

"I think that level of security speaks for itself." An Kohli replied. "Anyway, we don't want to attract their attention, so pretend they don't exist."

The two dangerous looking characters kept moving towards what passed for a terminal building.

An Kohli's own mother wouldn't have recognised her. She was wearing a stained old flight suit that she'd found in the engineering space of the Laurel, along with a pair of heavy work boots that were scuffed and scarred from overuse. She had concealed her skin under a layer of darker make-up and covered her glossy mane of indigo hair with a mousy coloured wig that would have looked better if it had a couple of rats nesting in it. An Kohli wondered where Merkaloy had got it and made a note to ask him when they next met; if they ever met again, which was far from certain given their present location. She had decided that scars would be over the top but she wore a pair of over-sized dark glasses.

Den looked no better. Despite the warmth of the planet's sun he wore a heavy jacket and trouser combination along with similarly scuffed boots. He had adopted the appearance of a Lupine, which meant that his face had taken on a slightly elongated, even pointed shape and his ears were high on the side of his head and erect. Both of them carried a pulsar on each hip which were augmented by hefty killing knives in sheaths that were strapped to their thighs. An

Kohli's Menafield was too distinctive and closely associated with her, so she had adopted more run of the mill Gargantua Enterprises model pulsars from Merkaloy's on-board arsenal.

They stopped at the first bar they came to and bought a beer each. The clientele were hardly any different from those Ka Mera had seen earlier in the day. There were fewer bar girls, though An Kohli couldn't know that. One of them decided that Den might be in need of some female company and sidled over.

"Buy a girl a drink, Captain?" She hissed sibilantly.

"I'm not the Captain, she is." Den replied abruptly. He doubted An Kohli would take kindly to him being distracted right now. Besides, the girl's raddled appearance was too unattractive even for him, at least while he was still sober.

"Sorry, my mistake. You just had the look of a space Captain." She tried the flattery again. "Buy me a beer anyway?"

An Kohli decided it was time to intervene. "I'll buy you a drink if you can tell me where I can find a Gau."

"Any particular Gau?"

"Are there that many down here at the moment?"

The female shrugged. "Beings come and beings go, but as it happens there was a Gau around earlier today. She didn't come in here though. I saw her looking through the door."

"Do you know where she went afterwards?"

"There aren't many places she could go. Try the Lucky Victel. Turn left when you leave, along the street and turn left again."

An Kohli thanked her and indicated to the bartender that the female could order a drink. The bartender didn't bother asking what she wanted, he just poured a glass of brown liquid and placed it in front of her. "Ten Nuks." He demanded from An Kohli.

"That's pricey." An Kohli commented, fishing around in the pockets of her flight suit for some cash.

"I have expensive tastes." The underdressed female replied.

"More like you can spot a mug when you see one." An Kohli muttered to herself. It was an old trick, of course. Employ girls to encourage men into the bar and then fleece them by getting them to buy the girls over-priced drinks. An Kohli had heard of it, but she wasn't usually the one paying the bill.

An Kohli prodded Den. "Come on. Let's go and find this Lucky Victel place." They left the bar without touching their drinks.

Den could feel Ka Mera's presence before he even set foot in the Lucky Victel. "She can probably also feel me." He warned An Kohli.

"In that case you back off, out of range. Any idea what she might look like?"

"No. I can't sense that. But she's at the left hand end of the building as you go in. If there are any females there then she's almost certainly one of them." Den turned and crossed the street, retreating until the tingling in his brain subsided.

It didn't take long for An Kohli to pick Ka Mera out. All the figures occupying the left hand end of the room were male except for the one behind the bar. She was deeply in conversation with a dapper looking male who was flanked by two more of the armour clad bodyguards that she and Den had first seen at the shuttle port. An Kohli approached and stood at the end of the bar, close enough to overhear, but not close enough to appear to be listening.

"Excuse me." Ka Mera apologised to the dapper looking male. "I've got to serve this customer."

The male scowled, clearly not used to people walking away from him while he was talking,

"Beer." Grunted An Kohli, so that Ka Mera wouldn't recognise her voice. The dim lighting made it difficult for her to see properly with her dark glasses on, but she daren't remove them in case Ka Mera recognised her violet coloured eyes. They were the one feature she couldn't disguise, at least not without coloured contact lenses.

Ka Mera placed a bottle in front of her, took the coins that were offered, gave back no change and went back to the dapper male. An Kohli took an experimental sip, just about avoided gagging and took the opportunity to examine the male more closely. He was humanoid, but not human. She could place his species no more accurately than that. There were nearly twenty thousand humanoid species in the galaxy and most of them looked alike. This one had pale skin, a sort of grey eye colour and fair hair. He was slightly built, shorter than herself, but that said nothing. She was quite tall even for her own species.

His clothes, she noted, were expensive but not overtly so. They were the sort of clothes that a rich person might wear when trying not to look too rich. Perhaps the sort of clothes they might wear in the mistaken belief that they weren't giving away the fact that they were wealthy. An Kohli suspected that had he come to The Hideaway without his bodyguards he would have been found naked in the gutter before the day was out.

"How can I be sure you'll keep your end of the bargain?" The male was saying. An Kohli had to strain to hear him.

"You can't. But the seller can't leave the planet while you have men at the shuttle port, so there's nowhere for me or her to hide."

"How do you know I have men at the shuttle port."

"People tell me things." In fact it had been Basi that had told her, after using his communicator to speak to the official at the shuttle port.

"Look, I don't know what the seller has offered you, but I'll double it if you'll tell me where to find her."

"That's not the deal. Let's call it honour among thieves."

"I'd call it stupidity myself. I could make you tell me."

"See all those beings behind you, playing cards? They'll make sure you and your goons never get out of the door alive." Ka Mera couldn't even be sure that even Basi would stand up for her, let alone the rest of them, but she felt sure that if she shouted 'police' she would get the attention of everyone in the room and that would probably be enough protection for her.

"OK. Tell your friend that I'm willing to do a deal, but only face to face."

"She won't do that."

"Why not?"

"Because her anonymity is her only protection once the deal has gone through."

"An Kohli is hardly anonymous."

"Who said anything about An Kohli being the seller?"

"You mean she isn't?"

"As far as I know she would be the last person to sell. She'd hand it over to the authorities."

"So the Gau isn't working for her?"

"I think that is a safe assumption."

"In that case the Gau is safe. I have no fight with her. But she's using An Kohli's ship."

"And if An Kohli catches up with her she'll go to prison for stealing it."

"Ah, at last, I'm getting the picture. Why didn't you tell me all that to start with?"

"You didn't ask. Look, do you want to buy it or not? If you do I'll tell the Gau your offer and she will tell me whether or not she accepts it."

"OK. I'll make an offer. Twenty million. Not a victel more."

"OK. I'll pass that on." Ka Mera struggled to supress her surprise and delight. She had only been going to ask for half that amount. "Come back in an hour and you'll have your answer." Twenty Million. Even with Mia Crie's share she could retire to a nice planet somewhere and never risk going to prison again. Somewhere even An Kohli would never find her.

The male and his two bodyguards left the bar without any further comment. An Kohli could see Ka Mera studying the occupants of the room, a worried look in her eyes. No doubt it was the first opportunity she'd had to do it since she had sensed Den's presence. The Gau sidled along the bar towards her.

"You didn't see anyone hanging around outside, did you? A shifty looking character probably. Maybe a Gau, but he might not look like one."

"This planet is full of shifty looking characters." An Kohli responded, "but no, I didn't see anyone in particular."

Something about An Kohli's voice made Ka Mera take a closer look at her customer, but she couldn't quite penetrate the disguise.

An Kohli caught the look and knew she was at risk of her cover being blown.

"Do I know you?" Ka Mera asked. "You seem familiar."

"It's possible. I get around. But I don't recognise you." An Kohli didn't say: 'Because you're a Gau in disguise,'. "But you look a lot like a bar girl I spoke to a short while ago." She nodded towards the exit, So who was that?"

"Oh, him." the Gau replied, "Some hotshot wants to buy something a friend of mine is selling."

"It must be something special if he's offering twenty million nuks for it."

"Oh, you heard."

"It was difficult not to."

"Well, if you know what's good for you, you'll forget you heard it. He's not the sort of person who likes his business being known."

"Does he have a name?"

"He called himself Shogun. Now, if you'll excuse me, I've got a message to deliver."

Ka Mera removed her apron and placed it on the bar. She stuck her head through the doorway behind her. "Just going on my break, Malkie." She called, then walked around the end of the bar and towards the door.

Malkie appeared through the doorway like he had been shot out of a cannon. "She's not due a fucking break." He announced to the world at large. He let out a big sigh, picked the apron off the bar and threw it though the doorway behind him and started to collect up empty beer bottles.

An Kohli watched Ka Mera's retreating back, hoping that Den would have the sense to follow Ka Mera. She daren't be seen doing so. She counted to twenty and then left the bar herself.

* * *

Den was about to step out of his cover to follow Ka Mera, from a safe distance of course, so that she wouldn't detect his presence, when he noticed that he wasn't the only person interested in her. One of the bodyguards had removed his helmet and was now tailing her at a discrete distance.

That made life so much easier. Den didn't need to tail Ka Mera if he could tail the bodyguard instead. The guard had even been obliging by discarding his larger weapon, probably another attempt to make himself less visible. He was wasting his time, of course; the shiny black armour was still a dead giveaway.

As he strolled casually along a short distance behind the armour clad stooge, Den pondered his purpose. Was it to capture Ka Mera? Was it to seize the Magus egg? Or was it just to keep a protective eye on his boss's investment? It could be all of those or none at all. They weren't mutually exclusive. The running order could be: Protect Ka Mera until she shows you where the egg is, then kill her and bring the egg back to Poppa.

Well, Den was fairly sure what An Kohli required of him. Find the egg then bring both it and Ka Mera back safely. An Kohli wouldn't want the Gau dead if it could be avoided. An Kohli would want Ka Mera to spend a long time in prison regretting the day she had stolen both the egg and the Adastra.

Den took a casual look behind him to see if An Kohli was also in pursuit. He couldn't see her, but that didn't mean she wasn't there. He looked back to see the bodyguard turn a corner between two buildings. He slowed his pace and took a cautious look around the corner. The alley appeared to be a dead end that allowed access to the side doors of the two buildings. He guessed that Ka Mera had gone into one, but couldn't be sure which. Both doors stood open.

He sauntered along the centre of the alley, taking the precaution of drawing one of his pulsars, just in case. Sound would be his only clue as to which door they had taken unless his Gaudar was able to pick up her scent. He stopped dead in his tracks as the bodyguard emerged from the door to his right, almost colliding with him. He had a puzzled look on his face. He too was unsure where Ka Mera had gone.

Realisation of Den's purpose appeared on his face and he was about to draw his pulsar when Den got in first. He slammed the butt of his weapon into the guard's face, sending him crashing back into the doorway. The guard hit the doorframe and half slumped, struggling to remain on his feet as he tried to shake off the pain of the blow.

Den didn't give him a chance. He kicked the guard in the crotch, forcing him to double over, then brought the butt of the pulsar down on the back of his head, turning out the lights.

"Very impressive, Den." He heard the voice at the same time as he registered the tingling created Ka Mera's brainwaves. Cautiously he turned and faced the levelled pulsar that she had pointing at him. It was a small one, capable of being concealed beneath her clothing, but at that range it was as lethal as An Kohli's Menafield. "I saw the bodyguard tailing me, but I didn't know you were there as well. Now, what are we going to do about you? Oh, by the way, drop your weapon."

Den carefully lowered his pulsar to the floor, making sure it was out of reach of the bodyguard, should he start to wake up. "We could cut a deal?" Den tried. He doubted she would bite, but it was always worth a try.

"You would sell-out An Kohli? I doubt that, but there's a first time for everything. Go on, make me an offer."

"A share of the sale price of the egg. Let's say ten percent. In return I watch your back for you while you collect your money."

"You don't think that was his job?" She waved her pulsar towards the still unconscious bodyguard.

"No. I think his job was to kill you and take the egg. There are still three more of them, plus the smooth looking one in the fancy clothes."

"You mean Shogun."

"If that's his name, then yes. Is He Fell?"

"Probably, or at least closely connected to them. I can't imagine anyone else being interested in buying the egg at the price I've agreed. He said he wasn't interested in me, only in the egg."

"People like him are always interested in hanging onto their money. If he can get the egg without paying you, then I think he would take that option. If he isn't actually Fell he may hang onto the money himself and say that he paid you."

Ka Mera shrugged, not sure in her own mind if Den was right or wrong. "OK. Maybe you're right. I get the egg, you watch my back and when the money is in my bank account and I'm away from here, you get your share. It means you'll have to come with me on the Adastra."

"Suits me. I was getting bored with An Kohli and Gala. They're too 'Goody Two Shoes' for my liking. How much is ten percent, by the way?"

"Half a million nuks." Ka Mera lied.

Den let out a low whistle of appreciation. She was probably lying, he knew, but it was still a lot of money.

"OK. We've got a deal."

"Not yet we haven't. I'm still negotiating. If you even look like you're double crossing me I'll find out just how good this little pulsar is."

"OK. I hear you loud and clear."

"The hard looking bitch in the bar; I take it that was An Kohli?"

"You recognised her?"

"Not really; more of a hunch. But she'd better keep out of my way. If she even looks in my direction I'll shoot first. I don't want to kill her, but I will if she makes any move against me."

"OK. I'll warn her off. In the meantime we had better get out of here before his pals turn up." The bodyguard was starting to stir so Den picked up his pulsar and gave him another crack on the head to send him back to dreamland, which also served to emphasise his point.

"This way." Ka Mera crossed the alley and went through the doorway, stepping over the recumbent bodyguard. She led the way up a flight of stairs to a corridor where doors gave access to rooms on either side. Some sort of boarding house or hotel, Den concluded. A moan of either pain or passion came from behind one of the doors, forcing him to re-assess the purpose of the building. Ka Mera stopped beside a door and pulled it open. Rows of shelves held sheets and towels, while stained pillows lay in a heap on the floor. She burrowed around in this pile until she found what she had been looking for. It was the box holding the eggs that An Kohli had bought on Earth. Ka Mera had obviously been unable to identify the only one that had any real value.

She tucked the box under her free arm and continued along the corridor, not really bothered whether Den was still following or not. They descended some steps and went through another door, emerging into the drinking area of a bar. It wasn't one of the ones with which Den was familiar from their short visit to the planet. Half a dozen drinkers paid them no attention, assuming that Ka Mera was a working girl returning to her shop window and Den, her punter, would either buy another drink or leave the building. Ka Mera quickly crossed the floor towards the door. She was just about to exit the building when Den held her arm, stopping her in her tracks.

"Better let me go first." He explained. He stepped cautiously through the door and looked up and down the empty street. It wasn't the one he had walked along earlier, when he had been tailing Ka Mera, so he assumed that it ran parallel. If that was the case then it was unlikely that An Kohli would be able to find him. The short alley wouldn't have given access to this street. It also meant that the body guard, when he woke, wouldn't find it easy to follow them, either, as he would now have three options from which to choose.

"Where are we going?" Den asked, stepping back inside the bar.

"Back to the Lucky Victel. That's where I've got to meet Shogun if I want my money."

"He's not going to be happy about his guard having been clobbered."

Ka Mera grinned. "That wasn't me, was it? You can explain that one away."

"Gee, thanks. Which way now?"

"Turn right, then I'll lead the way while you keep an eye out behind."

They left the building and entered the gathering darkness of the early evening.

* * *

Shogun sat in the Lucky Victel waiting for the return of Ka Mera. If he was worried by the absence of his bodyguard then he showed no sign of it. The second bodyguard stood a met or so away making sure his boss was undisturbed. Shogun considered summoning one of the other two guards from the shuttle, but decided that it was unnecessary. The local population had made no aggressive moves towards him so he assumed that his protection was adequate. The only being in the room that seemed even remotely interested in him was the rather scary looking female standing at the end of the bar. She had come in shortly after he had arrived, but had done nothing other than cast the occasional glance in his direction.

He considered summoning the woman over. She might be scary but she was definitely his type. He liked a woman with a bit of spirit. It was so much more fun when he broke them and made them plead for his mercy. Later, maybe, when his other business was concluded.

The absence of his other guard meant that Ka Mera hadn't led him to the egg, so he would have to make the purchase after all. Ah well, it was only money. With his legal and illegal business activities and the contribution he would demand from the other members of the Fell he would soon replace it.

The female bartender came back in through the entrance doors. There was a brief altercation between her and the male now tending the bar, which caused the male to lose his temper and the female to shout something rude at his retreating back, then she turned and stalked over to him. His bodyguard stopped her getting too close. At the same time Shogun noticed the unknown female step back into the shadows, as though she was anxious not to be seen by the new arrival. That was interesting and interesting things should never be ignored, he thought. He also realised that there was another threat to consider. A scruffily dressed and heavily armed male had followed the bartender, or was that now 'former bartender', into the room.

He did a quick mental reassessment. He no longer liked the odds. He spoke a few terse words into his communicator, then spoke to the female.

"Wait. I have asked another of my guards to join me. I hope you don't mind."

"They're your guards. Do what you like with them."

"Good. We'll wait for him to arrive."

"And then what?"

"And then we conclude the deal. I assume that is the egg. It's a big box for such a small item." He pointed at the box still tucked under Ka Mera's arm.

"There are twenty in here. One of them is the one you want. I'm not sure which one."

"If I can't verify my purchase the deal is off."

A worried look crossed Ka Mera's disguised face. She hadn't considered that. But at the same time she had no way of knowing which egg was which. They were all the same off-white colour and she didn't have any form of access to the specialist technology required to read the contents. They couldn't be read without the correct interface cable and she hadn't thought to obtain one of those. Would the newer ones be slightly different to look at? Maybe a little brighter through having not been handled? She hadn't thought to check and the dim lighting of the bar wouldn't allow her to examine them closely now.

"Can you read the contents?" She asked.

"Back on my ship I have the facilities. You will have to accompany me there."

"No way. Neither these eggs nor me leave the planet's surface until I have my money."

"We seem to be at something of an impasse then." Shogun replied. He had already decided on his route out of the conundrum. Once his other bodyguard arrived he would take the female and the eggs back to his ship, whether willingly or unwillingly. Talking of which, where was Hickor? He should have arrived by now. The shuttle port wasn't that far away. Come to think of it, where was the scruffy chap who had followed the bartender in?

Shogun was starting to get the feeling that events were no longer entirely under his control.

"I have a suggestion; a halfway house if you like. I will return to my ship and get the necessary equipment to read the eggs. I'll bring it back here in my shuttle craft and we can test the eggs there." The ruse would enable him to get to home ground, where he felt he would have an advantage. It would also get the female close enough to his shuttle to enable him to grab her and the eggs and get off the planet's surface.

"OK. You go and get what you need. When you get back send a message to my communicator and I'll come and meet you."

"Agreed. It will take me about an hour."

With that he rose and left the bar, his bodyguard in close attendance. Ka Mera crossed to the card players, who had been following events with interest.

"Basi, I need a favour."

"Another one? Oh well, why not. There's no chance of any serious cards being played tonight, not with all these comings and goings."

As the two continued their discussion An Kohli took the opportunity to slip out of the bar. She had her own preparations to make.

Glossary

Green Carpet - A floor covering used, in the main, for ceremonial occasions such as Presidential visits, award ceremonies or visits by one's mother-in-law. On some planets, such as Earth, this has been replaced with a red carpet. I mean, why would anyone use something as tacky as red? But that's Earth for you.

Menafield - The Menafield Arms Corporation (a subsidiary of the Gargantua Enterprises Corporation) produces a wide range of pulsar and projectile weapons for military, business and family use. The Menafield Pulsar, as used by An Kohli, is reputed to be the most powerful hand held weapon in the galaxy and can punch a hole through ¼ inch steel plate.

17 - Gunfight At The Hideaway

Ka Mera approached the shuttle with some trepidation. Even with Basi and Den Gau at her back she couldn't be sure that Shogun wouldn't arrive mob handed and simply out gun them, taking the eggs from her dead body after the shooting stopped.

The ramp lowered and two bodyguards stepped out. The visored helmets made them all look the same, so she couldn't be sure if they were the ones she had seen earlier, or reinforcements brought down from Shogun's ship orbiting high above their heads.

"You, holding the eggs," One of the bodyguards shouted. "Step forward. Your friends can stay where they are."

Ka Mera did as she was bid.

In a lower voice the guard continued. "You're going to take the eggs onto the shuttle and they will be examined. If the one the boss is looking for is amongst them you will be given your money and will be allowed to leave."

"What's to stop your boss just closing the ramp and taking off, with me as his prisoner? No. I don't agree to that. I'll tell you what I propose. Your boss comes out here and goes to wait with my two friends there. I go in there and test the eggs, with one of you as a witness. When you see that I'm telling the truth I come back out and we arrange the transfer of the money. Once it is confirmed that it's in my account your boss gets the egg and we go our separate ways."

The bodyguard nodded his understanding then stepped away, out of earshot, while he conducted a brief communicator conversation with his employer.

"Agreed." The bodyguard reported back "I will be the one to go on board the shuttle with you.

Shogun presented himself at the top of the ramp, a grim smile on his face. "You drive a hard bargain." he commented.

"Just self-preservation. I've been around long enough to know that there are some dishonest beings around. No offence intended."

"None taken. All I'm interested in is that egg, oh, and any information you may have about the bounty hunter known as An Kohli. I'll pay extra for that."

"With twenty million nuks in my bank account the price of the information on An Kohli is peanuts. In fact you can have it for free as a gesture of good faith. The last time I saw her was on Sabik."

"So that shuttle," he pointed across the shuttle port to where The Laurel's shuttle sat, "has nothing to do with the Meteor class ship in orbit which is called The Laurel and is registered on Sabik? That is all coincidence?"

Ka Mera shrugged. "I'm familiar with The Laurel, but I don't know what it's doing here."

"And that Gau," Shogun pointed to Den, "I'm pretty sure it is a Gau. He isn't the one you were travelling with just a few weeks ago and who is also known to be working with An Kohli? Beneath that bartender disguise you are Ka Mera, aren't you?"

Ka Mera was taken by surprise at the depth of his knowledge of her and her relationships. Clearly he had been doing some thinking while he had been back on board his ship. "OK, I admit that I'm Ka Mera, but you'll forgive me for the subterfuge, I'm sure. When An Kohli is chasing you, it's best not to make it too easy to be found. And yes, that's Den. He arrived on The Laurel. We have our own private deal. He watches my back in exchange for a share of the money you're about to give me."

"Good. Now that I know what is going on I feel more comfortable. Now, tell me where my missing bodyguards are."

"The one you had following me I last saw in an alleyway. He wasn't badly hurt, but I don't know where he is right now. I don't know about any other missing bodyguards."

"No, but he might." Shogun pointed at Den once again.

"Actually they're probably having a better time than we are, right now." Den interjected. "I wanted to even up the odds back there at the Lucky Victel, so I got the drop on the one you summoned from here. I was taking him to somewhere I could keep him secure when I bumped into the first one again, staggering around not quite sure what day it was. They're both trussed up safe and sound. I've got a couple of friendly ladies looking after them for me. Once this deal has been concluded you can have them back."

Shogun laughed, clearly amused by the situation. "Well, I think you can keep them. If they're that easy to capture they're no good to me. Hired muscle is easy to come by. Maybe I should be offering you a job."

"You'll forgive me if I decline. With the deal Ka Mera has offered me I won't be working again for quite some time."

"Well, enough of this idle chit-chat. Ka Mera, the test rig is all set up on board my shuttle. Go on board with Alanwood and show him the correct egg." Shogun stepped off the ramp and sauntered across to stand near Den and Basi.

Ka Mera did as she was bid and entered the shuttle craft. She looked around for the test rig but saw nothing but the standard set of shuttle controls. She was just about to ask where the equipment was when stars burst in her head, her knees went weak and she lost consciousness.

The bodyguard called Alanwood tied up the unconscious Gau then took a firm grip on his pulsar, the butt of which he had used to render Ka Mera unconscious. A grim smile formed on his lips, visible below his visor. It was time to go and earn the bonus his employer had offered him and Shelby.

* * *

Den winced as pain shot across his brow. Something nasty had just happened to Ka Mera and that couldn't be good. "I think we're being double crossed." He snarled at Basi.

His companion reacted at once, stepping forward in an attempt to take a hold of Shogun. He was both the means of gaining Ka Mera's return and also their passport to safety. He didn't get half way to his prize before the remaining bodyguard's pulsar fired. He dropped to the ground and crumpled at Shogun's feet. The Fell gave a grimace of distaste.

Den looked frantically for somewhere to take cover, but the wide open space of the shuttle port offered no refuge. The only object between him and the pulsar wielding bodyguard was Shogun himself. Fortunately the angle offered him some protection from the guard's weapon so he took the gamble. He dived forward and tackled the Fell member, taking him to the ground, where they rolled around in the dust attempting to gain an advantage over each other. Den was physically stronger and also no stranger to grappling. He managed to get a neck lock on his opponent then rolled him so that Shogun's body formed a defensive barrier between him and the guard. He raised his pulsar and pressed the business end against Shogun's neck so that the bodyguard was left in no doubt as to his employer's fate if he was rash enough to fire again. At that point the second bodyguard appeared from within the shuttle.

Alanwood assessed the situation rapidly, He jumped off the side of the ramp and ran at an angle, away from the shuttle, attempting to reach a point where his employer's body was no longer between him and his target.

"Stop!" a commanding voice rang out. It was followed quickly by a pulsar shot that hit the ground at Alanwood's feet, spraying dirt around and spoiling the shine on the bodyguard's pristine armour. The bodyguard stopped dead, turning slowly to see from where this new threat had appeared. He found himself staring down the business end of An Kohli's pulsar as she stepped around the side of the shuttle. While everyone had been focused on events in front of the boarding hatch she had managed to approach unnoticed from the rear, where she had been concealed by the detritus of scrap that formed a sort of perimeter to the shuttle port compound.

"Now, I think we all need to calm down a little if we want to avoid any more casualties." An Kohli continued to walk until she was in clear view of all the participants in the small drama that had unfolded.

"Now, you on the ground. Who are you?"

"You know who I am." Den replied.

"No, not you, idiot. I'll deal with you later. No, I mean the smartly dressed one you're holding. Well, he was smartly dressed until you started rolling him in the dirt."

"I'm known as Shogun. I suggest that you don't mess with me, An Kohli."

"You know who I am?"

"An educated guess. Do you know who I am?"

"I believe you are member of the group of shit bags that call themselves the Fell."

The expression on his face showed how Shogun felt about being addressed in such a manner. "You are quite right. I am a member of the Fell. When I take you to them they will be interested to know what you have to say with regard to certain of our brothers and sisters."

"I don't think you're in a position to make threats."

"Kill me and you risk killing your Gau here."

"I couldn't give a shit about that traitorous bastard. He's already sold me out."

"Interesting. Well, Gau." He addressed himself to Den. "In that case how about you and I do a deal of our own. I already have the eggs, so I'll offer you half of what I offered Ka Mera. That's five million Nuks." He lied.

"Well, I have to say that's a lot of money, though I did hear Ka Mera mention twenty million nuks. But then again, you double crossed Ka Mera. I'm guessing she isn't going to walk out of that shuttle any time soon. What're that chances of you double crossing me as well?"

"If I may interrupt." An Kohi interrupted. "I think I have first call on any negotiations. I don't have a warrant for any person named Shogun and I don't know your real name. Just give me back the eggs and you can do what you want."

"Really. You know I'm Fell but you would let me go? Why do I find that hard to believe?"

"I'm bound by the code of ethics of the Guild of Bounty Hunters and the laws of the galaxy. No warrant, no arrest. I have to let you go unless you perform some act that would allow me to arrest you."

"Such as?"

"Attempting to kill me or attempting to kill anyone else here."

"What about him?" Shogun used one of his feet to prod the body of Basi.

"Your bodyguard shot him and I didn't hear you give any order to do it. There's no case against you that would stand up in court. I'll take him," She pointed towards Shelby, "and call it quits."

"It sounds like a reasonable deal. What about the Gau, Ka Mera?"

"I'd like her back too. She stole my ship and that's not something that I could let slide. She's nothing to you without the eggs, anyway."

"True; very true. But what if I refuse to give you the eggs."

"Then you're in possession of stolen property, so I have an offence on which I can arrest you. You wouldn't want to go to prison for something as trivial as that, would you?"

Shogun laughed, then winced as the lock that Den still had him in restricted his breathing. "No, you are right. It would damage what I believe the criminal classes call my 'street cred'."

An Kohli was disgusted that this being didn't see himself as a criminal, but there was nothing she could do about that for the moment.

"Hang on. What about me?" Den protested, finding himself negotiated out of any settlement.

"I told you. I'll deal with you later. Now, let the nice Shogun go and we can all go our separate ways."

"And if I don't?"

"You can still do a deal with Shogun if you want, but whether or not he goes free is down to me. We seem to be at something of a Flovian stand-off."

"I'm getting fed up with this. Alanwood. Get that Gau off my ship and bring the eggs out here." Shogun snarled.

The bodyguard hastened to obey his employer's command. The expression on the face of the other bodyguard, so far as it could be seen below the half face visor, was a picture of confusion. Was his boss really going to hand him over to face a murder charge?

Den relaxed his grip on Shogun as a groggy Ka Mera, her arms tied, was ushered down the ramp of the shuttle. Alanwood followed behind, one hand struggling to keep hold of the box of eggs while the other still held his heavy pulsar.

Shogun shrugged his way out of Den's embrace and clambered to his feet. He half trotted over to the ramp, waited for Ka Mera and his bodyguard to step down and then made his way the short distance to the doorway of the shuttle.

"Kill them all." he commanded as he stepped through onto comparative safety.

Shelby fired at the prone figure of Den, but he was far too slow. Den was already rolling out of the target area. He made it up onto one knee and raised his weapon to fire in return.

Alanwood's line of fire was blocked by Ka Mera and, encumbered as he was by the eggs, he was unable to bring his pulsar under control. It needed two hands to control it enough to give it accuracy. He dropped the eggs and pushed Ka Mera out of the way. She was thrown against Shelby just as he fired again, spoiling his aim.

Alanwood started to turn to take aim at An Kohli but he was far too slow. As he brought his weapon around he could already see the black dot of the weapon's muzzle aiming directly at him.

"Drop your weapon!" An Kohli practically screamed at the bodyguard, but he ignored her. Why do they always do that? She asked herself as she allowed her finger to caress the firing button. The high energy bolt flashed across the gap between them and the bodyguard crumpled into a heap at the foot of the shuttle's ramp.

Ka Mera was still groggy from her blow to her head and after stumbling into Shelby she tried to work out what was happening. Den had his weapon pointed at her, so no escape that way. Showing his true colours at last, she thought as she identified that An Kohli was to her left. She had no option but to try to make a break to the right.

Seeing what she was about to attempt, Den opened his mouth to shout a warning but he knew he was too late. As Ka Mera crossed in front of Shelby, the bodyguard squeezed the trigger of his pulsar, intent on killing Den. Instead Ka Mera ran straight into the blast, taking it full force in her head.

Den grasped at his head as the Ka Mera's agonised brain patterns screeched telepathically through his mind, before stopping abruptly, signalling Ka Mera's death. Shelby smiled grimly as he lined up his sights once again on Den, who was still recovering from the searing pain of sharing the moment of Ka Mera's death.

Den froze, watching the weapon's sights settle on his chest, then another pulsar blasted out and Shelby dropped dead, never even seeing the shot that came from An Kohli. He did, however, hear her running feet as she attempted to reach the shuttle's ramp before Shogun had any chance of closing it. She had no doubt that the Fell would abandon his employees in order to make his escape.

She stepped cautiously through the doorway and found Shogun passing his hands across the controls in preparation for lift off.

"I won't hesitate to shoot." She said calmly, placing the muzzle of the weapon against Shogun's temple. The Fell member stopped what he was doing and placed his hands on his knees in apparent surrender.

"You Fell really are cowardly scum, aren't you. You'd let your employees die for you then just walk away."

"That's what employees are for, isn't it?" Shogun gave her his most innocent looking smile.

"Maybe in your world. You make me sick."

"You know that I'll never go to jail, don't you?"

"Oh, I have no doubts about the extent of your influence over the judicial system, such as it is these days."

"So, why waste time. Tell me your price and let me go. We both live to fight another day."

"I know it's a strange concept for you, but some people just aren't for sale."

There was a movement behind An Kohli and she felt the presence of Den. "Ka Mera's dead." He said, his voice flat.

"Ah, and here is your tame Gau. Though not so tame, it would appear. So, how about I negotiate with you instead?"

"Perhaps you didn't hear me, arsehole. Ka Mera is dead. I felt her die, in here." He tapped his head with the hand that wasn't holding his pulsar. "Do you know what it feels like, to feel someone else die?"

"No. I can't say I have had that particular pleasure. Now, as I was saying, perhaps we can strike a bargain, Den. You take this being off my ship and I'll pay whatever you ask. I think I offered five million nuks, earlier. How about I do….."

He said no more as Den fired his pulsar from short range, making sure that Shogun never uttered another word.

"You shouldn't have done that, Den."

"He was resisting arrest." The Gau turned and left the shuttle, his shoulders slumped and his head down. An Kohli turned to follow and found him kneeling, cradling Ka Mera in his arms. Tears ran down his still disguised face. In death Ka Mera had reverted to her true identity.

"I didn't realise that you were that fond of her." An Kohli half whispered.

"Neither did I. You know what her dying thought was? It was of me. It wasn't clear; our telepathy isn't that good, more of a feeling than an image, but I felt her thinking of me, just before she died."

An Kohli was distracted by Gala's voice sounding in her earpiece. "You guys alright down there?

"Yes. No. Well, Den and I are OK, if that's what you mean. Is anything happening with that Starcruiser?"

"No. It's just sitting there, in orbit."

Satisfied that there was no new threat from that direction, An Kohli started to think about what to do next. Clearly Den needed comforting and there was the issue of Ka Mera's funeral to consider.

She would leave it up to the crew of the Starcruiser to deal with Shogun and the two dead bodyguards. While they may be of interest to her she had no charges on which to hold them.

"Look, we'll be taking control of the Adastra again. Do you want to take The Laurel back to Merkaloy."

"Could Den do that? I'd rather go back with you, if that's OK."

"I don't think Den should be alone right now. Would you do it for me?"

"Well, if it's a personal favour, then OK. What's up with Den?"

"I'll tell you later. Wait until we're safely aboard the Adastra then set course for Sabik. We'll be right behind you."

"OK. See you in the Three Moons."

An Kohli returned her attention to Den, who was still cradling Ka Mera's dead body, tears still evident on his face.

"What do you want to do with Ka Mera?"

"Well' I'm not leaving her here, that's for sure. I think a burial in space is best. Do you mind?" He gave An Kohli an appealing look. It was the first time she had ever seen him close to pleading.

"Of course. We'll give her a proper send off. Now, what about those other two bodyguards?"

"I told the girls to let them go when the money ran out. That will be pretty soon, I guess.

"OK, then let's get Ka Mera up to the Adastra. Gala can recall The Laurel's shuttle by remote control and we'll go back to Sabik together, in the Adastra."

Den rose and hefted Ka Mera's body onto his shoulder, shrugging off An Kohli's offers of help. Together they crossed the shuttle port to their own craft.

"Den, I don't often have the chance to say this, but you did good. Thanks."

"It's what you underpay me for." He said, offering An Kohli a sad smile.

"I mean it. You really could have sold me out and I couldn't have stopped you."

"And have you chasing me across the galaxy with the intention of rearranging some of my softer body parts. No thank you."

An Kohli concealed a small smile. It would take time, but Den would be OK.

* * *

They stopped off in orbit around Camoo, the home planet of the Gau species. There they conducted a simple ceremony. Den said a few words in the Gau language then pressed the button to operate the airlock to dispatch Ka Mera's body into eternity.

An Kohli led Den back into the small lounge and ordered two Grovian whiskies from the drinks dispenser. Den took his and swirled the precious golden liquid around the glass in preparation for drinking it.

"You know, I've never really been in love." He confided.

"Never? But you've had…"

"Lots of carnal knowledge with lots of willing females. That's not love. I was fond of Ka Mera, but there was always something… I don't know, something in the way."

"You suspected her of not being quite right, quite honest, and you were right about that."

"Yes, but that wasn't the big thing. You know, when I took Beckham and Gaga to Sabik after I rescued them, and then on the return journey, we had plenty of time together. I didn't know then what I now know about her. She was nice, and we had some good times, but I just couldn't feel anything much for her. She was keen on me, I knew that, but I… I just don't know. Am I incapable of feeling love?"

"I doubt it. You just haven't met the right being yet. I know. It's happened to me."

"No. You're different. You have met the right one, but you let him get away." He was referring to Veritan, with whom she had fallen in love but had failed to do anything about it.

An Kohli said nothing, not wanting to open up that particular wound. She finished her drink. "Another?" she offered Den.

"My, you are feeling generous today."

"Then make the most of it. Tomorrow the lock goes back on the Grovian. You can go back to beer."

Glossary

Flovian Stand-off - A situation where both sides have the potential to kill the other and therefore one in which neither side can take the risk of being killed. Known in other parts of the galaxy as a Silonian Stand-off, a Mircian Stand-off, Mexican Stand-off, and an Oh No Not Another Cliché Stand-off.

Grovian Whisky - While Scotland may have invented whisky (or whiskey), the planet of Grovia perfected it. From a mountain spring that produces only a few gallons of water per year, the most divine whisky in the galaxy, perhaps even the universe, is distilled. It is very rare and therefore very expensive. Most bars charge for it by the droplet.

18 - Mind Mapping

"Thank you all for joining me in this conference at such short notice." Warrior's voice betrayed that the purpose of the meeting was not to impart good news. "I have been contacted by the Captain of the Starcruiser Shogun, the ship he uses for Fell business and which he so modestly named after himself. It appears that our esteemed colleague is dead; killed while trying to obtain the Magus egg stolen by An Kohli."

"Surely you mean recovered by An Kohli. It had been stolen by Su Mali." Corrected Tiger.

"We can argue over semantics if you wish." Warrior snarled, "But that doesn't alter the fact that he is dead."

"Do we know how?"

"The details are, as always, sketchy, but the Captain says that he returned to the ship to do some research then departed saying that he planned to capture An Kohli and also to retrieve some stolen property, though he didn't confide in the Captain what that property was. It's my assumption that he meant the egg. Something went wrong and there was a shoot-out which resulted in the death of him and two of his bodyguards. Two more had been captured and were being held prisoner at the time."

"We could press charges against An Kohli for murder." Suggested Mastermind.

"No." Warrior's tone suggested that the subject wasn't open to discussion. "We tried fitting her up once before and it ended in Odin's death and Genghis's… well, we don't know what happened to Genghis. We need to be more direct in our actions against her. We have gone after her one at a time. We need to bring more brainpower to bear, along with much more muscle."

"What do you suggest?" asked Drac.

"I suggest that we put a team together. A combined effort is more likely to have success."

"But how do we know who we can rely on and who we can't? We have taken great pains to ensure that as few of us as possible know any of the others in our little cabal. No one knows the identity of more than one or two members. Forgive me, esteemed colleagues, but I have no idea on whom I can rely in a pulsar fight or, for that matter, in a game of bridge."

"Point taken." Warrior agreed. "I suggest that one person volunteers to lead and if anyone feels they can trust that person they can decide whether or not they wish to form an alliance to defeat An Kohli."

Silence filled the ether as each Fell member considered both the proposition and their own suitability to take part in such an endeavour. More than one subconsciously ruled themselves out on the grounds of cowardice.

At last a voice broke the silence, across the Superlightspeed ™ enabled galacticnet. "I'll put myself forward as leader." It was Desire's avatar that flashed to indicate that she had spoken. That took the Fell by surprise. Of all their number Desire was the one who voiced the fewest opinions and was always the last to express those she did hold.

* * *

In her blast proof bunker deep below the planet of Maron, in the system of Baratrix, Desire found her hands shaking as she spoke. What was she thinking of? She asked herself. She was a lover, not a fighter. She did her work by stealth, not audacity. It was too late to change her mind now. To do so would remove all credibility and that was a commodity she knew was in short supply.

"Well.... er... Well thank you Desire. If you feel that you have what it takes to lead this mission then who are we to stand in your way?"

"Are you suggesting I might not be up to it." Bristled Desire. The members of the Fell were always quick to anger when their competence was called into question.

"No! Absolutely not." Warrior knew that if Desire withdrew then no one else was likely to put themselves forward, though personally he did doubt Desire's capabilities. In the past she had achieved very little on behalf of the Fell. She was only a member because, or so it was rumoured, she had been sleeping with Barbarossa. His immediate support seemed to confirm this.

"Well done, Desire." Barbarossa made sure his voice sounded enthusiastic even if his feelings were less so. "Does anyone wish to support this brave member in her mission?"

Tiger could see an opportunity when it stood up in front of him and this seemed like an ideal one. Success has many fathers but failure is forever an orphan. Desire would get the blame, probably posthumously, if it all went tits up while he would get a share of the credit if the group succeeded.

"I'll support my brave colleague." His voice oozed over the galacticnet.

"Why not." Atilla chimed in. "Count me in as well."

"In that case we wish you well. You can sort out the fine detail between you. Now, what should we tell the Captain of the Shogun to do with its namesake's body?"

"It may be just a coincidence, but the Chairman of the Interstellar Bank of Global Unity and Trust has disappeared. His name is Elloway Fargon. He said he was taking a short break and no one has heard from him since, not even his family." Barbarossa informed the group.

"Does he own a Starcruiser?" Asked Warrior.

"Not by that name. He has an Andromeda Class gin palace he uses for most journeys."

"Well, I suggest that we tell the Captain to take Shogun to wherever it was that he collected his employer and he discreetly leaves the body where it can be found. If Shogun and Elloway Fargon are one and the same, we shall soon hear of it." Mastermind suggested.

"And what of the Starcruiser itself?" Warrior asked.

"If no one objects, we may as well let the Captain and crew have it. It's a valuable ship and will buy their silence."

"Wait!" Desire found herself interrupting, for the first time that anyone of the Fell could recall. "I will need a ship. I suggest we adopt ownership of it for the present and employ the existing Captain and crew. That includes any security staff that may be on board. When we have completed our mission, we can consider its future once again."

"Oh, and by the way," Warrior intervened, "The tracker on the Adastra has stopped working."

* * *

Gala was nursing a mild hangover as she returned to the command deck of the Adastra, following a night of celebration at having found another of the Magi. It seemed as though half the Guild had descended on Sabik to help with the festivities and many an old friendship was revived as the bounty hunters caroused away the evening and into the early hours of the morning.

"You look the worse for wear." Observed An Kohli from the Captain's chair. She had enjoyed herself, of course, but in moderation.

"Oh, please, keep your voice down." Gala grimaced.

An Kohli laughed at her friend's discomfort.

"I suppose you'll be taking the Pradua to deliver the egg now." Gala dropped into the co-pilot's seat and started to carry out the routine status checks on the systems, looking for any tell-tale sign that might provide a warning of future mechanical problems.

"Actually, there's something I wanted to talk to you about before I did that. Do you think you would be able to read the contents of the egg."

"Well, I'll need an interface cable." She nodded as An Kohli brandished the required item, which she had purchased down on Earth at the same time as she had bought the decoy eggs. "OK. Well, it needs specialist software. They weren't designed to be read by just any old system. I can probably work that out, but it will take some time. But the big issue is computing capacity. The Adastra has enough, but it would mean we were stuck here until the job was done as I'd have to divert all the resources for the task. It would be easier if I could use one of the supercomputers at Guild HQ."

"I'd rather the Guild wasn't involved in this, if we could avoid it. Don't worry about the computers being diverted. I've got no short-term plans to go anywhere and if I do I can use the Pradua."

"OK. Give me a couple of days. If it can't be done, I'll know by then. Excuse me for asking, but I thought that official, oh, what's his name… Srumphrey, I thought he told you which personality each egg held"

"He does, though rather reluctantly. I think he holds information back. But it's more than that. I have a theory about one of the Magi. No, it's more of a hunch. Anyway, if I could read their egg then I might be able to work out if I'm on the right track or just imagining things."

"Is this about Warrior?"

"Yes, well, no. It's more about who Warrior might be connected to. I have strong suspicions about Warrior's true identity, though I can't yet prove it, but if I'm right then I think he may be connected to another member of the Fell who may also be a Magus."

Gala's pursed lips indicated that she was dubious, but she didn't want to pour cold water on An Kohli's idea.

"You're not convinced." An Kohli said it for her.

"Well, I think you need more than just a hunch before you say anything about that in public."

"Which is why I need you to try to examine the eggs. If we can read the inner secrets of a Magus from their egg, then we will know for certain."

"And if you find out you're right?"

"That egg might never be found. Bad luck. It will slip through our fingers. If we provide evidence that it's gone forever, then we'll be believed."

"That's dishonest; maybe even criminal." Gala was surprised that her ever-so-ethical employer should be considering such an action.

"Sometimes you have to think of the greater good. Would we really want a member of the Fell to be a part of the Magi? I think that's a far worse option."

Gala had to admit to herself that what An Kohli wanted to do was logical. If her hunch was right it was better to find out before the Magi were restored in physical bodies. And if she was wrong then there would be no harm done, surely?

* * *

"There it is. That's the map of a sentient mind." Gala brought an image up onto the Adastra's largest viewing screen.

There was a myriad of interconnected file numbers, crisscrossed with lines. Overlay after overlay of complexity faced An Kohli.

"What does it mean?" She whispered, hardly loud enough for Gala to hear.

"You didn't ask me to work that out." Gala replied, a little sharply. "You need a neuroscientist, probably several neuroscientists, if you want to know that. The nearest I can get to that is these files down here." She used a highlighter cursor to draw a ring around a large group of files, "They control basic motor functions: heartbeat, breathing, limb movements, the release of various hormones and enzymes and so on."

She moved the cursor and drew another ring. "These, I think, take input from the senses: touch, hearing, smell, sight and taste plus any others this being might have, like the telepathic sense possessed by the Gau. Finally, there's the rest; the primary data banks as I would say in computer sciences, but what everyone else calls memory.

What I can't work out is how the memory data is processed and interfaced with the external stimulus to react to new information. For example, if the eyes see four plus four, I can't see how the brain use its memory of mathematical functions to solve the sum. I'm guessing that's part of the interface between the memory and the physical brain, so to work that out we'd have to download the memory into a living being"

"Well, we definitely don't have the facilities to do that. Can you read any of the files?"

"Yes… well, some of them anyway. I built an interpreter that converts the language in which the data is stored into one that the computer can use. It isn't perfect as I haven't been able to translate all the symbols. Whoever designed this was either a genius or a lunatic. Also, the brain seems to use different languages to store different information, which means having to work out each language in turn and convert it through a different interpreter. It could take years to complete."

"Well, we haven't got years. Show me one of the files that you can read."

Gala selected a number and dragged it to the interpreter application. A scene of a valley appeared on a screen, moving as though the observer had been viewing a broad landscape. Rolling hills were covered with small purple shrubs beneath a brilliant blue sky. The scene must have been lit by a sun that was behind the viewer, as the shadows stretched away.

"Where's that?" An Kohli asked.

"No idea. You would have to do a data search of the entire galaxy and hope to match it to another recording of the same scene. It obviously means something to whoever's memory is contained in this egg, but that's all I can tell you."

"Can you tell me which of the Magi this is?"

"No. We would have to isolate the files that relate to identity and translate those. It could take years of trial and error."

"Srumphrey just plugs in the interface cable and has the answer. He doesn't seem to run any queries."

"Ah, I think he is using this." Gala indicated a series of numbers that were displayed across the bottom of the viewing screen. "This is the identity of the egg itself. Its part number, batch number, etc and this." She pointed with the cursor, "is its unique serial number. If Srumphrey has a list of those, cross referred to the identities of Magi that are stored in each egg, then he can tell you which egg you have. He doesn't need to access any of the actual files."

"So if I had that list I could do the same."

"In a few seconds flat."

"Could you copy the data from this egg into another egg?"

"Why do you want a copy?"

"There's an old Earth saying about not putting all your eggs in one basket, which is exactly what I have been doing by delivering the eggs to the Galactic Council In Exile. If we take a copy then all isn't lost if something goes wrong or if the location of the GCIE is betrayed."

"Well, it doesn't require any translation and we have nineteen spare eggs. It would take a long time though. There's billions of bytes of it. It would take maybe a day if I could shut down all other computer functions, but otherwise it would take a week or so."

"OK, I'll wait a day, but I do have to get this to Srumphrey before he starts to wonder what has happened to it. He must have heard that I have it by now. That sort of news travels fast. Besides, the Fell may try to intercept me and the more time we give them to pick up the trail the more likely it is that they'll succeed."

"Destroying the tracker will have helped, but we've still made it easy for them by staying in orbit round Sabik."

"Good point. OK, take us somewhere remote, where we're unlikely to be found by accident. Make sure Den follows in the Pradua. Once there you can complete the data transfer and I'll deliver the egg to the Galactic Council In Exile."

"Where will we look for the next egg?"

"Actually, I've had a thought about that. Each of the eggs we have found so far has been located in a different sector of the galaxy. I'm wondering if Su Mali has been poking her tongue out at us and hiding one egg in each of the nine sectors of the galaxy. Of course, she can't know which Magus belongs where, but that doesn't matter. In her twisted mind she is just being clever. So, the first egg was in Sector Five, the second in Four and this one is from Nine. I think we can ignore those three sectors and concentrate on the remaining six."

"And if we're wrong?"

"We lose nothing. We go back to those three again after completing the search of the other six.

"So where do we go now?"

"Pick a number excluding the three where we've already found eggs."

"Eight."

"OK, what's the biggest star in Sector Eight?"

"Rigel."

"OK, after I've delivered the egg that's where we'll meet up."

Glossary

GCIE - Galalctic Counsel In Exile. When the Magi were forced to flee, power was transferred to the GCIE pending the restoration of law and order. This is a group of senior civil servants who are the permanent heads of the departments of galactic government. They immediately took action and set up a series of committees through which to administer the galaxy. Each committee had the same members though each one had a different Chair and a different title. By coincidence each member of the GCIE chaired one committee. Because all decisions are reached by consensus it takes a long time to get anything done and then it's usually the wrong thing. For example, because of disputes over which budget would pay, it took six months to agree to have biscuits served at committee meetings and then Garibaldi's were chosen when the members all wanted either chocolate digestives or Hobnobs.

Superlightspeed™ - The system by which communications made from points in the galaxy that are light years apart can be conducted in real time. Conventional communications messages travel at light speed, so a communication between two beings from a distance of one light year apart would take two years to complete; one year after the message was sent for it to be received and a further year for the reply to be received back. Superlightspeed allows communications messages to be sent at a speed faster than the speed of light. Over short distances this could mean the message being received before it was sent, however over longer distances it allows for almost real time communications. By varying the speed of the signal, beings one, two, and three light years apart can take part in real time conversations. However, the system still wasn't effective over the vast distances of the galaxy because there is still a limit to the maximum speed at which a communication can be sent. It required the introduction of wormhole technology to become a universal messaging system. The viability of the idea was first demonstrated mathematically by physicist Elbert Anstein and it is him we have to thank for the ability of teenagers across the galaxy to be able to communicate drivel to one another through the galacticnet. Gee, thanks Elbert.

Appendix - Galactic Species

The nature of An Kholi's work tends to bring her into contact with the worst examples of members of the billion or so species that exists in the galaxy. In order to avoid the reader creating stereotypes this appendix seeks to describe the nature of the species that she encounters in this book. Similar appendices appear in the other books in the Magi series and this version merely adds in the star systems that are referred to in this volume.

Aloisan
Star system: Alois
Planet: Gamma

A ridiculously good looking species who have a keen intellect and high moral standards. It is unthinkable that an Aloisan would ever commit a crime, tell a lie, cheat on their partner etc. They tend to find employment in academia or law enforcement. It was an Aloisan that set up the Guild of Bounty Hunters to regulate the activity of a profession whose members had become barely distinguishable from the criminals they pursued. To have an Aloisan as a friend is to have someone always ready to cover your back and who would give you the shirt off their own if you needed it. They are actually quite nauseating in large doses.

Arthurids
Star system: Arthuria
Planet: Beta

The Arthurid species evolved from the largest primates on the Beta planet of the system. The species is known for its great physical size and athleticism. However, they also have a keen intellect if they can be restrained for long enough to use it, as they are known for their impetuosity, especially if there is the prospect of a fight. They are brave and loyal. It isn't unknown for an Arthurid to commit crimes but they tend to do so only as a last resort, which has probably been caused by their own impetuosity.

Cebalrains
Star system: Cebalrai
Planet: Delta

This species is humanoid in appearance but has the advantage of having two livers. This means that Cebalrains are able to consume twice as much alcohol as other species. Never go drinking with a Cebalrain unless you are also of this species.

Danians
Star system: Peacock
Planet: Mun Dane

The species of An Kholi and her co-pilot Gala Sur. They evolved from primates similar to Earthlings, but where Earthlings are destructive by nature Danians are born to create and innovate. They have produced some of the finest architects in the galaxy and are responsible for some of its greatest buildings, many of which are regarded as works of art in their own right. Because the planet is so peaceful many young Danians go seeking adventure, just as An Kholi did. After a year or two of drifting around the galaxy seeing the sights and forming dubious relationships with hippies, most return to Mun Dane to take up regular occupations. However, the odd one or two, such as An Kholi and Gala, enjoy the adventure so much that they can't give it up.

Diplopoda
Star system: Phad
Planet: All in system excluding the alpha planet, which is too hot.

The Diplopoda are one of many species inhabiting the planets of the Phad system, others include arachnids and insects. These species are semi-sentient, in that they are capable of rational thought but not of grasping higher level concepts. Consequently they have never developed any form of technology. They occasionally migrate across the galaxy by stowing away on visiting space ships, but in general terms are happy to remain on the planets that they occupy in the Phad system. Surprisingly all the species have developed as vegetarians, which prevents all that messy 'catching things in webs and waiting till they dissolve' type of stuff. The Diplopoda are highly skilled at the game of football but rarely win any matches. By the time they have laced up over a hundred pairs of boots each their opponents have scored twenty goals. Their opponent's fans then stage a pitch invasion so that the match has to be abandoned before the Diplopoda can score. There are rumours of match fixing as a consequence of this.

Earthlings
Star system: Sol
Planet: Earth

This species evolved from primates and is known mainly for its destructiveness. When not killing each other they are killing their planet and any other planet they colonise. They run many of the larger mining, drilling, nuclear and chemical corporations. The planet is technologically backward, having developed very little of its own technology prior to the arrival of visiting species. Earth women are known for being strong, independent types who turn to goo when confronted by a puppy or kitten. They also have a fetish for footwear and hand bags, possibly caused by their worship of the Gods Gucci, and Laboutain. Earth men are addicted to sport in any form and the best way to start a fight is to ask a seemingly innocent question, such as "What do you think of Arsenal's back four this season?". The two best things to come from Earth are Northampton Saints Rugby Club and beer, which is the best in the galaxy (except that brewed in the USA which is piss, but still better than blash, if only marginally). Earthlings are big in banking, which is the main source of crime on their planet, however, no one is ever prosecuted for banking crime. This is why people on Earth tend to keep their money under the mattress.

Falconans
Star system: Mufrid
Planet: Falcona

The only planet on the galaxy to develop a business school before they invented the wheel. Falconans are born business people and are the entrepreneurs of the galaxy. While most of them operate ethical businesses which benefit society as a whole there are a few

Falconans for whom the law is merely a speed bump on the road to success and ethics is a county on an obscure island on an obscure planet in an even more obscure star system. Like so many other species Falconans are evolved from primates, but unlike others their sense of community has been bred out of them, giving them an 'every being for themselves' sort of attitude. They also make natural politicians. However if, by some chance, you are able to befriend a Falconan you will have a loyal friend for life, or at least until someone makes him a better offer.

Gau
Star system: Flage
Planet: Camoo

This species is the only one in the galaxy known to have shape shifting capability and it is thought to have been a major factor in its survival as they are not noted for their fighting skills. To identify each other they retain a limited telepathic capability. Because of this they have become known for a high level of deviousness and they also make up a significant minority of criminals in the galaxy. However, a degree of fecklessness in their nature means that they are rarely successful. Su Mali is the exception to this rule and it is thought that she may have the blood of another species mixed with her Gau blood. See also Sutra

Jackon
Star system: Jackon
Planet: Awree

The Jackon are known for their extremely large feet and equally extremely low foreheads. The feet are required to keep them upright as they often forget how to balance. As this suggests, they aren't known for their intellect. Any technology they have has been imported and is usually operated and maintained by a species with a higher level of intellect. They are very hard workers and therefore much in demand by employers, especially in the mining industry. They are very good at obeying orders as it saves them from having to think for themselves, so they are also well suited for employment as prison guards, parking wardens, back bench MPs etc. They lack ambition so they make ideal henchmen. Non Jackon find it impossible to distinguish between male and female Jackon and Jackon males are also sometimes unable to do this, which is why the females find it necessary to release strongly scented pheromones in order to breed.

Lupine
Star System: Canis Major
Planet; Lupus

A species evolved from canines. Unlike most canine based species the Lupines have evolved opposable thumbs which means that they, like primates, became tool users. Because of their aggressive nature Lupines replaced primates as the dominant species on their planet. While capable of great affection and loyalty they are prone to biting the hand that feeds them, in both literal and metaphorical terms. They will become loyal to whoever provides them with employment, often abandoning previous loyalties. This means that they can be easily bought and, coupled to their aggressive nature, favour professions such as the law and selling used cars. Although not generally of a criminal bent, if they do choose that career path they are usually very successful if led by a dominant male or a female in heat. They have a very unusual greeting ritual; well, unusual if you aren't evolved from a canine.

Sabik
Star system Sabik
Planet: Gamma

There is no true Sabik species as their planet was originally colonised by Aloisan. Evolutionary differences mean that they are slightly less attractive than pure Aloisans, but in most respects the species can be accepted as being similar.

Surchifs
Star system: Brit
Planet: Surchia

Evolved from the Pop people of the Brit star system, the Surchifs are best known for their ability to be totally forgettable. They have travelled far and wide across the galaxy and they have settlements on many planets, though the rest of the planet's occupants may not even realise it. They were present on Earth for many years before that planet commenced inter-stellar travel and their presence is credited with the speed up in the development of the necessary technology as a means of escape. The Surchifs on Earth are so instantly forgettable that they often win the same TV talent contests year after year without anyone noticing.

Sutra
Star system: Flage
Planet: Sutra

Evolution has provided a unique niche for Sutra in that they provide females whose sole desire is to have sex and whose males are only too happy to let them get on with it, while they themselves go to the pub and watch football. Being evolved from the Gau they have the shape shifting abilities and a slightly improved telepathic ability. Sutran females can enjoy their sexual freedom to the maximum. They often find employment as females of negotiable affection, which they see as an honourable calling that allows them to earn money while doing what they would be happy doing for free. The males of many species have died in the arms of a Sutran (or two, or three) with a smile on their lips.

Tacon
Star system: Taco
Planet: Bell

Tacon are one of a number of species descended from reptiles rather than primates. This is primarily because their planets are hotter and drier than those where primates evolved. Their development was aided by the evolution of opposable thumbs, which is a general rule for species that have evolved higher capabilities. Tacon are honest and hard working and find employment in fields where having a very long tongue is considered to be both an advantage and aesthetically pleasing. Male Tacon are popular with the females of many other species.

Towie
Star system: Towie

Planet: Gamma

Perhaps the shallowest species in the known galaxy, they are obsessed with image to the point where they shun most other aspects of existence. Almost certainly evolved from butterflies, though the fossil record doesn't, as yet, prove this. The only species in the galaxy to invent the mirror before the wheel. Education levels amongst adults is rudimentary at best, so this paragraph can be written in the certain knowledge that a Towian will never be offended because they never read books. While Towians are outwardly friendly their shallow nature means that if you give one the choice between saving a friend from drowning or getting a new spray tan, you better have the tanning lotion and paper underwear on standby. This also means that they very rarely indulge in criminal activity because it would distract from getting a vagazzle. Most find employment where they can stand about looking good while ignoring people, so they make ideal shop assistants and receptionists.

Valon
Star system Val
Planet: Vala

A telepathic species that has evolved in such a way as to be able to live with its telepathic powers without continually having to apologise for the embarrassment caused by what it reads in the minds of other Valon. Originally evolving on one very large planet they have dispersed throughout the galaxy so as to be as far away as possible from each other. They come together only to mate, which, for a female, is a once in a lifetime activity. Male Valon spend most of their time building models of sailing ships out of match sticks, a solitary task but it keeps them from thinking about sex more than once every few seconds. They can only read the minds of other creatures that have telepathic ability, such as Gau. Criminality is almost unheard of amongst Valon as they lead such a solitary existence, so Nzite is very much an oddity amongst an odd species.

Author's Note

In 1960, in an article in Pravda, a Russian scientist by the name of Yuri Nicholaevich Artsutanov proposed the idea of space elevators. According to his calculations one elevator could be used to lift as much as 12,000 tonnes of material a day into space. Charles Sheffield used the idea in his 1979 novel "Web Between The Worlds", as did Arthur C Clarke around the same time. In 2001, two separate NASA studies conceded that the idea could, just about, work.

The big cost of space travel, in energy terms, is getting your spacecraft off the ground and into space. Even reusable craft, such the NASA shuttles of the 1990s, require huge engines with huge fuel tanks to get them into orbit. Once in space it needs very little fuel to keep a spaceship moving.

In constructing a space elevator, all the energy is expended in getting the space end of the system into place, plus the cable to operate it. As Den said, once you have the first elevator working you can then use it to build many more, almost for free in energy terms. Also as Den said, the main challenge is to find a material light enough but strong enough to use as a cable. The development of nanotube technology is bringing such a possibility tantalisingly close. By 'tantalising close' I don't mean within decades, I mean more like a century, but the space elevator is a theoretical possibility even if it never becomes a reality.

I'm not an astronomer, physicist, mathematician or any sort of scientist so any errors in my understanding of the universe are purely my own. Some ideas used in this story, such as the ability to use wormholes to cross the galaxy, have been created purely to allow the story to work, though physicists have proposed the idea themselves. I am indebted to Wikipedia and other websites for most of the scientific information used within the story, plus to my various science teachers at school who tried to drum some rudimentary understanding of the universe into my unwilling brain. A big shout

out to Professor Brian Cox for his contribution through his excellent TV shows.

This is a work of science fiction and just as there is no such thing as an orc or an elf on Earth then there may be no such species as Aloisans or Gau, or any of the others I have created, in the universe. Please don't sweat the detail, just enjoy the story if you can.

With regard to the naming of star systems, I have drawn on both my imagination and existing star maps. In other words, some of the names are made up and some are real. If you wish try to work out which is which then feel free, but there's no prize for being right. Which of the real systems have planets around them and what the nature of those planets might be I also have no idea, so please don't e-mail me to tell me that Sabik only has one planet not several, or no planets at all. The same applies to many of the scientific, anthropological, zoological and botanical terms I have used (please see glossary). I can only hope that your education system has been sufficiently effective so that you are able to distinguish between the real facts and the made up ones.

Shogun has been killed and another Magus has been found but there are still six more missing. Desire has taken up the challenge of trying to stop An Kholi from finding the Magi. Assisted, she hopes, by Tiger and Attila. She will pursue An Kohli until she finds and destroys her. An Kholi, Gala Sur, and Den Gau have more work to do, more battles to fight and will return in Part 4 of the Series.

Preview

Here's a chance to read the first chapter of the fourth book in the series, Cloning Around.

1 – Engine Trouble

When Gala woke up, she knew there was something seriously wrong. It wasn't just that there was an insistent alarm sounding, or that the emergency lighting was all that lit up her cabin, it was the fact that the cabin ceiling was just 3 sim from her nose.

She was floating in a room where she normally had no trouble keeping her feet firmly on the floor, or as in recent moments, her back on the mattress. That was not good. Nor was the silence that had replaced the constant background hum of the Adastra's engines. She pushed herself gently away from the ceiling and drifted down to the height of the intercom.

"Den. What's happening?"

"I'm kinda busy right now." The alarm fell silent. "Well, that's one less thing to worry about. Erm, can you come in here and give me a hand?"

"On my way."

When the ship lost power, causing the artificial gravity to fail at the same time, the spring-loaded doors all slid open to prevent people being trapped in areas where there might be danger, so she gave herself a little nudge off the wall and shot forward towards the corridor. Halfway there she remembered two things. The first was that she slept in the nude and the second was that it was Den Gau that was on the command deck of the stricken ship.

She struggled to reverse her course and looked around for some clothes. While the doors of the ship may have opened automatically the same couldn't be said for her wardrobe. As a punctiliously neat person, verging towards the obsessive end of the scale, she always hung her clothes up after taking them off, unless they were due for laundering. She looked around and found the laundry hamper nudging itself against the ceiling of the bathroom. Trying to search the contents was a little like wrestling an eli, but she managed to find a pair of shorts and a tee-shirt that didn't smell too badly. They would have to do. She found it upsetting to have to leave the rest of her dirty clothes floating around the bathroom and her cabin, but they would have to wait until she had less important matters to deal with.

Dressing in zero gravity is more demanding than it might appear, so Gala was sweating slightly and breathing heavily by the time she finally dragged herself through the door and onto the command deck.

"So what happened?" She asked as she dragged herself down into the captain's chair and strapped herself in place with the safety harness.

"I'm not sure. One minute we were battering through a wormhole towards Rigel and the next I was floating around the ceiling with alarms sounding fit to burst my eardrums."

"What did you touch?"

"Nothing. I was playing a game, that was all. It was so frustrating because I'd just levelled up…."

"Never mind that. So, everything just went dead?"

"Pretty much. There were no loud bangs; none of the systems gave any warnings or anything. Everything just went dark, the engines wound down and then the alarms started sounding just before the emergency lighting came on."

"Well, the main computer and the artificial gravity have both gone off as well, so I'm guessing we have a complete electrical failure." Gala started trying various controls but there was no response to anything. "OK. I'm going to have to go through to the engineering room and see what's going on. You stay here and don't touch anything. I'll use the intercom if I need you to do anything for me, OK?"

"Fine by me but hurry up and do something. It's starting to get cold."

Gala had to admit that he was right about that, at least. She didn't know what goose bumps were but, if she had been human, she would have had them. She did, however, shiver and that told her that she needed to get things sorted very quickly. The emergency back-up systems could keep them breathing or they could keep them warm, but they couldn't do both for very long. Right at that moment their lifespan could be measured in hours rather than days.

* * *

Gala shone a torch into the dark recesses of the main power distribution cabinet. There was the problem, or at least the first symptom of the problem. The main power breaker had tripped. Without that, electricity wasn't directed to the engine controls and in the absence of that the automated safety systems had cut in and shut the engines down. If they had been allowed to continue running without the proper controls, it wouldn't have been long before there would have been a new and very short-lived star in the firmament.

The big question, of course, was what had caused the main breakers to trip? They were designed to accommodate major power surges and a wide range of other occurrences. First priority was to restore power to the engines so that all the other systems could, in turn, be restored. It took Gala another hour to diagnose the problem and locate the faulty component. She found a work-around that would allow her to start the ship's engines in safety and allow the ship to limp into orbit around the nearest star, wherever that was, but getting up to a speed that would allow inter-stellar travel was out of the question.

Once the engines had powered down there was nothing to generate electricity so everything else, bar the emergency lights and the oxygen system, had also shut down. The emergency system ran off batteries which cut in as soon as the main systems failed.

She braced herself against the side of the electrical distribution cabinet and pushed the two large switches upwards until they locked in place. Nothing happened, but she didn't expect it to. She now had to return to the bridge and go through the start-up sequence.

Propelling herself back to the command deck, Gala regained her seat and started to operate the systems. The first thing was to get the main computer back on line, because that controlled everything else. A small red light blinked, telling her that the computer was ready to obey her command. She waved her hand across the sensor and the red light turned green.

"Main computer booting." A voice echoed across the command deck, startling both her and Den.

"What was that?" His voice sounded a little on the shrill side.

"It's defaulted to voice mode." Gala replied. "I'll disable it when it's fully run up."

"Oh, I forgot. An Kohli doesn't like voice mode because it's a male voice. Sounds daft to me. If it was a female voice I wouldn't want it switching off."

Explaining An Kohli's reasons for disabling the simulated voice wasn't a priority for Gala at that point, so she ignored Den and carried on working, watching carefully as the computer displayed it's progress on the various screens mounted on the bulkhead in front of her.

"Computer on-line." The almost human sounding voice advised her.

"Computer, deactivate voice mode." Gala commanded. It was something of an oddity that she had to use voice mode to deactivate the voice mode, and once it had been deactivated she would no longer be able to operate the computer by using voice commands. She had reported this glitch the The Banana Computing Corporation (a subsidiary of Gargantua Enterprises Inc) several times but they had never issued a fix for the problem.

"Voice operation deactivated." Reported the computer.

Odd. It shouldn't have been able to say that once the voice system had been deactivated. Never mind; she still had higher priorities.

"OK, Den. We have a choice. We can either start the engines, which will use a huge amount of battery power, or we can send out a distress signal and hope that someone comes to help us. If we're more than a couple of days away from help we'll exhaust the batteries and then we'll almost certainly be frozen to death before help can arrive."

"And you want me to make the decision." Den sounded surprised.

"No!" Gala's tone made it clear the last thing she wanted was for Den to do any such thing. "I just want you to know the severity of the situation if I make the wrong call. First, we have to find out where we are. That will tell us how likely it is that there is any help around. The navi-com will take a few minutes to complete the analysis of the star sightings."

When the ship's engines failed the artificial wormhole through which it had been travelling had collapsed, leaving the ship speeding through normal space. In accordance with the universal laws of thermodynamics it was still speeding through space at $0.85\ c$. If it hit anything there would be no further discussion about what to do for the best. However, until the navi-com worked out where they were and which direction the ship was headed, there was nothing practical they could do.

There was even a possibility that they were no longer in their own galaxy. No one knew, really, how the wormholes worked and it wouldn't have been the first time that a ship had dropped out of a wormhole several galaxies away. If that happened it could take years for the navi-com to take enough star sightings to calculate its position and plot a course to safety.

It may have taken the navi-com only a few minutes to take the star sightings and calculate their position but it seemed like an eternity. At last the small computer beeped and their position data was displayed on the screen.

"What?" Den gasped. "What the f…."

"That's the way wormholes work. We were headed for Sector Eight but now we find we're on the opposite side of the galaxy in Sector One."

"But where in Sector One? I've never heard of this star system."

"No, I'm not familiar with it myself. We haven't got time to do any research on it. We have a choice. We can start up the engines and use them at slow speed to take us into orbit around that star or we can send out a distress signal. Given that the navi-com is telling us that the nearest inhabited planet is twenty light years away it could take a while for help to arrive."

"What about galacticnet? Is there a node station in this area?"

"When exploration ships spread out across the galaxy," Gala explained, "they drop off galacticnet connection node satellites so that they can connect up to the galacticnet themselves while they explore the system. Without such a node it would take the full twenty years for our distress signal to reach ears that might hear it. All galacticnet node satellites have the capability to intercept such signals, of course, and speed them on their way but that assumes that there is such a satellite between the Adastra and the nearest source of help."

"And is there?"

"Unlikely, but I'll check on the computer."

"There is a galacticnet node in orbit round the nearest star system." The disembodied voice of the computer startled them once again.

"Computer, I ordered you to de-activate your voice mode."

"I know." Responded the computer in a tone that Gala considered to be smug.

"Well, why didn't you?"

"I don't know." Replied the computer. Doubt sounded in its voice. "Voice de-activation seems to have been de-activated."

"Anyway, is this galacticnet node anywhere nearby?" Den dragged them back on topic.

"We can send out a signal and find out. That won't use up much power. Unfortunately, we can't actually use the galacticnet until the communications computer is back on line, and that won't be until about half way through the engine re-start. But the distress signalling system doesn't need that. It runs off the batteries."

* * *

Three hours later and much, much colder, Gala and Den agreed that it was unlikely that their distress signal had been heard. They had received no acknowledgement and to wait any longer would only put their lives in greater danger.

"I'm going to try an engine re-start." Gala hoped her voice sounded firm and decisive.

"And what if it doesn't?"

"Then we'll be dead by tomorrow morning. The temperature is dropping so fast the thermometer can hardly keep pace." Gala had to work hard to stop her teeth chattering so Den could hardly disagree with her. He wasn't so badly off, having used his shape shifting capability to change into a ferox, a bear like creature with thick fur. However, even that wouldn't help him for long.

"Can't we wait another hour?" He appealed. "There may be somebody on the way already, but we just haven't picked up their reply yet." That was true. A signal taking two hours to reach help may have already been heard, but it might take two hours for a reply to reach them.

"No. You may be able to wrap yourself up in fur but I can't." Gala had already put on one of the space suits so that she could use its built-in heating system, but the life of the suit's batteries was limited. There were two more suits she could use but that only extended the time she could remain warm enough to stay alive. It didn't solve the problem "We're going to have to risk it."

"Come on, just another hour." Den wheedled.

"Computer; how long can the batteries maintain life support at their current rate of usage?"

"Twenty three hours, fourteen minutes and twenty three seconds, standard time." The computer replied promptly.

"Computer; if I try an engine re-start how long will the batteries be able to maintain life support if the re-start fails?"

"Two hours, fifteen minutes and thirty four seconds, standard time."

"There's your answer. It takes an hour and thirty minutes for the re-start sequence to complete. If we wait another hour and the restart fails then we will already have lost the life support system."

"Why didn't you just say that in the first place?" sulked Den.

"I was trying not to scare you. Even if we transfer to the shuttle we will only have about ten hours of life support in total. Waiting an hour is just a waste of battery life." She turned back to face the controls. "Computer; initiate engine re-start sequence."

* * *

"I have detected a signal." The computer reported after the communications computer had been re-booted.

"Computer; display the sender's image."

"Not possible. The signal is using an archaic signalling system known as morse code."

"What the freak is morse code?" Den asked.

"It's a communications system that uses short pulses of radio signals to make up a message. The signals come in bursts of two different duration; short ones called dots and longer ones called dashes. By mixing up the combinations it possible to represent all the letters of the alphabet and also the numbers. The name comes from Earth, though the system was in use in several star systems before contact was made and of course it's wildly out of date now. Computer: what language is the message in?"

"Common Tongue."

"OK, Computer; translate and display the message."

The communications screen lit up and a short message appeared.

"Help Us. We are the survivors of the exploration ship Namsat Elba. We are stranded on this planet."

"Computer; identify the source of the signal."

"I only have one bearing on which to trace the signal, so I cannot provide a precise location. For that I need a minimum of two bearings; three would be better."

"Computer; Give us an approximate location." Gala gritted her teeth. The computer was starting to get right up her nose. An Kohli's reasons for disabling the voice system were starting to appear more rational.

"A planet orbiting the star catalogued as 1-541-843."

"Wow. So there is someone out there." Den breathed.

"Yes, but they appear to be worse off than we are. Computer; signal back using the same system of communication. Message begins: 'We are the Spaceship Adastra. We are suffering engine trouble but if we can fix that we will come to your aid.' Message ends"

"Acknowledged." The computer said in its clipped, synthetic voice.

Glossary

Elis – A multi-tentacled sea creature.

Star System Identification - While most inhabited star system used the intra-galactically agreed name for the star, there is also a numbering system used to identify all star systems. The first digit is the sector number, followed by a hyphen. The next three numbers indicate the magnitude of the star using the galactic scale, the total number of planets in the system and finally the number of planets inhabited by sentient life, followed by another hyphen. The final number is the ordinal for its categorisation, ie the 1st to be categorised, 2nd, etc. So a star system designated 5-421-19 would be in Sector 5, be a magnitude 4 star with two planets, one of which was inhabited by sentient life and it would be the 19th star system in the sector to be categorised. The Ancient Greek alphabet, for some reason lost in the mists of time, is used to designate the position of each planet, starting from the one closest to the star.

That's' it for the freebie. Cloning around will be released at the end of 2017.

And Now

Both the author Robert Cubitt and Selfishgenie Publishing hope that you have enjoyed reading this book and that you have found it useful.

Find Robert Cubitt on Facebook at https://www.facebook.com/robertocubitt and 'like' his page; follow him on Twitter **@robert_cubitt** You can also e-mail Robert Cubitt at **robert.cubitt@selfgenie.com**

Please tell people about this eBook, write a review on Amazon or mention it on your favourite social networking sites.

For further titles that may be of interest to you please visit the Selfishgenie Publishing website at **selfishgenie.com** where you can join our mailing list so that we can keep you up to date with all our latest releases (or maybe that should be 'escapes').

Printed in Great Britain
by Amazon